How to get Magically POPULAR

To my mum, for teaching me to meditate

First published in the UK in 2025 by Usborne Publishing Limited, Usborne House, 83-85 Saffron Hill, London EC1N 8RT, England, usborne.com

Usborne Verlag, Usborne Publishing Limited, Prüfeninger Str. 20, 93049 Regensburg, Deutschland, VK Nr. 17560.

Text © Radhika Sanghani, 2025.

The right of Radhika Sanghani to be identified as the author of this work has been asserted by her in accordance with the Copyright, Designs and Patents Act, 1988.

Cover art by Mimi Moffie © Usborne Publishing, 2025.

Author photo by SEBC Photography.

The name Usborne and the Balloon logo are Trade Marks of Usborne Publishing Limited.

All rights reserved. No part of this publication may be reproduced or used in any manner for the purpose of training artificial intelligence technologies or systems (including for text or data mining), stored in retrieval systems or transmitted in any form or by any means without prior permission of the publisher

This is a work of fiction. The characters, incidents, and dialogues are products of the author's imagination and are not to be construed as real. Any resemblance to actual events or persons, living or dead, is entirely coincidental.

A CIP catalogue record for this book is available from the British Library.

ISBN 9781805318286 9458/1 JFMAM JASOND/25

Printed and bound using 100% renewable energy at CPI Group (UK) Ltd, Croydon, CR0 4YY.

RADHIKA SANGHANI

How to get Magically POPULAR

USBORNE

Chapter 1

Sabina Patel sat on her own in the far corner of the dining hall. In her old school, they'd just called it the canteen, and she used to sit right in the middle of its plastic brightness with her best friends – Harry and Ria – talking non-stop as they shared their packed lunches. Soft white-bread sandwiches from Harry's mum, complicated South Indian food from Ria's dad and whatever new health-food recipe that Sabina's mum had decided to make for dinner the night before. Always eaten in that order, because life – or at least their lunch break – was too short to save the best for last.

But things were very different now that Sabina was at Marlstone Girls' School with its wood-panelled halls and high ceilings. Not only was there absolutely no white bread in sight – the freshly-baked counter only sold sourdough – but Sabina seemed to be the only person who brought packed lunch

(the students who ordered in pizza with their parents' credit cards didn't count). Seeing as she was also just one of five girls of colour in her year – and the only Indian girl – it meant that Sabina stood out a mile off. Especially when she had curry in her lunchbox. It was the complete opposite of her old school, where most people had been from diverse backgrounds, meaning everyone was so different that in the end, nobody stood out at all. But that wasn't the worst thing about MG. The worst was that there was no Harry and there was no Ria.

Sabina had spent the entire summer arguing with her mum about the new school, even making a four-minute video to prove that staying at Hackney High was the most conducive option to her having a successful future. But Sabina's mum had been resolute in her decision: they were moving to a village an entire hour away from London. It would be a brilliant opportunity for the both of them. Her mum was going to achieve her dream of opening a beauty salon (apparently villages had cheaper rent than London) and Sabina would be going to the exclusive girls' grammar school nearby, because there was finally an opening.

It didn't matter to her mum that this meant Sabina would turn up to a brand-new school for the start of Year Eight – a whole year after everyone had already made their friendship groups – or that they'd have to leave the city they'd always lived in for some weird *village*. Sabina had googled it and it didn't even have a train station! Or a Nando's! But all Sabina's

mum cared about was that the new school had an amazing academic record. She was hoping that this would make up for the fact that Sabina came from a single-parent household – something she worried would hold her daughter back, no matter how much Sabina's video had tried to convince her otherwise.

It was why Sabina was now sitting alone in MG's overly fancy dining hall, trying to video call Harry and Ria. Exactly like she'd done every single day since she arrived an entire month ago.

She'd always known it would be bad to go to a new school without her best friends – but she hadn't thought it would be *this* bad. Back at Hackney High, she hadn't been in the most popular crew, but she'd had her best friends, she'd never been picked last for PE, and if Harry and Ria were off sick, she always had other people she could have lunch with. Even though Sabina had been against moving to MG, when her mum had said it was definitely happening, she'd kind of just assumed the same thing would happen there. Part of her – a very tiny part that even Harry and Ria didn't know about – had secretly hoped that she might even become *popular*. The kind of popular where everyone would be desperate to hang out with her and she'd walk down the hallways feeling like a celebrity. After all, she was from London – the actual capital city – surely that would make her cooler than these village girls?

It mortified Sabina now to think of just how wrong and naïve she'd been. Her classmates had wanted to know about her life in London – but not life at Hackney High, or the local skate park near Sabina's house, or the falafel place she loved. They'd stared at Sabina blankly when she'd talked about these things, until she'd eventually trailed off, embarrassed. That was when her new classmates had started reeling off lists of cool restaurants and shops they'd visited in London, wanting to know how often Sabina went to them. When it became evident she hadn't even *heard* of them, they'd lost all interest.

Sabina had spent the rest of her first week at MG awkwardly hovering on the edge of conversations as her classmates chattered rapidly about their summer holidays to places she hadn't known existed. She'd always thought she was quite good at geography, but the Hackney High syllabus hadn't included Caribbean islands. The one time she'd worked up the courage to ask where St Lucia actually *was,* they'd all completely ignored her. Sabina had felt so invisible that she'd decided to just accept her status as an outcast and stop trying. It was less painful that way.

Her mum kept telling her things would change with time, but it had been an entire month and Sabina was *still* "the new girl". If it wasn't for her daily calls to Harry and Ria, she'd have no friends at all.

"Look who it is," said Harry, raising his perfectly arched eyebrow as he and Ria finally answered the group call. "Again."

"I've been waiting ages for you guys to answer," complained Sabina, adjusting her headphones.

"Sorry, we only just got out of double maths with Mr Carter," said Ria with an apologetic smile. "And the canteen was packed, so we had to kick some Year Sevens out of our seats."

Sabina sighed longingly. "I miss the word canteen. I even miss double maths with the world's most boring teacher." Her eyes widened as she saw what her friends were eating. "And I *really* miss your mum's sandwiches, Harry. Is that—"

"Egg mayo," he said, his mouth still full. "Your fave. Soz."

"Is that Katniss on the table behind you?" asked Ria. "I still can't believe your school has its own cat – that's so cool!"

Sabina couldn't help smiling. Katniss Evermean was the best thing about MG. She belonged to the headteacher Mr Grant – who had a house next door to the school – and wandered around MG like she owned it. Which she basically did. She was as sassy, spoiled and mean as her name suggested, but it just made everyone love her more. Sabina was slightly in awe of her – this cat had levels of confidence she could only aspire to.

"Who are the girls feeding her?" asked Harry, squinting at the screen. "They've got *style*."

Sabina turned to see the silky black cat with green eyes sprawled out on a table while two girls with perfect make-up and shiny hair hand-fed her sushi, filming the whole thing on

their phones. "The Leeshes, obviously. Remember I told you about them?"

The Leeshes were Alicia Johnson and Felicia James. Like most of the girls at MG, they had names that ended in "ah". But Alicia and Felicia also happened to be the most popular, pretty and privileged girls in Year Eight. They went everywhere together, had the same haircut (Alicia was blond and Felicia was brunette), and both accessorized their navy school uniform with identical overpriced trainers, gold jewellery and acrylic nails – even though anybody else would have got detention for flouting the dress code. They even had the same nickname, calling each other "Leesh", which was why the whole school knew them as the "Leeshes". Though Sabina privately thought of them as the "Leeches" because they were always stuck to each other's sides.

The only apparent difference between the Leeches was that Felicia was in an on-off relationship with Alexis, the best lacrosse player in the year – a weird posh sport that Sabina hated but the entire of MG was obsessed with. While Alicia had a constant stream of boyfriends from Marlstone Boys' School next door. When it came to romance – as with everything else in their lives – the Leeches were always winning.

"Who could forget the *Leeches*?" cried Harry. "Not when they look like that! They're even more perfect than you described!"

"Why are they hanging with Katniss?" asked Ria. "I thought you and her had a special bond. It was so cute when she licked peanut butter off your fingers on your first day!"

"I thought so too," admitted Sabina. "Till I realized she'll hang with anyone who feeds her. And seeing as the Leeches always have the best food, obviously they get Katniss priority. Katniss is amazing, but she's not mine – *everyone* wants to be friends with her."

"Awkward that the cat's more popular than you," said Harry, accurately reading Sabina's thoughts.

"Harry!" admonished Ria. "Have you...made any friends at all yet?"

Sabina shook her head sadly. "Nope. And I'm starting to lose hope I ever will."

"Just give it some time, Sabs," said Ria encouragingly. "Honestly, I can't believe people aren't lining up to be your friend already! I mean, you're really funny. And you're smart! Though you aren't great at physics... But you're generous! Unless it comes to sharing dessert. I still can't believe you made us use a *ruler* to divide your birthday cake."

"That *was* generous of me!" protested Sabina. "I could have given myself an extra big birthday slice! And I'm not that bad at physics!"

"Ria's right," interrupted Harry. "Just be yourself, and they'll all come running. If they don't, they're the problem, not you."

If only it was that easy. Sabina could be herself with Harry and Ria because they'd been best friends for as long as she could remember. It wasn't so easy with the girls at MG – they were all so different to her with their credit cards and expensive clothes. She already felt like such an alien around them that the thought of being her true self felt completely impossible. Besides, it wasn't like anybody even spoke to her, so she had no idea how she'd ever get the chance to try.

"In fact," continued Harry, "I'm going to end this call right now so you can start the heartbreaking but essential process of replacing us."

"You can't just hang up on her!" hissed Ria. "She's eating alone!"

"And she'll be eating alone for ever if she doesn't make some new friends," retorted Harry. "Which is not going to happen if she keeps video calling us every lunch break!"

"Could you both please stop talking about me like I'm not right here?" asked Sabina. "It's not helping the whole self-confidence thing."

"Sorry, Sabs. It's only because we love you!" said Ria.

"Exactly," said Harry. "So we're going to love you and leave you. Maybe someone will come say hi to you when we're gone? Update us later. Byeeee!"

"Wait, I—" But the call cut off before Sabina could finish her sentence. She sighed, looking down at her phone. The screensaver was a selfie of her, Harry and Ria from their last school trip to Hackney City Farm. They were all baring their teeth like the goats they'd just seen because Harry had demanded they channel their inner bovids. The photo made Sabina laugh every time she saw it – they were not natural bovids – but right now it was also making her realize she didn't *want* to replace her friends. All she wanted was for things to go back to the way they were.

"He-eeeyy! Cute glasses!" A sing-song voice cut through Sabina's thoughts. She looked up, startled, to see the Leeches beaming at her. Katniss was sitting by their feet, licking her paws and completely ignoring Sabina, even though she'd given her a chunk of tuna the day before.

The Leeches had *never* spoken to Sabina – at least, not since she'd revealed that she hadn't ever shopped in Selfridges. But as she smiled back at them, self-consciously adjusting her plastic tortoiseshell glasses, she wondered if Harry was right and all it took for her to make new friends was to get off the phone to her old ones?

"What's the new girl's name again?" Alicia loud-whispered to Felicia.

Or maybe not.

"Wait, I have it here somewhere," said Felicia, scrolling through her phone. "Oh! Sabrina! Hey, girl!"

"*Such* a cute name," said Alicia. "So, Sabrina, I wanted to personally tell you I'm running for form prefect, and I'd *love* your vote."

"All the info is here," said Felicia, pressing a flier into Sabina's hand. "But basically, we're focusing on improving recycling, and making the canteen vegan. You're vegan, right, Sabrina?"

"Uh..." Sabina blinked, dazed. This was the longest conversation she'd had with a single person at MG to date – the nurse who'd made her fill out a health form didn't count – and it was with the *Leeches.* The only problem was they were calling her by the wrong name. "I'm not. But also my na—"

"It's, like, way better for the planet," said Felicia. "You should totally consider it. Anyway – vote for Leesh and we'll make MG a better place!"

"Thanks for your vote, Sabrina!" said Alicia, spinning on her heel and automatically linking arms with Felicia, giving Sabina a presidential wave. "Come on, Katniss, let's go for dessert! There's vegan ice cream!" Katniss followed the Leeches without looking back at Sabina.

She stared after the Leeches in angst, knowing if she didn't say anything now, she'd have to spend the rest of her school life being called by the wrong name. She wished Harry and Ria were there to do it for her. But then she glanced down at her phone screensaver and felt a surge of empowerment. She'd do it for herself and make her friends proud!

"Wait!" she cried out. Her voice came out way louder than she expected, and the Leeches turned in surprise. Even Katniss looked affronted.

"Um, sorry, it's just that my name's not actually Sabrina," she said haltingly. "It's Sab*ina*. Without the R."

Felicia blinked at her. "Why?"

"Uh…I'm sorry, what?" replied Sabina in confusion.

"Why is there no R in your name?" asked Felicia slowly.

Sabina stared from Felicia's expectant brown eyes to Alicia's matching hazel ones. She'd never had to *explain* her name before – it was just her name! But the Leeches were clearly waiting for an answer, so she tried to supply one. "That's…the way my mum chose it?"

"I totally respect that," said Alicia. "But I think Sabrina sounds cuter, so you don't mind if we call you that, do you?"

Felicia nodded. "I'm never going to remember to drop the R anyway. It's too confusing."

"I mean…" Sabina tried to think of a way to say she very much did mind.

But the Leeches just looped their arms together and beamed at her. "See you later, Sabrina!"

Sabina stared after them, wondering if she'd hallucinated that entire conversation. She couldn't believe that after she'd worked up the courage to correct the Leeches, they were still calling her by the wrong name! Shaking her head, she pulled out her phone to call Harry and Ria again as she walked to maths – they needed to know every sentence of that interaction before she forgot it – and was so engrossed that she didn't notice the girl striding towards her.

"Owww!" yelled Sabina, as she crashed into her.

"You really shouldn't use your phone in the corridor," said a serious voice. It was Faye Collins. The smartest girl in their year and the only other girl of colour in Sabina's form.

"Sorry!" said Sabina, nursing her bruised arm. "Forget dangerous driving – clearly dangerous walking is worse!"

"I doubt it," said Faye, her brown eyes serious. She was black with long braids, glasses similar to Sabina's, and pretty silver hoop earrings in her ears. "The speed of a car would lead to much more damage on impact."

Sabina blinked, wondering why nobody in this school responded like a normal person. But Faye carried on, unperturbed. "I saw you speaking to the Leeshes earlier so I want to say that before you vote for Alicia, you should consider voting for me instead. Her policies aren't based on clear research. Veganism is better for the environment, yes, but what about the fact that the canteen's vegan food comes in plastic? Also, why don't we give our school's leftover food to those in need? These are things I care about – as well as improving diversity."

"You said canteen!" cried Sabina.

Faye looked at her like she was deranged.

"Sorry, it's just…that's what we said in my old school."

"Ri-ight. Well, if you want more info on my policies, you can visit my website – fayecollinsforformprefect.com." She looked down at the piece of paper Sabina was holding.

"Fliers aren't great for the environment."

"Oh, sorry."

"You apologize way too much," remarked Faye. "Anyway, see you around."

Sabina waved awkwardly in response. She couldn't believe she'd spoken to not one, but *three* of her classmates! As much as it annoyed her to admit it, Harry was right. Not being on the phone to her old friends had given her a chance to make new ones. And okay, the Leeches weren't calling her by her actual name, and Faye thought she said sorry too much, but this was still a solid start. If she carried on at this rate, she might have an actual human being to have lunch with by the end of term!

Chapter 2

When school was finally over and she'd walked home, Sabina ran up the stairs to their new flat, hurriedly unlocking the door. "Mum?!" she called out impatiently, dumping her bag on the kitchen table before walking into the sitting room. She was hoping to find her mum curled up on her floral armchair, reading the newspaper with a cup of chai and an inevitably soggy biscuit.

But Sabina's shoulders fell when she saw there was nobody there. She trudged up the stairs to check if her mum was in her large airy bedroom, or in Sabina's smaller cosy attic room, tidying up the clothes she should have put away the night before. Sabina would have happily accepted a lecture on her messy room if it meant her mum was there, but she wasn't. The flat was empty, just like it had been most evenings since they'd moved there.

Sabina collapsed on her soft peach bedspread (her mum called it pink, but Sabina insisted it was peach) feeling disappointment flood her body. She knew it was embarrassing that a thirteen-year-old was so desperate to spend the evening with her mum, but Sabina had been excited to tell her about her lunch break. Not only had she finally spoken to the terrifying Leeches but she'd also looked at Faye's website, which was the coolest thing ever! She was definitely going to vote for her for form prefect – Alicia's flier had nothing on Faye's interactive site. It even had an inbuilt video game that simulated MG's canteen and its plastic problem.

Only Sabina's mum wasn't there. Again. She must still be working at Beauties, her brand-new salon. She'd told Sabina that she'd named it after the two of them because they were the original beauties. Sabina had rolled her eyes at how cringe her mum was, but she'd secretly loved it. Besides, the salon was seriously cool. There were chairs that gave you massages while you had a pedicure, private rooms for waxing and facials, and the largest selection of nail polishes Sabina had seen in her life. On her mum's first day in the salon, she'd given Sabina a full mani-pedi in her new chair – she'd chosen "posh purple" in honour of their new surroundings – and Sabina had almost burst with pride for her.

But back then she hadn't realized how much things would change with her mum owning a salon. Before, she'd worked as a freelance beauty therapist, and most of her appointments had taken place in the daytime while Sabina was at school. But with Beauties, she had to work late, accepting evening appointments so she could bolster her client base and earn enough money to cover all their new costs. It made sense and Sabina knew it wasn't her mum's *fault* that she wasn't there any more. But she still missed her. Her mum hadn't even painted her nails since the posh purple day, and that was before school had started!

Before the big move, her mum had given her weekly manicures (though she was only allowed boring school-appropriate colours during term time) and Sabina had loved it. But that was only one of their evening rituals. They also had their daily catch-ups while her mum made dinner, and Sabina would describe her day at school like it was a TV episode in the series that was her life. And then they had their breathing ritual…

This was Sabina's absolute favourite thing to do with her mum. It always started with simple stretches that they'd do together in the living room, which would inevitably end in laughter when Sabina fell over mid-balance in a complicated stretch or, even better, if her mum had eaten beans at dinner and farted mid-bend. When they'd calmed down, they'd sit cross-legged on the floor, sliding cushions under their bums. That was when they'd do their relaxing breathing ritual: focusing on their breathing, in and out of their noses, imagining a bright white light in the middle of their eyebrows.

Sabina loved it. It was so peaceful sitting by her mum's side, hearing her steady breath, and then eventually, getting so focused on her own breath and white light that she'd forget where she was. Her mind would go blank, and no matter what had happened that day, it would all fade away. By the time her mum would gently shake her shoulder, all her worries would be gone. That was precisely why her mum had started the ritual, back when Sabina was five years old...

She'd come back from her first week at school in tears, after their teacher had asked them to draw a family tree.

"Everyone has a dad," Sabina had sobbed into her mum's arms. "I know not everyone's dad lives in their house. Ben's dad is divorced. And Meera's dad is dead. But I don't have one at ALL!"

Her mum stroked her hair as she gently explained the story Sabina knew off by heart. But this time, she added in more details. "*Beta,* you had a dad as well. He was strong and kind and handsome. I loved him. But...he wasn't ready to settle down and have a family. He went back to India, and unfortunately, he never got in touch with me again."

"Did he...not love me?"

"He never met you, baby," said her mum softly. "But I know he always loved you – he just had to do it from afar. And you know how much *I* love you, right? I love you..."

"Infinity!" they both said at the same time, smiling.

"Can I see the photo of Daddy again?" asked Sabina.

Her mum pulled out the faded photo – the only one she had – and Sabina stared at the image of her parents back when they were twenty-one. They'd never married, which was something her grandma and mum still fought about, but they looked happy. Her mum's face was lit up with love, while her dad had his arm around her protectively. He had a strong jaw, dark brown eyes and a thick moustache.

Sabina felt a mix of deep longing and sadness when she looked at it. She knew she loved him even though she'd never met him – so why didn't he love her? She wished he'd stayed to be a proper dad, like Harry and Ria's dads, and she couldn't help but think that the reason he'd left was because of her. Because she wasn't the daughter he wanted.

"I'm still sad," she admitted to her mum, putting the photo back in the Drawer of Important Things.

"That's okay. It's normal to feel sad sometimes. But I know something that might help you feel a bit better if you want to try it out?"

That was when they'd begun their breathing ritual.

Sabina still remembered how soothed she'd felt by the magic white light, and how loved she'd felt by her mum. After everything that had happened today with the Leeches, she wished her mum was there right now to do the ritual with her. Tears pricked her eyelids and she shook her head. This was ridiculous! She was too old to miss her mum like this. She should make the most of her freedom and spend the evening playing games with Harry and Ria. But when she pulled out her phone, she saw they'd already messaged her to say they had so much homework from Mr Carter that they couldn't speak. The lump of disappointment in Sabina's throat grew. But she swallowed it down. It was fine. She could do her homework too! And if she kept her phone screensaver on, she could pretend that Harry and Ria were right there doing theirs with her.

Chapter 3

The next morning, Sabina reluctantly walked out of the toilet cubicle in her fleece and tracksuit bottoms. Having lacrosse first thing was the worst. No matter how many hours she spent running across a field in the freezing cold, she still didn't fully understand this weird game, beyond a vague comprehension that you were meant to use long sticks with nets on the end to hurl heavy balls at each other. To the frustration of their teacher, Sabina always spent the entire lesson trying to avoid those balls hitting her in the face.

"*That's* what you're wearing for yoga?" Alicia – who was standing in the middle of the changing room in her pastel-green underwear – looked Sabina up and down, an expression of amusement on her face.

Sabina flushed, unsure where to look. Not only was a Leech speaking to her for the second day in a row – after weeks of ignoring her – but she was doing it half-naked. Back at her old school, privacy had been a thing. They'd all changed in toilet cubicles or manoeuvred shorts under their skirts. But at MG, it was all about body confidence, which apparently meant taking off your clothes at every opportunity.

"I...thought we had lacrosse?" Sabina managed, firmly staring at Alicia's fuchsia toenails.

"Nope – we have yoga and meditation," said Felicia, pulling on a pair of yellow leggings with a matching top. "It's part of MG's new wellness programme, which is totally on Leesh's agenda if – I mean *when* – she's form prefect."

Alicia shot her an irritated look. "Yes. And I have been doing yoga since nursery, so this is *very* on brand for me. I'm guessing you've done it too, what with it coming from your culture?"

Sabina shook her head. "I've never gone to a yoga class before. Or meditated. I didn't even know it was happening today."

"It's the free taster session," explained Felicia. "But afterwards, our parents will have to pay for it. It's going to be an optional paid extra-curric, but I mean, whose parents *won't* want to invest in their wellness?"

Sabina's face fell. As much as she preferred the idea of yoga to running around in the cold for lacrosse, extra costs meant extra hours at work for her mum.

"Leesh, let's take a selfie!" Alicia, who was now wearing electric blue leggings with a hot pink crop top, pulled out her phone. Instantly, Felicia was by her side, posing with namaste hands. "Oh, the lighting isn't great. Let's try the corridor!"

Sabina took advantage of the Leeches' absence to change into her plain black leggings. She tied her long hair into a ponytail, adjusted her glasses in the mirror with an encouraging smile at her reflection, and, feeling marginally better about herself, walked towards the gymnasium.

She pushed the door open then halted in surprise. It looked completely different! The bright halogen lights had been swapped for tiny candles dotted around the corners of the room, and the blue gym mats had been arranged into a circle. Right in the centre was a woman sitting cross-legged, eyes closed, oblivious to the girls staring at her.

"Sabrina, look, the teacher's Indian too!" loud-whispered Alicia. "Maybe you both know each other?!"

Sabina laughed awkwardly. Was Alicia for real? Or was that a joke? Either way, she had no idea how to respond. For the millionth time, she wished Harry and Ria were there; they'd know *exactly* what to say.

"Newsflash, not every person of colour knows each other." Sabina jerked her head up to see who'd spoken. It was Faye. "Also, her name's Sabi*na*. Without the R."

Sabina gasped aloud. Someone at this school knew her name! Her *actual* name.

"Uh, we know, and she doesn't mind us calling her Sabrina, do you, babe?" retorted Felicia.

Sabina shook her head uncomfortably, avoiding eye contact with Faye. She knew Faye was trying to help, and the fact she knew her name meant the world to her. But she couldn't alienate the most popular girls in the year. Not when she still had zero friends and counting.

"In Hindu mythology, Sabina means 'knowing' and 'wise'." The whole room spun round to face their yoga teacher. Her voice was soft, but it cut through the gymnasium, commanding everyone's attention. "Names are powerful. And Sabina is a strong one."

Sabina gaped at her. She'd never known what her name meant – and she was pretty sure her mum hadn't either. "Knowing" and "wise" weren't exactly the top adjectives her mum would use to describe her – "fun" and "messy" would be more accurate.

"I love that!" cried Alicia. "What does Alicia mean?"

"And Felicia!"

But the teacher just shrugged at the Leeches. "I only know the meaning of Sanskrit-based names. You'll have to google yours."

The Leeches didn't look pleased about this. But they didn't have time to respond because the teacher suddenly stood up. She was tall and lithe, wearing loose yoga clothes, and her dark hair was streaked with gold. She gestured for everyone to sit down.

"My name is Diva, which means light. I try to bring light

into everything I do, and everywhere I go." She raised an eyebrow. "Even Marlstone Girls' School."

Sabina grinned, deciding she liked Diva already.

"Now," said Diva. "Today's class is going to involve a fifteen-minute meditation."

There were gasps around the room, echoing: "Fifteen minutes?!"

"But what about the yoga?" demanded Alicia. "We can't sit still for that long!"

"We'll do some yoga first," said Diva nonchalantly. "But the most important part of our practice is the meditation. That's how you access the energy within you and balance your chakras." Her words were met with blank silence. "Does anyone know what a chakra is?"

Felicia put her hand up. "Are they, like, crystals?"

Diva shook her head. "No, but crystals *are* said to have powers that can help us tap into our different chakras, so you're not fully wrong." She gestured to her spine. "We all have seven main chakras, or energy centres, in the body, going from the bottom of the spine – where the root chakra is – to the top of our heads – the crown chakra. In our meditation, I'll explain what each one does, and what colour it is. We'll use that information to try and focus on the chakra, using the power of our minds to balance and heal it. Any questions?"

"Several," said Faye authoritatively. "What's the scientific proof for these chakras? How do we know they're real? And what's the point in balancing them?"

"Maybe she should just google it," whispered Alicia to Felicia. They erupted into giggles, but when Diva lifted her hand, they instantly fell silent. Sabina's eyes widened in awe. If balancing her chakras would give her power like that, she was *so* down.

"Thank you for your questions," said Diva. "The idea of chakras comes from ancient Eastern spiritual texts. There is some scientific proof behind them, but to me the biggest proof is in our own experiences. As you meditate, you'll *notice* the energy vibrating and moving inside you. Try to feel it and listen to what it's telling you."

"What if it tells me I need to stop meditating and get back to a downward dog instead?" asked Alicia.

"Then maybe listen a little harder," said Diva sweetly.

Sabina's mouth dropped open. She'd never heard anyone stand up to a Leesh before – let alone a teacher! But it was becoming very clear that Diva was not an ordinary teacher.

Diva clapped her hands loudly and the sound reverberated around the room. "Now. Sit cross-legged on your cushions. Hips higher than the knees. Eyes closed. And…we begin."

When Sabina had told the Leeches she'd never meditated or done yoga before, she'd thought she'd been telling the truth.

But she'd been wrong. Because when Diva started leading them through some simple stretches, Sabina realized they were the *exact* same ones she did with her mum! In fact, they were even easier than the ones she did with her mum, and she noticed the Leeches looking at her with confused appreciation when she managed to stay for a whole minute in a one-legged balance – or a "warrior three" as Diva called it – without wobbling. Neither of the Leeches had been able to stay still for more than a few seconds, and the one time they tried, Felicia crashed into Alicia so loudly that the whole class lost their concentration and tumbled down like dominoes. Except for Sabina. She had plenty of practice not falling over whilst laughing on one leg, especially when her mum had eaten beans.

But the part Sabina was most shocked by was the meditation. She'd always thought that her and her mum's breathing ritual was something only they did – a private two-person activity with a magic light her mum had invented to cheer up a younger Sabina. But when Diva started to guide them through the meditation, telling them to focus on breathing deeply in and out of their noses, and to imagine a white light in the middle of their eyebrows, Sabina almost cried out in shock. This was EXACTLY what she did with her mum! She opened her eyes then, looking around the room in disbelief. When she locked eyes with Diva, she could have sworn her teacher winked at her.

She quickly closed her eyes, and slowly, as she focused on her breathing, she found herself relaxing. Her thoughts started to disappear, until it was just her and the white light, with vague sounds of her classmates breathing far away in the distance. She felt the same soothing peace that she did with her mum when they did it at home. But then Diva started to mix things up.

"Now we're going to start imagining the colours of the rainbow along our spine," said Diva. "They represent the seven chakras. Let's start with red at the base of our spine, which symbolizes safety. Breathe into it, let the red grow super bright. And then we're going to move to our tummies, below the belly button, where we have orange for pleasure, joy and creativity." She spoke slowly as she guided them through the remaining five.

"Yellow in our centres for power...green in our hearts for love...blue in our throats for communication and honesty... indigo in between our eyebrows for insight and intuition... and finally, violet at the very top of our heads to symbolize our connection to others."

Sabina was so engrossed in the meditation that she didn't even fully associate the words as Diva's. They just appeared in her head, and she did exactly what they said, connecting with all seven of her chakras. With each one, she felt the thing it symbolized suffuse her whole body. Like when Diva told them the heart chakra represented love, and Sabina imagined a green light shining through her entire body, until she could feel her toes tingling with love. By the time she reached the final chakras, she felt like she was practically floating, with all the colours of the rainbow radiating around her. She was used to just focusing on one bright light with her mum, but here, there were seven. And Sabina felt seven times as good.

Until a sudden sound shattered her serenity. She blinked open her eyes to see the Leeches giggling at her. Sabina's peace instantly evaporated as she jerked her head around the room to see that *everybody* was staring at her; even Diva was smiling sympathetically. She must have told them to stop, but Sabina hadn't heard a thing! She wondered how long she'd carried on meditating after everyone else had opened their eyes.

"You were really into that," said Alicia, suspicious. "I thought you'd never done it before?"

"I...didn't think I had," said Sabina, embarrassed by the sudden attention.

"You were practically vibrating," said Felicia, staring at her like she was a circus attraction.

"Could I check your stats next time we meditate, Sabina?" asked Faye enthusiastically. "Just your heart rate and blood sugar, that kind of thing." Her face lit up. "I could do my next science project on you! To investigate the effects of meditation and whether chakra energy is real!"

"Uh..." Sabina looked from Faye to the Leeches helplessly.

She really didn't want to be a science project; she just wanted to get through the rest of Year Eight without humiliating herself, and ideally, making a friend or two. "I was just... breathing?"

Diva clapped her hands again and everyone jumped. "Class is over. Everyone, go and get changed. Sabina, I'd like to speak to you, please. Alone."

Everyone trudged out of the room, including a reluctant Faye. Sabina felt her heart racing as everybody left – had she done something wrong? Was she already in trouble with the only teacher at MG she liked?

But Diva beamed at her. "You have a gift, Sabina. Your meditation practice is very strong."

Sabina laughed in shock. "Uh, no, I... It's just something I do with my mum. I didn't even know it was meditation! And it's not a gift – anyone can do it."

"Yes, but you're a natural. And with a bit more practice and guidance, you could take your meditating to new levels."

"I'm not sure what that means. But I *really* don't need more reasons to stand out here."

Diva settled her unusually grey eyes on Sabina's dark brown ones. "Maybe you were born to stand out. Maybe it's in your destiny."

Sabina shook her head quickly. "No, no. The Leeches, I mean the Leeshes, are born to stand out. I'm just...me."

Diva smiled mysteriously and pulled something out of her

pocket. She gestured at Sabina to open up her palm, then placed something cold and heavy onto her soft skin. A dark purple stone, with shades of indigo and grey running through it. Sabina exclaimed as it caught the light. It was *beautiful*.

"It's an amethyst," explained Diva. "A very powerful crystal that can help open up the third eye chakra – that's the one between our eyebrows that represents insight and intuition."

"What does that mean?"

"It's all about understanding things better and seeing things clearly. It's why I want you to have this crystal – I think it will help you."

"You're giving it to me? But...why?"

"I think your third eye chakra is close to opening, Sabina. If you keep meditating – just like we did today, going through all the chakras – but with the use of this crystal, your chakra could completely open up." Diva paused dramatically. "It could change your life."

"Right," said Sabina. "By making sure I become Faye's next science experiment and nobody here ever wants to be my friend?"

"Or by unlocking powers in you that help you to live the life you were always destined for." Diva raised her brows enigmatically as she closed Sabina's fingers around the crystal. "Good luck."

Sabina frowned down at the crystal. "Wait, what do you want me to do with it? I don't understand!"

"You'll know what to do with it when the time comes," said Diva, before turning around to her candles, clearly dismissing her.

Sabina walked away in confusion. She had no idea what Diva had been going on about. What even *was* this third eye chakra? And what did she mean by powers?! She gazed down at the crystal – it was undeniably beautiful, but it was also just a rock. She very much doubted it had the power to change her life. If she wanted to make friends, she was better off doing less meditating, not more. Because Diva was wrong; she needed to fit in, not stand out.

Chapter 4

"... And *this* is what they wore to yoga," said Sabina, tapping her screen to send Harry and Ria links to the Leeches' Instagram profiles.

Ria's eyes widened on Sabina's screen. "Wow, they're so glamorous! They look like Year Tens!"

"And so colour-coordinated." Harry sighed longingly. "I wish you two took my fashion advice more. Then you could look as good as the Leeches."

"I doubt it," said Sabina. "And it doesn't matter, because I won't be doing yoga again."

"But I thought you liked it!" said Ria. "It sounds like it went really well!

"I'm sorry, did you not hear what I said?" asked Sabina. "I meditated through the end of the lesson. When I opened my eyes, everyone was staring at me like I had an *actual* third eye in the middle of my forehead."

"Wait, *that's* why you're not continuing?" asked Ria. "Sabina, don't let the Leeches stop you from doing something you're good at. Besides, it comes from your heritage, not theirs!"

Sabina shrugged. "It doesn't matter anyway. It's too expensive. And I can't make my mum pay for it when she's already working so hard."

"I miss your mum," said Harry. "She's a woman who knows her colour palette. Though she's not so great with her taste palate…"

Sabina sighed. "I wish you were both here. I don't know if I can get through this year without you."

"We're coming in the holidays!" said Ria. "That's not *that* far away. And it sounds like you're making friends. Okay, not the Leeches, maybe. But Faye sounds cool! I played her canteen game twice."

"Not as cool as us," said Harry, putting up a warning finger. "But, agreed. We're pro Faye."

Sabina bit her lip. "I guess now we just need to find out if Faye is pro me…"

When Sabina had ended the video call with her friends, she padded downstairs to see if her mum was finally back for dinner. She wasn't. As if on cue, her phone beeped with a message.

> Hi honey, working late again, sorry… But there is a dhal in the freezer! You just need to stick it in the microwave to defrost it. Save some for me – I'll try and join you soon!!

Sabina felt her shoulders sag in disappointment. It was at times like this that she really wished she had a dad. If he was around, she wouldn't have to be alone so much. They could spend the evening together, and maybe he'd play games with her like Harry's dad did, or take her to the cinema for dad-daughter movie nights, like Ria's dad did. Sabina desperately longed to have a dad who'd do these things with her and would support her mum so she didn't have to work crazy hard. But most importantly of all, Sabina wished she had a dad who loved her.

She knew she was beyond lucky to have such an amazing mum who loved her infinity, but it hurt to know that her dad hadn't loved her at all. He hadn't even tried. He'd left before she was born, and it made Sabina feel like there was something wrong with her – why else would he have abandoned them like that? She knew that rationally this didn't make total sense – her dad hadn't even met her so how could he not like her? – but she still couldn't get it out of her head. It had been there for as long as she could remember. She'd always felt she wasn't quite good enough, and the only thing that would make her believe otherwise would be her dad coming back.

But that was never going to happen and it was ridiculous to think it ever would. Her mum had kept the same phone number for all these years in case her dad called, but he hadn't. Not even once. And he'd changed his contact details so she couldn't even get in touch with him if she wanted to. Her dad was officially AWOL and there was no point in Sabina thinking about him all the time. She should just focus on what she did have – a mum who loved her and a dinner to heat up.

With a sense of newfound determination, Sabina pulled open the freezer and took out the hard yellow lump of dhal in its transparent Tupperware. Like most things her mum cooked, it did not look particularly appetizing. But it was either that or toast. So she stuck it in the microwave, knowing she'd probably end up taking the rest of it to school for lunch the next day. The Leeches would definitely have something to say about that if they saw her with it. She could imagine it now: "That smells *super* authentic!" She felt a tingle of shame, then remembered it wasn't real. The Leeches hardly ever spoke to her anyway, and they weren't there; nobody was. It was just her and a sad defrosted dhal for company.

With an air of resignation, Sabina collapsed onto the sofa and turned on the TV. She may as well try that new prom thriller everyone was watching – at least that way she'd have something to say if any of her classmates ever asked her if she'd seen it.

By the time her mum came home, the leftover dhal was cold, Sabina had worked out that the murderer in the TV show was the victim's prom date (obviously) *and* she'd finished all her homework.

"Mum! Finally!"

"I'm so sorry," her mum apologized, dumping down a bunch of bags on the kitchen counter. "Today was ridiculously busy. And I thought I'd do a quick food shop on the way back. I bought apology crisps!"

"Your dinner is officially cold," Sabina informed her.

"Don't worry – you can take it for lunch tomorrow!" said her mum, exactly as Sabina had predicted, peeling off her giant puffer coat. "I grabbed a sandwich in the supermarket. Do you mind...?"

Sabina rolled her eyes as she began to help unload the bags her mum was gesturing to. "Fine. I guess it's good you were so busy today – it means that Beauties is popular with the locals!"

Her mum crossed her fingers. "I hope so! Though it might still be a while before I earn enough to hire more people to help out. I may have spent more on the refurbishment than I should have..."

"It's worth it," said Sabina confidently. "The salon looks great! Now, please can I give you the latest update in *Sabina*

Survives MG? That's what we're calling this new stage of my life."

"Oh, I thought it was *Sabina's Mum Ruins Her Life*." Her mum grinned at her, tucking her brown curly hair behind her ears as her dark green eyes sparkled. She was beautiful, even when she was so exhausted that she had tiny lines on her forehead and her hair was shiny with sweat.

"I thought my version was a bit catchier," said Sabina, placing her mum's coffee capsules in the drawer. "And today's episode is called: *The Opening of the Third Eye Chakra*."

Her mum turned to her in disbelief. "You learned about the third eye chakra at school? Wow, things have really changed since I was your age!"

"A yoga teacher came in to teach us. Diva. Her name means light."

"Oh yes, I saw an email about that! How did it go?"

"It was interesting... Mainly because you never told me that our breathing ritual – that we have been doing for seven whole years – is actually *meditating*. And the stretches are yoga," said Sabina in an accusatory voice.

Her mum shrugged as she placed tins of chopped tomatoes in the cupboard. "I guess they are. But I never thought of them like that – they were simply things I did growing up. With my mum."

Sabina's mouth gaped at this new information. "I'm sorry – you and Ba, who you spend every second arguing with every time we visit, used to *breathe* together?"

Her mum turned away to unload the cereal. "Yes. She didn't call it meditating either. It was…a normal part of life. Though she *did* teach me about the chakras, but I couldn't remember the details, sorry. That's why I skipped that bit with you."

Sabina pulled herself up on the counter to face her mum. "Whoa. I did *not* see that coming. Can you tell me more?"

Her mum's phone started vibrating. "Sorry, darling. It's a client. I won't be a minute!"

Sabina kicked her legs against the counter as she waited for the conversation to end. She couldn't wait to find out more about her mum meditating with Ba. Her grandma was the fanciest woman she knew. She sat upright and only ever on stiff chairs. The thought of her cross-legged on the floor with her mum, a cushion under her bum, breathing into a magic white light…nope. Sabina could *not* imagine it.

"Don't hate me," said her mum, hanging up the call. "But…"

"No!" cried Sabina in disappointment. "You have to work now?"

"My new client needs an emergency manicure for a brunch date tomorrow morning. I'm sorry, Sabs. But I don't want to lose this client."

"But you were supposed to give *me* a manicure," said Sabina quietly. She didn't want to sound needy, but she'd been looking forward to it. Not just because she missed her time with her mum, but because she'd been hoping that if she went to school with amazing nails – albeit school appropriate ones – it might help her make friends. The Leeches always had their nails done and they were the most popular girls in the entire school!

"I know, I'm sorry," apologized her mum, racing to grab her bag. "I'll make it up to you, I promise. And, Sabs, I'm so proud of you for today's episode. I *love* that you're learning more about the chakras at school. You can teach me everything I've forgotten!"

"But I won't be continuing the class," said Sabina. "I mean, it's a paid for extra-curric. There's no point spending money on stretching and breathing when we can do that at home!"

Her mum put her bag down and faced Sabina, suddenly serious. "Sabina, this is a good thing for you to do. You're learning about things I can't teach you, and it helps you connect with your culture."

Sabina's eyes widened in alarm. It hadn't occurred to her that her mum would *want* her to continue the overpriced activity that had led to her humiliation. "But…it's so expensive! And…I love lacrosse!"

Her mum put one hand in the air to silence her. "Sabina Patel. Do not try and out-parent me, your actual parent. I know perfectly well how you feel about lacrosse. And I am not doing late-night manicures for nothing. I can afford it. What's the real reason you don't want to do this?"

Sabina sighed. Her mum knew her too well. "Fine. I meditated way longer than everyone else and now they all think I'm weird."

"And since when do we care what people think?" asked her mum hotly. "That's no excuse! You are going to learn about the chakras, and you're going to update me on *The Opening of The Third Eye Chakra*. Which means you're signing up for the whole course, no discussion."

Sabina gave up. There was no arguing with her mum when she'd made her mind up like this. "You sound like Diva right now," she said begrudgingly. "She even gave me a crystal to help me open my chakra. Whatever *that* means."

"Oooh, fun! I like the sound of Diva. And it looks like you've got some evening plans of your own now. Don't stay up too late with your crystal!"

Sabina made a face at her mum. "As if!"

Her mum winked at her whilst putting her puffer back on and simultaneously sliding into her trainers. "You never know – you might end up surprising yourself. Love you—"

"Infinity," finished Sabina reluctantly.

The door slammed shut after her mum and the flat suddenly felt empty again. Sabina glanced at the IKEA clock. 8 p.m. She could try and call Ria and Harry? But she had a feeling that five calls a day was definitely over their limit... She could watch more episodes of *A Prom to Die For*. But now she'd guessed who the killer was, she was already over it.

Her eyes landed on her navy blazer, draped over the chair instead of the hook it was meant to be on. Sabina reached into the front pocket for the crystal. It felt oddly satisfying in her hand. Smooth, heavy, cold. Sabina rolled it around, enjoying the sensation of the rock against her skin. It had been beyond mortifying when everyone had looked at her in the meditation class today. But before that had happened, she'd actually been enjoying the meditation. With Diva's guidance, she'd felt even more relaxed than she did when she breathed with her mum.

Maybe she *should* try another chakra meditation now, alone, at home? Her mum had been more positive about it than she'd thought she'd be. And it was something she'd done with Ba when *she* was younger. It might help Sabina feel closer to her mum while she was out. Or at the very least, it would give her something to update her mum on. She could imagine the episode title already: *Sabina and the Crystal Meditation*.

Sabina sat cross-legged on her pillow in front of a candle. She held the crystal in her right palm, hoping this was what Diva meant by "you'll know what to do". She'd googled it but so many different options had come up that she'd been overwhelmed – how was she meant to know whether her crystal needed a moonlight bath or if a specific part of her body was "called to connect with it"? In the end, she'd picked the least weird option she'd seen – to hold it in her hand while she meditated. She had no idea if this was right, but it wasn't like Diva was there to grade her on it. Besides, what was the worst that could happen? It was only breathing.

Sabina began how she always did with her mum – breathing slowly, feeling her bum nestle into the cushion, her knees resting on the floor. Her thoughts gradually began to fade, until even the hard lump of loneliness in her throat started to soften. Her breathing deepened as she focused on her chakras.

She started at the bottom with the red root chakra for safety. She imagined feeling safe and warm. Her mum's arms around her, giving her double love to make up for her lack of a dad. The smell of home-cooked food. A hot cup of tea. The more she felt the feelings, the more the red light at the bottom of her spine grew brighter in her mind's eye, until she could practically feel it throbbing.

Then it was time for the orange one which represented... she couldn't actually remember. Sabina peeked open an eye, unsure whether she should pause for a quick google. But then it came to her. The sacral chakra. For joy. Creativity. Pleasure. Laughing with Harry and Ria. Helping Harry design his Lady Gaga outfit for Halloween. The cakes Ria's mum made them. She felt warm with an orange glow.

Now the solar plexus. Bright yellow in the middle of her body. For power. Self-confidence. Self-esteem. Sabina felt herself grow taller as she remembered how she'd felt winning the "best all-rounder" prize at her old school the year before. Seeing Harry and Ria clapping in the audience. Her mum cheering loudly.

She moved onto the green heart chakra without even thinking. Her body started to vibrate with love for her mum and her best friends. She'd do *anything* for them. She felt tears slide down her cheeks – but they weren't sad tears. They felt natural. Loving. She was so lucky to have the best people in her life. She just wished she got to see them more often...

Then she felt a warmth in her throat for the next chakra. The blue throat chakra. Sabina could almost *see* a blue light in her throat. She didn't understand it, but it was there, glowing bright. The feelings associated with it instantly washed over her. Trust. Honesty. Good communication. All the words made Sabina think of her mum. They were always honest with each other – they told each other everything. And their relationship made her feel safe, happy, strong and loved.

Sabina let the feelings wrap around her in a deep hug, and somehow, she knew that all her other chakras were shining bright. Her eyes were closed, but it was almost like she had light bulbs going down her spine, and five of them were switched on – red, orange, yellow, green and blue.

Sabina moved onto the next chakra – the third eye in the middle of her forehead. A distant voice in her head wanted to giggle at how dramatic the name was. But Sabina was so in the zone that she continued breathing, imagining a bright indigo light switching on in the middle of her eyebrows. She felt her mind completely quieten. There were no memories or thoughts here at this chakra. Just stillness. Sabina suddenly became aware of the crystal in her right hand as it started to *throb* in time to her breath. It no longer felt cool in her hand – it was so warm it almost felt alive! Without knowing what she was doing or why, Sabina found herself lifting her right hand to her forehead. She kept the crystal there, in the middle of her eyebrows, as she continued her meditation.

That was when she felt the crown chakra activate in the top of her head. The final light bulb – it was a mystical violet colour. Sabina could somehow *feel* this pale, violet light heating up the top of her head, just like the other chakras were shining down her spine. But this one was different. Sabina felt the light illuminate brighter than she'd thought possible – she could visualize it even though her eyes were closed – and the light started to trickle out from the top of her head, washing over her, like she was having some kind of magical light shower.

Sabina gasped out loud. This was crazy! She was used to visualizing a bright white light in between her eyebrows when she meditated with her mum, and sometimes it felt warm there. But this chakra meditation was a whole other level! There were seven rainbow-coloured lights shining down her body – from the base of her spine to the top of her head – and they were all glowing brightly.

She could feel all the feelings associated with them too – safety, pleasure, confidence, love, trust, clarity and now, with the crown chakra, connection. She was connected to her mum, Harry and Ria, even Faye and...the Leeches?! Somehow, Sabina felt a connection with every single person she'd ever met, even the ones she found annoying, and the strangest part was that she didn't mind. She felt at peace, knowing there was something connecting her with the whole world, and a slow smile spread across her lips.

Sabina had no idea how long she stayed there, breathing. But it didn't matter because there were no classmates to make fun of her. So she kept going, visualizing all seven bright lights, when she noticed the crystal start to vibrate. In normal circumstances, Sabina would have freaked out. But she felt so zen right now that she wasn't fazed. She already had seven rainbow light bulbs down her spine, so a vibrating crystal on her forehead didn't seem like a big deal. The gentle vibrating buzz of the crystal spread through her whole body, and Sabina felt her body practically humming as it radiated out rainbow lights. This was the most intense meditation she had *ever* done – but it felt amazing. Who knew that breathing could be so powerful?

Eventually, the sensations started to fade. Sabina wasn't sure how much time had passed, but it had to have been over half an hour because she was starting to get cramps in her legs. Slowly, she noticed the vibrations had stopped and the chakra lights had dimmed. Sabina opened her eyes.

Everything was exactly the same as it was when she'd started meditating – her clothes were crumpled on the floor, her homework was on her bed, and her phone was by her side in case Harry and Ria rang – but Sabina felt completely different. Her body was floaty, like she was drifting in space. She glanced at her reflection in the mirror on the wall, and realized she looked different too! Her eyes – boring black eyes that she always wished looked more like her mum's unusual green ones – were alive with colour. There were flecks of shining gold in her irises that she'd never noticed before, and they were catching the light in a way that made them look... beautiful.

In that moment, Sabina suddenly realized how exhausted she was. She collapsed straight into bed, pulled the cosy blanket over her body, and curled up into a ball, warm and happy. She fell asleep almost instantly, not realizing she was still clutching the crystal in her right hand...

Chapter 5

Sabina jerked awake as her alarm blared. She fumbled around for her glasses. She needed them so she could find her phone and turn the alarm off – the same disorganized chain of actions she did every morning. She knew it would be easier to leave her phone and glasses by her bed like a normal person, but 1) she always forgot, and 2) where was the fun in that?

Her fingers brushed against the solid frames of her glasses from underneath her hoody on the stool, and she put them on, still half-asleep. Sabina blinked slowly, searching the room for her phone while her eyes adjusted to the bright light, and when she could see clearly, she gasped aloud.

"Whaaaaat?!"

Sabina rubbed her eyes, making sure she wasn't still dreaming. But no. She was wide awake and there was something *seriously* wrong with her eyes.

Because, somehow, she could see absolutely *everything*. Not just the cosy mess of her room, with its armchair covered in clothes, the bedside table drowning in books, and polaroids of her, Harry and Ria stuck above her bed. She could see SO much more than that – things that no human eye should be able to see!

A minuscule crack on the ceiling she'd never noticed before because it was so minute. A tiny spider crawling across the window on the other side of the room – a really, *really* tiny spider. And a speck of *dirt* on her mirror, which was at least five metres away from her!

This did NOT make sense. She always needed her glasses to see properly – without them, everything was a fuzzy blur, and they helped her see things clearly. Sabina was used to that. What she wasn't used to was the fact that she could see to a level that was practically microscopic!

Everything around her was magnified. The colours, the textures, the outlines. Sabina almost felt dizzy as she moved her eyes around the room, realizing she could see things she'd only normally be able to see if she was right up close to them. She pulled off her glasses, and her vision was the same as it always was. Blurry and fuzzy. But when she put them back on, she could see absolutely everything again. Was this how normal people saw and she'd been missing out all these years? Or had she somehow gained some kind of...super vision?!

"Mum!" Sabina called out, running down to the kitchen.

She paused as she realized she could see every single swirl of the patterned navy wallpaper in the stairway, not to mention the fibres of the carpet. She turned her head to face the front door, and even though it was an entire flight of stairs and hallway away, she could make out every item of clothing draped on the hooks by the door. Which meant she could see her mum's puffer coat was missing.

Sabina walked into the kitchen in resignation, knowing what she'd find before she even looked: her lunchbox filled with dhal, with a Post-it note on top.

Left early for a client. Can't wait to hear about your crystal meditation!! Love you infinity.

Disappointment flooded her body as Sabina picked up the note. She wished her mum was there to help her. But all she had was this yellow piece of paper with a tea stain on it.

As she moved to put the Post-it back down on the counter, some kind of electric current ran through every cell of her body. Sabina froze in shock, still clutching the note in her hand as the odd sensation started to fade. She didn't move, but everything in front of her *did.* The bowl of fruit on the kitchen counter started spinning and then so did the counter, the stove, and the entire room – until suddenly everything around Sabina whirled faster and faster into a blur! She held her breath in terror, gripping the note tight, until finally, everything stopped moving.

But Sabina was no longer in the kitchen. She was...

standing on the street right outside Beauties! She recognized the white and purple sign that she'd helped her mum select, and the colourful display of nail polishes in the window. Sabina yelped in shock. This couldn't be happening! One second ago she was in the kitchen, in her pyjamas, but now she was in those very same pyjamas, standing on the side of the road!

Just then her mum walked out of the salon in her puffer coat, holding her shiny leather handbag. Sabina's heart sank in relief – her mum was there. Everything would be fine now. She raced over to her, calling out: "Mum!"

But her mum didn't turn around. She didn't react, not even when Sabina waved her arms wildly. It was like she couldn't see Sabina. She simply continued her walk to her car, smiling to herself as she pulled her favourite egg mayo sandwich out of her bag. When she reached her red Ford Fiesta, the smile dropped off her face. She reached out for something yellow on the car's windscreen and cried out in dismay. She was holding a parking ticket.

Sabina blinked, and found herself back in the kitchen, standing bare-footed, still holding her mum's note. She steadied herself against the counter. WHAT had just happened?! Had she given herself some kind of electric shock? But she hadn't touched anything electric – just the note. And why had she imagined her mum getting a parking ticket? It wasn't like it was a memory – she'd never seen that before in real life! Had she been dreaming? It was such a strange thing to dream about. And it had felt so *real*...

Sabina shook her head, simultaneously noticing and ignoring a shrivelled-up pea on the floor, poking out from underneath the bin on the other side of the kitchen (something she *never* would have been able to see before this morning). She had no idea what was going on. But there had to be a rational explanation. She was probably sleep-deprived. Or dehydrated. Or both. She simply needed to have breakfast, shower and get to school. By then, she was sure that everything would be normal again.

Sabina had been at school for two hours and things were very much *not* normal. She could still see things she didn't want to see in absolute detail – like the tiny pus-filled pimple on the corner of Mr Grant's face that had throbbed throughout his assembly, and the meme that Ms Baker had sent her friend when she was meant to be teaching them geography. Her phone screen was angled towards them, but it was so far away nobody would have been able to see what was on her screen – except Sabina. She could fully see the picture of the cat with a phone that said *If cats could text you, they wouldn't*. And she couldn't stop thinking about how weird it had been when she'd seen her mum getting a parking ticket. It hadn't been a normal daydream or even a memory – it had genuinely felt like she'd been transported to the street, watching her mum in real-time. Sabina could have sworn she'd even felt the chill of the wind...

She'd messaged her mum just to check it had all been a figment of her imagination. She hadn't wanted to freak her out so instead of asking if she'd happened to see Sabina standing in her pyjamas by her car, she'd asked how her day was going. Her mum still hadn't replied.

"So, I thought I'd give you all a surprise quiz," said Ms Baker, who had decided to stop sending memes and start teaching again. "Multiple choice, focusing on the different types of erosion."

The whole class groaned and Sabina crashed right back to reality. This was not good news. She couldn't remember a *thing* about erosion, and judging by the faces around her, she wasn't the only one. Actually, that wasn't true. Faye was sitting upright, a look of focused determination on her face, as though she was getting ready for a battle she knew she'd win. But the Leeches were making gagging gestures at each other, which was more in line with how Sabina felt.

"Here you go," said Ms Baker, handing out the sheets. "You have ten minutes – you'll be glad to know it's a short quiz! In silence, please."

Sabina looked at her sheet, panic rising in her chest. She couldn't fail geography – her mum would be so disappointed in her. She picked up the sheet to turn it over so she could begin – but before she could put it down, her entire body jerked with an electric jolt. It was the *exact* sensation she'd had in the kitchen!

Everything around her started whirling; the desks, her classmates, even the classroom walls. And then, finally, it all slowed down. Sabina opened her eyes in trepidation to see if she was back outside her mum's salon. But she wasn't. She was still in the geography classroom. To her relief, she saw that nothing had changed.

Except, as she looked back down at her quiz, she realized that it *had*! Her sheet was no longer blank. It was filled out – in her *own* writing. And someone had already corrected it! The sheet was full of purple marks explaining that the diagram showed "attrition" not "abrasion". And it was "hydraulic action" when water smashed into the riverbeds – not "wave action". Sabina inhaled sharply as she scanned the entire sheet, taking in the answers. She didn't understand. Had Ms Baker given her someone else's completed quiz by mistake? But it had been blank a moment ago – and the wrong answers were in her own writing!

Sabina blinked in confusion, and suddenly, her sheet was empty again! She gripped the edges of the desk in fear. Was she losing her mind?! She looked around to see if anyone else was having a similar experience, but they were all focused on their quizzes. Sabina swallowed as she realized her new improved eyesight meant she could clearly see their answers!

Alicia turned to her with narrowed eyes. Sabina quickly glanced away so she wouldn't get accused of cheating.

Instead, she faced the window, looking out at the headteacher's house, and the green fields stretching way into the distance. Katniss Evermean was sunning herself in the middle of a field, looking like a total queen. She'd caught a tiny fly, ripped its wings apart and was happily munching on them from her paws.

Eww! Sabina shuddered, then paused. It was NOT normal to be able to see Katniss eating a tiny fly when there were three fields and a car park between them!

She forced herself to breathe slowly, trying to calm down. There had to be an explanation for this. Maybe something had happened to her glasses that was affecting her sight? Though that couldn't explain the weird electric jolts... Let alone the fact that she'd just seen her corrected geography quiz! The only explanation that made sense was that she was officially losing her mind. But even if that was true, she couldn't hand in an empty quiz or she'd end up in detention. There was no way Ms Baker would accept "sorry, I lost my mind" as a legitimate reason for why she hadn't even tried to answer a single question of the quiz. So Sabina picked up her pen and copied down the answers she'd just seen written in purple pen on her sheet...

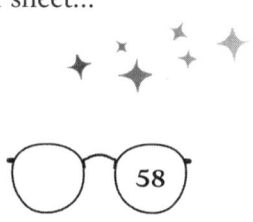

"Hello? Earth to Sabina!" Faye waved her hand at Sabina in the hallway.

"Oh, sorry. Hi, Faye." Sabina was still in a daze. When Ms Baker had asked them to mark each other's tests, she'd ended up getting one hundred per cent! She hadn't known a thing about erosion, but because those correct answers had somehow appeared on her sheet, she'd been the best in the class.

"Congrats on your geography quiz," said Faye. "It's not often somebody beats me. But my 90% is a reminder to not get complacent."

"Right," said Sabina, a guilty twinge in her stomach. She hadn't *meant* to cheat, but she hadn't exactly been able to un-remember all the answers she'd seen moments earlier.

"So...what do you think of my petition?" asked Faye, thrusting her iPad into Sabina's face.

Sabina obediently read the bold typeface: *Petition for MG's Science Department to Finally Teach Year Eight Everything About the Incredible Female Scientists Who Changed the World (and the TRUTH About the Male Ones Who Made It Worse)*.

"Um...it's quite long. Maybe you could condense it a bit?"

"I meant what do you think of the *content*? It's part of my campaign to become Form Prefect! You do agree with it, right?"

"Sure," replied Sabina. Then she remembered that if she wanted Faye to be her friend, she'd need to say something more impressive. "You know...we actually learned about Marie Curie in my old school! She sounded really cool."

"She was. But what about Margaret Sanger, the nurse who founded the birth control movement? Or NASA pioneer Katherine Johnson?"

"They...also sound cool?"

"We need to learn about them," said Faye passionately. "And we need to learn that men like Alexander Graham Bell—"

"The guy who invented the phone!" cried Sabina, grateful to finally recognize one of the names that Faye was referencing. She held up her phone with a grateful smile. "Thank God for him!"

"Thank *God* for the man who tried to ban sign language because he thought deaf people should try harder to be normal?!" Faye's eyes almost popped out of her face. "The man who thought deaf people shouldn't marry other deaf people because he was scared they'd give birth to more deaf people?" She took a deep breath. "Look, I know he cared about deaf people in his own way, and his wife and mum were deaf, but he also saw them as 'defective'! He was so against sign language that he stigmatized it for generations to come!"

Sabina swallowed, taken aback by the impromptu history lesson. "I'll...sign the petition."

Faye smiled triumphantly as Sabina scrawled her signature onto the iPad, before immediately going off to corner another group of unassuming students on their way to lunch. Sabina shook her head as she paused at the water fountain. She still felt dizzy. She wasn't sure if it was because she could literally see every hair follicle on everyone's head, or because she kept getting these weird visions. But she did know that none of it was conducive to her fitting in at MG and making friends.

Friends! That was what she needed. Harry and Ria would know *exactly* what to do!

She pulled out her phone despite her now very conflicted thoughts about its inventor, ready to message in the group chat. But before she could, she saw a message from her mum.

> Thanks for asking Sabs, but my day is officially a disaster. Just popped out with my sandwich and – look! ☹☹☹

There was an image accompanying it.

Sabina's breath tightened as she tapped open a photo to see her mum's red Ford Fiesta parked on the street outside her salon. With a bright yellow parking ticket on the windscreen.

Chapter 6

Sabina was following the mass of students into the canteen when she felt a jolt along the right side of her body. She froze, praying she wasn't about to get *another* weird vision. But when nothing started spinning, she realized she'd simply bumped into her English teacher.

"Oh, sorry, Mrs Fairweather!" she cried out in relief. "I was, um…"

"In your own world, it seems," remarked her teacher. "I hope you've prepared a spontaneous soliloquy for our class this afternoon?"

Sabina stared at her in confusion. "But…I thought we didn't have to prepare anything if they're spontaneous."

Her teacher raised a brow. "Sabina. Everyone will have prepared *something*. The spontaneity is more for added flourishes. I thought everyone knew that."

Sabina's heart sank. She was trying so hard to keep on top of everything, but it felt like there was a hidden system of doing things at MG that she didn't know about. Now she was probably going to end up doing the worst spontaneous soliloquy Mrs Fairweather had ever heard.

Mrs Fairweather tapped Sabina's shoulder, making her jump. "Would you mind passing me a tray? I can't resist when there's tiramisu for dessert!"

Sabina nodded, her chest tightening at the thought of humiliating herself with an awful soliloquy in front of the whole class. She was engrossed in her fears when she reached for the stack of trays and picked one up. Suddenly, her entire body jerked with a tingling sensation. She clutched the tray tight as she realized, to her dismay, that this time she *was* about to have a vision!

Everything around her whirled until she wasn't in the canteen any more. She was in the toilets with Mrs Fairweather. Only, they weren't the normal girls' toilets. The walls were pale pink instead of off-white, and there were actual soap dishes by the sinks, instead of plastic soap dispensers and the mirrors were framed by fancy light bulbs. Sabina's eyes widened in horror as she realized they were in the *staff toilets*. She would definitely get detention for being in there!

But...Mrs Fairweather didn't seem to notice that Sabina was there. She was too busy clutching her stomach and racing into a toilet cubicle. She locked herself inside, groaning loudly, then made a series of explosive sounds that left Sabina with no doubt that her teacher was currently experiencing a very bad bout of diarrhoea. Sabina gagged – gross!

Just then the bathroom door opened. Sabina tried to hide, but before she could lock herself into a cubicle, Ms Baker walked in. She looked right at Sabina but clearly couldn't see her. Instead, she called out to the cubicle that Mrs Fairweather was in.

"Mary, are you in there? Your English class are waiting for you. And they're not being very quiet about it."

"Sorry," gasped Mrs Fairweather. "I'm going to be here a while. I shouldn't have had the...tiramisu." There was another loud sound of Mrs Fairweather expelling her bowels, and Ms Baker wrinkled her nose at the accompanying smell. "I really should pay more attention to my dairy allergies."

"I'll...put a film on for them," said Ms Baker, quickly backing out of the room.

That was when Sabina blinked and found herself right back in the canteen clutching Mrs Fairweather's tray.

"Well?" asked Mrs Fairweather, holding out her hand impatiently. "Come on, Sabina. That tiramisu is calling out for me."

Sabina hesitated. "Um. Maybe you shouldn't have the tiramisu?"

Mrs Fairweather glared at her. "I know I've put on a few pounds lately, but what I eat is my prerogative."

"No!" squeaked Sabina in horror. She couldn't believe her teacher thought she was body shaming her. "That wasn't what I meant! I just..."

But Mrs Fairweather plucked the tray right out of Sabina's limp fingers, and walked off, shaking her head. "Students, honestly."

Sabina was left standing alone in the middle of the canteen wondering what on EARTH had just happened.

"Hey, Sabrina!" The Leeches walked up to Sabina with wide smiles on their fully made-up faces. They were both wearing patterned ribbons in their hair – Alicia's was pink and Felicia's was blue – and looked like they were on a mission. Alicia nudged Felicia sharply.

"We saw you signed Faye's petition," said Felicia. "We wanted to check that we're, uh, I mean, that Leesh is still getting your vote?"

Sabina forced herself to act normal. "I'm...still deciding. There's still time, right?"

"We vote in exactly one week," replied Felicia. "Next Wednesday morning in the school hall!"

"We totally understand you're taking your time," said Alicia smoothly. "Democracy is super important. But we wanted to remind you that if I win, I will be having a massive celebratory party. At my house, in our indoor pool. There'll be caterers. Vegan, obvs."

Sabina's eyes widened. Alicia had an indoor pool? Her new

classmates really were nothing like her old ones.

"It's going to be the party of the year," said Felicia eagerly. "You can't miss it. Alexis is going to DJ – she's amazing. I bet it will be better than the Winter Ball!"

Alicia frowned. "You can't compare my party with the Winter Ball. They're completely different events, Leesh."

"I know, I just meant they're both major! And yours comes first!"

"True," acknowledged Alicia. "Technically, they'll both be my parties anyway. As Form Prefect, I get to add the finishing touches to the Winter Ball!"

"What's the Winter Ball?" asked Sabina.

Both Leeches stared at her like she was an alien.

"Are you kidding?" asked Alicia finally. "The Winter Ball is *the* most important thing that happens at MG. It's basically our prom. But *bigger*. Think mocktails, a live band and couture dresses. It's even more high-profile than the Summer Ball."

"And we get to take dates," said Felicia eagerly. "They can be from Marlstone Boys' school – or in my case, Marlstone Girls'!"

Sabina's heart sank. She knew this was not a normal response to hearing about a very cool prom. But school dances were only fun if you had people to go with. And this one, where people took *dates,* would just prove how uncool and friendless Sabina Patel really was.

"When is it?" she asked, trying to work out if she'd have enough time to make a friend by then.

"Two weeks on Saturday!" cried Felicia. "Where have you been? There are posters everywhere!" She gestured to a black poster on the wall, with white avant-garde letters that spelled out *Saturday 5th December – be ready*.

"Oh, I wondered what those were for! Why don't they say 'Winter Ball'?"

Alicia rolled her eyes. "They don't need to. It's the event of the term. Other than my FP party, of course."

Sabina sighed, trying to keep track of it all. "There are *so* many events at MG."

Alicia smiled smugly. "We are a very active school. It's why there's such a long wait list for people to get in. You're lucky that Amelia Barnes got pneumonia."

Sabina paled. *That* was why there was an opening at MG?!

"Oh, she's fine now," said Felicia. "But she can't come to the Winter Ball – it's for existing students only. She's devastated. Her new school only does one ball a year – can you imagine?"

"Anyway, we'll see you in English," said Alicia. "We need to go prep our spontaneous soliloquies."

"You might not need to," said Sabina without thinking, glancing over to the teachers' table where Mrs Fairweather was eating a giant serving of tiramisu. "I think we'll be watching a movie today."

Alicia's eyes narrowed. "What? How do you know that? I haven't heard anything and I'm basically acting Form Prefect!"

Sabina realized her mistake. "Uh…just a…feeling? Anyway, I need to, um, make a call! Sorry."

The Leeches frowned as Sabina rushed away, clearly unused to someone ending a conversation with them. Harry had said she could only call during lunch if it was a real emergency, but she was pretty sure that witnessing her English teacher get diarrhoea counted. Especially considering she'd seen it in *an imaginary vision in her head!*

Chapter 7

Sabina smiled to herself as Mercutio was murdered on-screen. But she'd barely even registered the death of Romeo's bestie – she was too busy reliving her conversation with Harry and Ria. She'd finally managed to tell her best friends everything, and she felt *so* much better for it.

They had admittedly been concerned when she'd told them about her super sight. And that she'd been getting visions that transported her onto the other side of the village and into the staff toilets. But by the time she'd reached the end of her story and explained that everything she'd seen had come true in some way or another, they'd both calmed down.

"It sounds to me like you're just having a really intuitive day," Ria had said. "You know, tapped into everyone around you."

"I think it's probably in your head," Harry added. "Maybe you slept weird?"

"I actually slept amazingly," Sabina replied. "I meditated beforehand."

"See?" Ria cried. "It made you super connected to people! You're sensing what's happening to them."

"Or it's some kind of subconscious thing," Harry suggested. "My brother's learning about it in psychology. Maybe your subconscious already knew your teacher had a dairy allergy. And that your mum is so stressed she'd park badly. And some part of you even remembered the geography answers from before!"

"It's probably a combination of that *and* the energy stuff," Ria said knowingly. "But either way, you'll be back to normal before you know it."

"Totally," Harry agreed. "And you should go to the opticians too. A new prescription will sort you out. Ooh, maybe we can go glasses shopping again?"

Sabina had felt a million times better once they'd hung up. If Harry and Ria didn't think she was losing her mind, then maybe whatever was happening was just a blip. Now that she was safe in the English classroom watching a boring Shakespeare movie, she could almost believe that her overactive imagination had exaggerated things. That had to be it – Sabina refused to believe it was anything else.

Finally, the bell rang. Sabina jumped up, desperate to go home so she could fall asleep and wake up normal again. She gathered up her unopened books as her classmates chattered loudly. Normally, she felt lonely hearing everyone talking about their evening plans, but today, she was so full from her recent chat with Harry and Ria that she didn't mind.

"So how DID you know we'd be watching a movie today?" Alicia and Felicia appeared by Sabina's side.

Sabina froze, unsure how to respond. There was no way she could tell the Leeches about her weird visions. "Um…Mrs Fairweather. She…ate a tiramisu. And she has dairy allergies."

Alicia's eyebrows raised in intrigue. "She does? This is useful intel."

Sabina nodded, encouraged. "I figured it would make her sick so she wouldn't be able to teach."

"Sick like throwing up?" asked Felicia.

"Sick like diarrhoea," corrected Sabina.

The Leeches burst into peals of giggles, and Sabina couldn't help joining in. It was kind of funny.

"That is HILARIOUS," shrieked Alicia, looking at Sabina with newfound respect. "You figured out Mrs F got diarrhoea!"

"You're like Sherlock Holmes," said Felicia.

Alicia frowned. "Did you do some kind of sleuthing to get full marks in geography too?"

Sabina's laughter instantly died. "Um, no. I…should go."

She quickly turned away from the Leeches, shoving the rest of her things into her bag. She couldn't deal with this level of scrutiny – not when something so weird was happening to her. And it wasn't like this was the *only* weird thing that had happened lately. The day before, she'd zoned

out in Diva's class, making everyone laugh at her. And in her crystal meditation the night before, her body had literally lit up and vibrated!

Wait. That wasn't connected to what was happening to her now, was it?!

"Alexis is *dying* about Mrs F getting diarrhoea," said Felicia, typing fervently on her phone. "She's already told the whole lacrosse team!"

Sabina looked up, instantly distracted from her thoughts. Felicia was telling people? This was not good. She needed to focus on damage control with the Leeches, not thinking about last night. Besides, meditation was totally harmless – its only side effect was relaxation.

"You told the lacrosse team?" she asked.

"Technically Alexis did," said Felicia.

"But we're telling people too," added Alicia. "This is amazing gossip – it would be a crime not to."

"Okay, but...can you please not mention me?" asked Sabina. She wanted people at MG to know who she was – but not if it meant them finding out she imagined teachers in the toilet! And she *really* didn't want to think about how much trouble she'd be in if Mrs Fairweather found out she was behind a rumour like this!

"Don't worry, it's chill," said Alicia, sliding her phone away. "So, what *was* going on in geography? You looked kind of strange during the test."

Sabina grabbed her bag. "Nothing! Sorry, got to go!" She rushed past the Leeches, her arm accidentally brushing against Alicia's blazer. A familiar shock ran through Sabina's body. She inhaled, desperately praying to not have another vision.

But everything began spinning rapidly, until Sabina found herself standing outside the main school hall. There was loud music coming from inside, and there were people everywhere. Girls in long silk dresses, boys in tuxedos. They all looked like adults!

Sabina turned in a daze, looking at the twinkling fairy lights decorating the hall. What was happening?! Just then, Alicia – dressed in an incredible gold shimmery dress – sashayed past her, on the arm of a handsome tall boy. Sabina gasped as she realized who he was: Dillon Valia. Everyone knew of him – even Sabina. He went to Marlstone Boys' School and he was a model, which meant he had 900,000 TikTok followers and EVERYONE fancied him. He was half Indian with golden brown skin and dappled green eyes that were currently fixed on Alicia, who was glowing under his gaze.

They were standing next to her, but neither of them could see Sabina in her uniform – which was no different to a normal day at MG.

"You're so funny, Dillon!" giggled Alicia. "I'm so glad you asked me to come to the Winter Ball with you! Let's go dance!"

Sabina's eyes widened in recognition – *this* was the famous

Winter Ball! And Alicia's date was Dillon Valia!

"What about your friend?" asked Dillon, pointing to the corner. "Is she...okay?"

Alicia and Sabina both glanced over to see Felicia in a bright pink ballgown, sobbing loudly and clutching onto Alexis, who was trying to prise Felicia's fingers off her arm. Sabina stared in surprise; she'd thought that Felicia and Alexis were super in love, but right now, Alexis looked like she wanted to be anywhere but there!

Alicia shrugged. "They're always breaking up. Come on!"

Sabina blinked and found herself back inside the classroom. She was so shocked that she couldn't stop herself from blurting out: "Dillon Valia asked you to go to the Winter Ball?!"

Alicia shrieked. "Oh my God! He wants to go with me! How do you know? Tell me everything!"

Oh no. Sabina realized there was no way to explain what she'd seen without sounding completely and utterly insane. Even if it was her subconscious, the fact that it had recreated an entire scene in her mind was *seriously* strange – especially when it was of a Winter Ball she'd never been to! How could her mind even have imagined it when Hackney High's annual school disco had taken place in the gym with a few bowls of crisps and a teacher's phone plugged into the speakers?

"Um...I don't? Sorry. I've been...meaning to ask you? Out of, um, curiosity?"

Alicia frowned, until a look of understanding spread over

her face. "Oh my God, bless you! Do you *like* Dillon? Because I totally get that. But I can't imagine him and…you."

Sabina flushed. "No, it's not that! I swear!"

"They *are* both Indian," pointed out Felicia.

"God, Felicia, don't be so provincial! You don't have to be the same colour as someone to date them!"

"I know that, Leesh! Why did you just full-name me?"

Sabina saw her opportunity to leave. "I should go – bye!" She raced past them, desperate to get away. She didn't want to think about any of it – she just wanted everything to go back to normal.

"Mum, you're here!" Sabina wrapped her arms tight around her. She was so glad to find her at home, even if she was stirring something ominous on the stove.

"Careful!" reprimanded her mum. "I'm making a sweet potato and lentil stew I saw on the internet. Though theirs didn't look quite so brown…"

"It doesn't matter, I'm sure it'll be delicious," lied Sabina. "I'm *so* glad you're here! I have so much to tell you!"

"Me too," replied her mum, squeezing her arm. "I *really* need a relaxing evening at home with you! Today was a lot – especially with that parking ticket."

Sabina bit her lip. "That's one of the things I want to talk to you about…"

"Oh, it was my fault, really. I should have been more careful, but..." Her mum sniffed and to Sabina's horror, tears appeared in her eyes! "It's just such a lot to pay for a silly mistake. All the money I earned last night is gone now – it's such a waste."

"Oh, Mum!" cried out Sabina. "Don't be sad!"

Her mum quickly patted her eyes dry. "Don't worry, darling, I'm just tired. Long day. I'll be fine after a night in. Now – what did you want to talk to me about?"

Sabina looked away, trying not to overthink the fact she could see every tiny thread that made up the midnight-blue curtains, including a subtle woven pattern she had honestly never seen before. She didn't want to add to her mum's problems – not when she was already on the verge of tears. Harry and Ria were right; she was probably just having a weird day and would be back to normal tomorrow. There was no point stressing her mum out.

"Nothing much," said Sabina brightly. "I wondered if we could go to the opticians soon? I think I need a new prescription."

A look of apprehension flashed across her mum's face, and Sabina knew she was thinking about the cost. Thank goodness she hadn't confided in her about her visions! If a pair of new glasses made her look this worried, then who knew how she'd respond to what her daughter was *really* going through!

"Of course," said her mum. "Also...I was thinking maybe

we could do our breathing ritual, if you'd like? Or 'meditating', as you call it now."

Sabina hesitated as she remembered her intense meditation the night before. And suddenly, her earlier fears flooded back into her mind. What if her meditation *did* have something to do with her eyesight and visions? It didn't seem particularly likely, but she couldn't ignore the fact that everything had gone wrong the morning after she'd meditated with Diva's crystal.

The *crystal*!

What had Diva said to her when she'd given it to her? Something about the amethyst helping to open up her third eye chakra. Sabina's heart pounded as she desperately tried to remember what that chakra represented. It wasn't love, that was the heart one... Or communication, because that was the throat. And connection was the top one.

The third eye was...insight! And intuition. Diva had said it was about *seeing things clearly.*

Sabina froze. Her biggest problem right now was that she could see too much – things that hadn't even happened yet; things that no human eye should be able to see!

Could the crystal have done this? Sabina forced herself to think of exactly what Diva had said. She'd told Sabina that her third eye was close to opening – and then she'd said something about how the crystal could help her unlock her powers.

Powers! Could *this* be what was happening to her? Had the crystal unlocked her third eye chakra and given her powers that made her see things way too clearly?!

"Hello? Earth to Sabina?" asked her mum, waving a wooden spoon at her. Sabina could see a tiny crack in the middle of the spoon, even though her mum was on the other side of the kitchen. "Are you all right?"

Sabina tried to ignore the mild panic throbbing through her body. Nobody would ever want to be her friend now! The only person who'd want to speak to her would be Faye – and that would only be to turn Sabina into her science project!

She quicky shook her thoughts away so she could fake normality for her mum. "Sorry, all good! I'm just...distracted."

"Well in that case, it sounds like you really do need a meditation!" remarked her mum. "Shall we do one now? I need to leave the stew a bit longer anyway."

Sabina didn't know what to do. Everything in her was telling her to never, ever meditate again. If meditating with the crystal had caused her problems, it made sense to avoid them both for the rest of her life.

But – what if she could *undo* it all by meditating again? If she had unlocked her chakra by meditating with the crystal, then maybe if she meditated with it again, she could lock it back up? It wasn't exactly a foolproof plan – but it was the only one she had right now.

Sabina decided to risk it. She took a deep breath as she

faced her mum. "Okay. I'm ready. Let's do this. I'll…go and get my crystal."

"What's with all the dramatics?" asked her mum. "It's only a bit of meditating!"

Sabina looked at her seriously. "Meditating might be the most dramatic thing I have done in my entire life. Wish me luck."

Her mum shook her head in amusement as Sabina left the room. "Teenagers!"

Chapter 8

The next day, Sabina stared glumly at her reflection in the bright lights of the school bathroom. The meditation hadn't worked. She'd done it with her mum exactly like she had the night before. She'd even brought the crystal to her forehead when she got to the third eye chakra, and it had vibrated. It hadn't been *as* intense as the first time, but it had felt close enough. Sabina had gone to sleep hoping that when she woke in the morning, she'd finally be back to normal. Her chakras would be closed again, and the powers would be gone for good.

But when Sabina had woken up and put her glasses on, she'd instantly noticed a gossamer-thin spider web hanging in the furthest corner of her ceiling. If she'd had any remaining doubts that she still had her super sight, it had been confirmed in morning assembly when she'd seen Mr Grant's pimple from the back of the hall (he'd clearly tried to squeeze it, and it had left an angry red mark that resembled a still-active volcano). Not to mention how she'd suddenly become the class badminton champion in games, even though she'd never been able to hit the shuttlecock before. Now, she could see it so vividly that it was impossible *not* to hit it. Nobody understood how she'd suddenly got so good. Least of all, Sabina.

She scrunched up her face at her reflection. Being able to see every tiny pore as though she was looking at her skin through a magnifying glass was not helping her feel better. She didn't know what to do. Her super sight was still there, and even though she hadn't experienced a vision since she'd seen the Winter Ball, Sabina didn't know if that meant they'd stopped for ever – or if she was just being given a morning off.

"Found her!"

The bathroom door burst open to reveal the Leeches. They had both teased their hair into high ponytails and were wearing large hoop earrings, though Alicia also had a sparkly clip on the side of her hair. Sabina noticed Felicia glance at it longingly before she turned back to face her.

"We've been looking everywhere for you," said Felicia accusingly.

"For the vote? I'm...still deciding, sorry."

"Forget the vote," said Alicia, her blue eyes gleaming. "I'm here to talk about Dillon Valia. My official date for the Winter Ball, as of this morning."

Sabina's eyes widened. "He...asked you out?"

"Oh yes," confirmed Alicia. "At the bus stop in front of *everyone.* Well, not you. But everyone who lives on the nice side of the village."

"It was EPIC," added Felicia. "He asked Alicia out with a personalized dance and his friend filmed the whole thing. It's gone viral already."

Alicia shrugged nonchalantly. "It was cute. But..." Her eyes settled determinedly on Sabina's. "You knew that already, didn't you?"

"What...do you mean?" Sabina's voice faltered.

"You knew I'd go to the dance with him. In the same way you knew that Mrs F would get diarrhoea. And how you knew all those geography answers. I saw what happened in the quiz when you touched the sheet and your face went blank before you suddenly wrote down the answers. Your face did the exact same thing when you touched my blazer, *then* you wanted to know if Dillon had asked me to the Winter Ball."

Sabina paled. The Leeches were close to figuring out her secret. But she couldn't let them – it would be social suicide! She'd *never* make a single friend if people found out about her powers! She wouldn't even just be "the new girl" any more – she'd be "the seriously weird new girl". Those were adjectives that Sabina did *not* want added to her epithet.

"We've figured it all out," said Felicia proudly, as Sabina's heart raced in panic.

"Figured...what out?" she asked in a strangled voice, immediately regretting her question. She didn't want to give the Leeches the impression that she was hiding something. She quickly forced herself to laugh casually. "I mean, there's nothing *to* figure out! I just get a blank look on my face when I'm thinking. It's totally embarrassing."

"Oh really?" asked Alicia. "Because you didn't get it on your face when you were looking at the geography test – only when you touched it."

Sabina tried to raise an eyebrow nonchalantly. Why had the Leeches been *analysing* her during the quiz?! "It's weird you noticed that," she said, hoping it would threw them off her scent.

"Not as weird as you *doing* it," snapped back Alicia. "You know when you get that blank look, your eyes roll back into your face. It's creepy."

"It's exactly how you looked in the meditation when you were the only one still meditating!" chirped up Felicia.

Sabina gulped. She needed to stop the Leeches from thinking about her meditating – they were getting way too close to the truth. "Um, yeah. I'd...better go. Don't want to be late for physics!"

"Not yet," said Alicia, stepping forward to block Sabina from leaving. "We know your secret. And we need you to do it for us."

Her heart practically stopped. "I...don't know what you mean."

"Spell it out for her, Leesh," commanded Alicia.

Felicia nodded efficiently. "Sabrina. We know you're psychic and we need you to tell us the future."

Sabina made a choked sound. The Leeches *knew*.

Even she hadn't used that word to describe what was going on for her – she'd just thought of her problem as "powers". But...weren't the Leeches right? Psychics saw the future. And...so did Sabina. Like when she'd seen her mum get a parking ticket before it happened. And the geography answers that were filled out and marked. Mrs Fairweather's dairy problems. It did still remain to be seen whether Alicia would go to the dance with Dillon while Felicia and Alexis broke up next to her, but given his prom-posal, it now looked likely...

"It's not true," she said weakly. "That's crazy! There's no such thing as psychics!"

"There are loads on TikTok," said Alicia. "Leesh and I follow some. Once we used my dad's credit card to call one in Florida. That's how I recognized the expression on your face when you had a vision. But now we don't need to use them ever again. Because we have you!"

Sabina shook her head quickly. "No! I'm not psychic! I'm just..." She tried to think of what Harry and Ria had said. "Intuitive!"

Alicia scoffed. "Don't lie to us, Sabina. We've figured it out. And we need you to predict the future for us, so I know if I'll be Form Prefect."

"I can't!" said Sabina. This couldn't be happening. She wasn't even a real psychic! She was just...a girl with a crystal and seriously bad luck!

"Believe in yourself!" said Felicia. "Of course you can, you're a psychic!"

"I'm not!" protested Sabina.

"Then prove it," said Alicia calmly. She clicked her fingers and Felicia pulled a piece of paper out of her bag. It was Alicia's Form Prefect flier. "Touch this and see if you can see the future or not. That's how all psychics get their visions – by touching things."

"That's not true," said Sabina, backing away into the corner of the bathroom, desperately wishing she was *anywhere* but there.

"But didn't you get your vision about Alicia and Dillon when you touched her blazer?" asked Felicia. "And your geography results when you touched the quiz?"

Sabina hesitated. She'd seen her mum's parking ticket when she touched the note from her. And she'd seen Mrs Fairweather in the bathroom when she touched her tray. Were the Leeches right?

"Touch it," demanded Alicia. "It's the only way to prove you're not lying to us."

Sabina's heart was thudding. She really didn't want to touch it. If she got a vision in front of the Leeches, they'd know the truth. Her life would be more over than it already was.

But...their theory didn't make total sense. She touched things all the time and didn't get visions. She was literally touching her school bag right now and nothing was happening. She hoped this meant the Leeches were wrong. But she knew that either way, she had to touch the flier. There was no way the Leeches would leave her alone until she'd shown them she wasn't a psychic.

So, trying to look more confident than she felt, Sabina slowly reached her hand out to touch the flier. The second her fingertips touched the sharp paper edge, her entire body jerked and a shock ran through her veins. Oh no – it was happening! Everything around her revolved rapidly, spinning and whirling, until she wasn't in the bathroom any more.

She was in the assembly hall, and Mr Grant was speaking.

"...and so now we'll move on to the results for Year Eight. It was a very close race, but we do have a winner for Form Prefect." There was a dramatic pause as he looked around the room. Sabina's super sight meant she could see that his spot had faded, but it had left a dark red scar that was covered in something powdery and flesh-coloured. She grimaced as she realized he'd tried – and failed – to hide it with concealer. "And so, please welcome to the stage, the new Year Eight Form Prefect...Alicia Johnson!"

The entire hall erupted into applause and Sabina turned to see Alicia beaming as she strode down the aisle like it was a catwalk, waving regally at the room. Sabina blinked in shock and found herself right back in the bathroom, with the Leeches beaming at her.

"You did it!" cried Felicia. "You had a psychic vision!"

Alicia's eyes danced. "What did you see? Tell us EVERYTHING."

Sabina breathed heavily, wondering if she could run out of the bathroom. But the Leeches were blocking the exit and she was backed into the corner. "Um...nothing...I don't...I need..."

Alicia held up a warning hand. "Breathe," she ordered.

Sabina was startled into obeying, inhaling and exhaling through her nose. It helped.

"Now, tell us what you saw," said Alicia. "*All* of it." Sabina hesitated, trying to think of a way to lie her way out of this. But Alicia's eyes flashed. "Don't even think of pretending you didn't see the future – you got your weird look again. Your eyes went all funny."

Sabina's stomach sank. Her secret was out. And if the Leeches knew, it wouldn't be long before the *entire* school knew. Would her mum let her move school again? There had to be another one nearby. There was no way she could stay at MG as "the weird psychic new girl".

"Oh please," begged Felicia. "We're desperate to know! And you can have lunch with us tomorrow if you want!" Alicia frowned and Felicia faltered. "Um, if that's okay, Leesh?"

Alicia's face relaxed back into a smile. "Obvs! I would have suggested it anyway. Come on, Sabrina, tell us. Otherwise...

I'll have to speak to Ms Baker about the geography test. And I'm sure Mrs Fairweather won't be thrilled to hear you've told the whole year about her tiramisu-related diarrhoea."

"No!" cried Sabina. "Please!"

"Sorry," said Alicia, not sounding sorry at all. "You either tell us – or you tell the teachers. Your choice."

Sabina gulped, panic rising in her veins at the thought of trying to explain her visions to the teachers. They'd think she was insane – or maybe they'd think she'd actually followed Mrs F into the staff toilets, and cheated on her quiz! She couldn't bear the thought of getting into trouble and upsetting her mum.

She had no choice but to tell the Leeches the truth. "Okay. But if I tell you, will you promise to keep my secret?"

"We don't do ultimatums," said Alicia, even though they were giving Sabina one right now.

"Just tell us," said Felicia. "We're on your side! We love psychics!"

"Okay," said Sabina reluctantly. As much as she didn't want to, she had to trust the Leeches. "You were right, I had a vision. I...saw Mr Grant announcing the Form Prefect for Year Eight."

"And?!"

"Alicia won."

"EEEEEEEEKKKKK!" The Leeches' squeals were so loud and high-pitched that Sabina had to cover her ears.

"This is the best news EVER," cried Alicia. "Now I can plan

my victory outfit! Yay! We can discuss choices at lunch tomorrow! Bye!" She and Felicia linked arms, blowing Sabina a kiss as they strode back out.

Sabina was left alone, staring at her reflection. She'd thought her life was bad ten minutes ago, but now it was so much worse. She wasn't just a teenage psychic – she was a teenage psychic whose secret had been revealed to the most popular girls in the school. This was a total disaster!

Sabina sat in the maths classroom waiting for their teacher to arrive. She was fifteen minutes early, but she didn't know where else to go. She'd somehow got through physics and then spent all of break trying to call Harry and Ria, but their silence suggested they were stuck in lessons. Or Harry was enforcing his boundaries. Either way, Sabina had been left trying to process her newfound psychic abilities – and the fact that the Leeches knew about them – all on her own.

"Oh hi, Sabina." Faye entered the classroom, nodding at her. "I've come early too. I needed some quiet to work on my campaign."

Sabina felt a wave of guilt wash over her. She felt terrible knowing how hard Faye was working to be Form Prefect when she wouldn't win. "Faye, can I ask you a question?"

"You may, but I can't guarantee I'll answer it."

"Um, okay. Would you...still work so hard on your FP

campaign if you knew Alicia was going to win?"

Faye nodded vigorously. "Of course! I'm doing this to show the school what needs to change around here. Even if Alicia wins, I'll have shown Year Eight the importance of syllabus-based diversity, *and* I've made the canteen staff promise to stop using plastic packaging. That's going to happen whether I win or not – I made them sign a contract."

Sabina grinned. "Of course you did!" Thank goodness Faye wasn't obsessed with winning. And, who knew, maybe Sabina was wrong about Alicia's victory? After all, she'd had a vision of her terribly marked geography exam, but then she'd managed to get full marks in the real one. So perhaps the future could change?

"How are you?" asked Faye, observing her curiously. "You look worried."

Sabina was so surprised that one of her classmates was asking her how she was that she answered honestly. "I am. And stressed and anxious."

"You should talk to someone about that," remarked Faye. "Do you have friends?"

Sabina laughed out loud at Faye's directness. "Um, yes. Not here, obviously, which is probably why you asked... But I have two best friends from my old school."

Faye nodded. "I don't have best friends here either. And having best friends from an old school isn't applicable for me because I've been at MG since I was six."

"Oh." Sabina didn't know what to say. "I'm sorry?"

"If you want to tell me why you're worried, stressed and anxious, then...I have some time now," said Faye. "My campaign can wait."

Sabina paused. She *really* needed someone to talk to, and the thought of having a possible friend in Faye made her feel embarrassing levels of excitement. She might even end up with someone to have lunch with – she was pretty sure the Leeches had already forgotten their offer about tomorrow – and maybe they could go to the Winter Ball together! Besides, out of everyone she'd met so far at MG, Faye was the one person she could see becoming a real friend.

But telling her the truth *would* also mean somebody else at MG knowing about her...situation. Would Faye even WANT to hang out with Sabina once she knew?

"You don't have to though," said Faye, pulling her blazer tightly around her. "I know people can find me weird, and if you're one of them, then that's fine. We can keep our relationship to strictly classmates."

"No way! *I'm* the weird one," burst out Sabina. "I think something's happened to me...something really bad. And I don't know what to do about it."

Faye scrutinized Sabina for a second, as though she was deciding whether to believe her or not. Then she sprang into action, pulling out a notepad and pen. "I'll take notes. Start at the beginning. And don't miss out *a thing.*"

Chapter 9

Sabina paused as she unlocked her front door, suddenly remembering that, like most of the girls at MG, Faye lived on the nice side of the village and might not think too much of the two-bedroom apartment she was about to walk into. "It's...quite small," she said apologetically.

"Good; small is energy efficient," said Faye, pushing past Sabina into the hallway. "Is your mum here?"

Sabina shook her head, quickly following Faye. "She messaged to say she'll be home later. But there's food we can heat up for dinner."

"Great," said Faye. "That gives us the space we need to discuss your alleged psychic powers. I presume you've not confided in your mum?"

Sabina shook her head. "I wanted to. But she's stressed about work so I didn't want to add to her worries."

Faye pulled up a chair at the small kitchen table as though she'd lived there all her life. "Sounds sensible. We can work out exactly what's going on and then consider telling her once we have enough information. Parents tend to over-worry when their children are involved." She looked up at Sabina. "Can I have something to drink, please?"

"Oh, sorry!" Sabina rushed to pour out juice for her and Faye. It had been a while since she'd had a friend round, and she'd had no idea that her pre-maths conversation with Faye would lead to her coming over! But then again, it hadn't exactly been a normal conversation.

Faye had listened attentively to everything Sabina had said, interrupting only to ask questions. She hadn't once revealed what she personally thought of it all – not even asking Sabina if she was serious. She'd just assumed that Sabina was telling the truth and had squeezed as many details out of her as she could before maths. There hadn't been time to finish everything, so, to Sabina's delight, Faye had suggested they continue their conversation at her house after school.

"Thanks," said Faye, taking the juice from Sabina. "So, I think I've got enough information from you to make an initial hypothesis. Want to hear it?"

"Yes, please!" said Sabina, hoping a hypothesis meant she was *finally* going to hear Faye's thoughts.

Faye cleared her throat and flicked through her notepad. "Right. So, the change we are investigating is the fact that you woke up altered on Wednesday morning. When you put your glasses on, you had abnormal super sight, and you started getting psychic visions about the future – some of which have already come true."

Sabina gulped. It sounded so serious when Faye laid it out science-style.

"You have a theory that you've unblocked your third eye chakra and gained psychic powers – powers that Diva alluded to," continued Faye. "And this happened during your crystal meditation on Tuesday night."

"Yes. Do you...think I'm right?" asked Sabina. A tiny part of her was still hoping that none of this was true.

Faye nodded decisively. "Yes."

Sabina's face fell. If Faye thought it was true, it had to be. Her psychic status had been confirmed by science.

Faye was oblivious to Sabina's angst. "Luckily for you, I did loads of research into chakras right after our lesson with Diva. I don't like not knowing things, you see. And I found out that all human beings are believed to have powers deep down – but they never access them because they don't have enough energy. The only way to change that is to strengthen our energy centres – our chakras. It doesn't work for everyone, but a very small percentage of people – like you – are able to unlock their powers!"

Sabina hadn't understood every word of Faye's science speak but she got the last part – she had really bad luck.

"I think your third eye chakra was close to opening – as Diva said – because of all the meditation you did with your mum," continued Faye, in her element. "Anyone could see in class that your energy levels were already high. But the added electromagnetic charge of the amethyst – along with the chakra-specific meditation that Diva taught us – pushed your energy levels to an all-time high. Now you've unlocked super sight *and* the ability to tap into energy waves across all time planes, which effectively means you can see the future!"

Sabina slumped down into her chair. "Great."

"I have to admit this surprised me," said Faye. "My research already showed me this inner energy is real – but I never thought someone could actually get powers from it! Let alone someone I know!"

"Do you know how I can get rid of them?" asked Sabina anxiously. "I tried doing the same meditation again, to reverse it, but it didn't work."

"Of course not – that would simply increase the energy and strengthen your powers," said Faye, as Sabina's face crumpled. Her attempt to be normal had just made things worse!

"This is a nightmare," burst out Sabina. "And the worst part is the Leeches – oops, I mean the Leeshes – know about it."

Faye giggled. "The Leeches! They do leech off each other."

Sabina couldn't help but smile back. "It's my private name for them."

"I like it," said Faye. "But it's important we don't underestimate them. They're cleverer than they look if they managed to work out you're psychic so quickly!"

Sabina shivered as she remembered how awful it had been when they'd made her touch the flier in the bathroom. She never wanted to think about it again.

"Can you tell me more about what happened when they figured it out in the bathroom?" asked Faye.

Sabina stared at her in angst. Faye was the last person she could speak to about the vision she'd had then! She tried to think quickly. "Um...so...they made me touch a flier. Their Form Prefect flier. And I saw...everyone voting! On Wednesday morning!"

"Interesting. Well, I think we can definitely assume that every time you touch an object and it sparks a vision, the vision will always be linked to the object."

"But why doesn't it happen every time I touch something?" asked Sabina, relieved to be on safer ground.

"I imagine it's linked to the energetic charge of the item, but I'll look into it," said Faye, taking notes. "So, tell me more about the visions – what exactly happens when you get one?"

"Everything whirls around me until I end up at the scene of the vision," explained Sabina. "Nobody can see me. But I can see them. Then when the vision ends, I find myself back wherever I was."

"Are all the visions an equal length?"

Sabina paused. "I don't *think* so. At the Winter Ball I saw loads, but with my mum's ticket, it was only a moment, then I blinked and I was back."

"You blinked?" Faye started scribbling madly. "Did you blink in the other visions too?"

Sabina thought about it. "I suppose I did! Always at the end! Do you think that's what makes the visions stop?"

"It must be."

Sabina looked at Faye in excitement. "So, if I want to make the visions stop, I just have to blink?"

"I assume so."

"And if I want to make sure I don't get a vision? Ever again?"

Faye looked at her in surprise. "You don't *want* your powers?"

"Of course not!" cried Sabina. "I don't want to watch my teachers get diarrhoea or my new friend fail— Um, nothing... I just don't want to see things I'm not supposed to. Like...the geography answers! You should have been top of the class – not me!"

"That's true," agreed Faye. "Cheating is amoral, even if it's unintentionally caused by your powers. Though you could also do a lot of good with them – they'd be incredibly useful with scientific cures." Her eyes lit up. "You could be the new Marie Curie! Or some kind of scientific Wonder Woman!"

"But I'm not a scientist!" exclaimed Sabina. "I'm just a

thirteen-year-old who meditated too much. I don't want to be psychic any more – I want to be normal!"

Faye sighed. "I suppose it is your choice. Well, we'll just have to keep investigating. I think the first thing we need to do is speak to Diva."

"We?!" echoed Sabina, her eyes shining with hope. "You'll help me?"

Faye studiously looked down at her notepad, avoiding Sabina's gaze. "If you'll have me. Though you'd be silly not to, considering I'm the best scientist in school."

"Oh, thank you so much!" Sabina wrapped her arms around Faye tightly. "I couldn't do it without you."

Faye blushed. "You're welcome. Although…there is something I'd like to ask you in exchange."

Sabina's blood ran cold. She couldn't predict the Form Prefect winner for Faye – she just couldn't! Even if Faye claimed not to mind who won, Sabina knew she'd be devastated.

But Faye didn't say anything about Form Prefect. Or any vision at all. Instead, she nervously asked: "Will you let me submit an anonymous thesis on you for my Science Summer Camp application?"

Sabina's shoulders sagged in relief. "Yes! Of course! Whatever you need."

Faye smiled. "Great! Now, where's this dinner you promised you'd heat up?"

Chapter 10

The next morning, Sabina walked out of assembly feeling queasy. Mr Grant's spot was now in the peeling stage, which meant she'd been able to see dry skin flake off it every time he nodded. Unfortunately for her, he'd nodded twenty-five times. She'd counted.

"There you are!" said Faye, appearing by her side.

Sabina smiled shyly. "Hi!"

Faye had stayed at her house for two hours the night before, and they'd talked about everything from Sabina's crisis to *A Prom to Die For* (Faye had also guessed the murderer in the first episode and given up instantly. Sabina regretted sticking with it for another two.) They'd even spoken about the Winter Ball – Faye had been the year before, and her fun stories of dancing with people from advanced chemistry had made Sabina desperate to go. And then – without a word from Sabina – Faye had suggested that they go to the Ball together! Sabina had practically exploded with excitement. It was everything she'd wanted – who cared about her silly secret fantasy of being popular? She didn't need to be like the Leeches when she could have a real friend like Faye!

She'd been having so much fun with her that for the first time since she'd left London, Sabina had gone an entire evening without missing Harry and Ria. They'd both been so shocked by her lack of calls that they'd called *her*. Sabina had told Faye all about her best friends, and when she'd gone home, Sabina had even allowed herself to dream of a time where she could hang out with all three of them together.

The dream had been temporarily shattered when she'd called Harry and Ria back to tell them how Faye had confirmed she'd unlocked ancient energetic powers within her. They'd instantly declared that Sabina was losing the plot and were on the verge of emergency evacuating her from the countryside back to London. It had only been when she'd forwarded them Faye's hypothesis that they'd finally believed her.

After they'd recovered from the shock of having a psychic for a best friend, they'd both promised to be there for her on every step of her journey. And when Sabina had said that Faye had effectively promised to do the same – and wanted to go to the Winter Ball together – they'd shrieked so loudly that Sabina had been forced to pull her headphones out. It was typical of Harry and Ria to be more excited about her befriending Faye

than the fact that she'd gained magical powers.

"We'd better go find Diva," said Faye. "Before class starts."

Sabina nodded as she followed her. "And you still think I should tell her the truth? Even though it sounds crazy?"

"You don't have anything to lose," pointed out Faye. "I mean, other than your reputation as a normal person."

"I'm nervous," admitted Sabina. "I feel like telling a teacher makes it real."

"Can you read that tiny writing on the noticeboard at the very end of the corridor?" asked Faye, pointing to it.

Sabina read it aloud without even squinting: "Rolling up your skirts is NOT feminist expression. Anyone found doing so WILL get detention."

"Then I'm afraid it's already real," said Faye. "I have 20:20 vision with my glasses and all I can see is a black smudge." They stopped outside the gym door. "Ready?"

Sabina sighed. "I guess so." She pushed open the door to enter the candlelit gym, where Diva was sitting on her mat, eyes closed. Faye strode over to Diva, with Sabina following.

"Diva?" asked Faye, her voice clear and crisp. "Sorry to interrupt, but it's me, Faye Collins, and I'm with Sabina Patel. We have a question for you. An urgent one."

Diva slowly opened one eye. She looked from Faye to Sabina, then closed her eyes again. She breathed deeply for a few more moments, while Faye and Sabina glanced at each other uncertainly. Finally, Diva fluttered open her eyes.

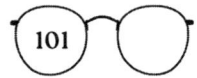

"Namaste, girls. How can I help?"

Sabina spoke reluctantly. "Um...so...I did the meditation on Tuesday when I got home. With the crystal you gave me. And when I woke up the next day...things...I mean..."

"She woke up with super sight and the ability to see the future," finished Faye.

Diva's expression didn't change. She just nodded serenely. "I see."

"*That's* your reaction?!" burst out Sabina. "I've been having electric shocks and visions that come out of nowhere! I've been seeing things that *haven't happened yet*."

"It sounds like you've managed to access the infinite power of consciousness," said Diva. "Only a very small number of yogis are able to do this, Sabina. For you to do it at your age is incredible."

"Incredible? It's a nightmare! And if it hardly happens to anyone, why has it happened to me?"

"Because of your breathing rituals with your mum," said Faye, pulling out her notepad to take notes. "That is right, Diva, isn't it?"

Diva nodded. "Sabina, you've been meditating your whole life without realizing it. This was always in your destiny."

Sabina shook her head. "But it only happened once I meditated with your crystal! That's what gave me the powers!"

"It might have helped open your third eye, but your gifts didn't come from the crystal – they were already inside you," said Diva. The expression on Sabina's face clearly suggested she did not think of her powers as gifts. Diva's voice softened. "It must be hard if your powers are still unpredictable. But the more you do your chakra meditations, the more you'll learn to control them."

Faye looked up at this. "Control them? How can she do that? Is it even possible?"

"Of course," said Diva. "The powers aren't coming from an external source like a magic bangle or something. They're coming from *within* which means they can definitely be controlled."

"How?" asked Faye.

"The same way you got these powers," said Diva, turning to Sabina as though she'd asked the question. "By breathing. Meditation will help you control the powers and sustain them."

"But I don't want to do that – I want to get rid of them!" cried Sabina in frustration.

For the first time in this entire conversation, Diva looked shocked. "But Sabina, these powers have come to you for a reason. They've chosen you. You don't need to get rid of them – you need to work with them."

"Why? They've just made me a freak."

"Aren't we all freaks?" replied Diva, as Faye let out a bark of laughter in agreement. "It's perspective. A freak, a guru, a girl – they're just labels. You can see this as a curse, or you can see it as a gift. If you accept it and receive it, you can work with it, and who knows what will change for you?"

"I don't *want* to," whispered Sabina. "I want things to be how they used to be. Before I even came to MG."

"Ah," said Diva knowingly. "Longing for the past. Almost as dangerous as worrying about the future! All we have is the present moment, Sabina. You can't go backwards. So just be where you are. And make sure you keep meditating to help you focus on today – rather than worrying about yesterday or tomorrow."

"How will the breathing help with controlling the powers?" asked Faye. "And how long should she meditate for?"

"As long as need be," said Diva enigmatically. "Meditation helps calm the mind. And when we're calm and focused, we can tap into our powers. The more we meditate, the more we can control those powers, aligning them for our highest purpose."

Faye was about to ask another question, but Sabina didn't let her. "Wait, so if I stop meditating, this could all go away?"

Diva frowned. "No, Sabina, stopping your meditations would be dangerous. There's a lot of energy inside you now. Meditating is the only way to channel it. If you stopped, especially suddenly, it could be perilous."

"Because it could cause electromagnetic build-up?" asked Faye. "And potentially death?"

Sabina gulped in fear, but Diva shook her head, smiling. "No, no, nothing like that! I just mean it could be overwhelming for you emotionally, Sabina. You have strong powers and they need to be treated carefully, with honour and respect. Work with them, not against them."

"And if I don't?"

Her teacher's voice was gentle. "This is your path. You can resist it and suffer. Or you can accept it and grow. Though I can't promise that path will be free of suffering either. Now, run along and get changed. Class starts in two minutes."

"Great," sighed Sabina to Faye as they walked to the changing room. "Option A, suffering. Option B, suffering. Can't *wait*."

That lunchtime, Sabina walked into the canteen, nervously scanning the room for Faye. They'd arranged to meet there but Sabina was scared that Faye would forget, or worse, cancel. She knew she was making too big a deal of their lunch, but this was her first time having social plans at MG, which meant it kind of *was* a big deal.

She forced herself to relax as she took a seat at her usual table. Faye would show up. And in the meantime, she could take some time to process everything that was happening to her. Like the fact she'd managed to get through Diva's class without any major drama. Sabina had spent the beginning half-resisting the meditation in case she ended up with even *more* powers afterwards, but Diva's warning of it being dangerous to stop had got into her head. So eventually, she'd found herself breathing deeply, letting her chakras light up one by one. The same warm peace from before had infused her body and she'd felt super relaxed. Until Diva had rung a loud gong to signal them to stop (Sabina couldn't help thinking she'd brought it just for her).

"Sorry I'm late," said Faye, sliding into the seat opposite her with a tray. "Advanced chem went over."

"That's okay," said Sabina, trying to stop herself from grinning too much. "What have you got for lunch?"

Faye raised an eyebrow as she looked down at the plate of fish and chips right in front of her. "Fish and chips. Obviously."

"Right." Sabina blushed and busied herself by opening her lunchbox. "I imagine I'll have something awful and homemade – oh! It's an egg mayo sandwich." She smiled brightly, but as she picked it up, a note floated down onto the table. Sabina shrieked, dropping the sandwich.

"What's wrong?" asked Faye. "Are you gluten intolerant?"

"It's a *note*," whispered Sabina. "From my mum."

Faye's eyes widened in understanding. "This is good! We can try out my new hypothesis!"

"We...can?"

"I've had a theory about how your powers work. So you're going to need to touch your mum's note."

Sabina breathed in sharply. "But what if I get a vision?"

"Hopefully you won't. But first, you have to do a mini meditation and breathe, like Diva said."

"In the canteen? What if people see?"

"Who cares?"

"Me!"

Faye rolled her eyes. "Fine. I'll tell you if anyone notices."

Sabina gazed around the canteen to check nobody was looking at her. As always, they weren't. She turned back to Faye reluctantly. "Okay. I'll do it." She closed her eyes. Her mind was worried about her freak status at school being cemented even further, but as she exhaled deeply, her thoughts started to slow down.

Faye spoke gently. "Do you feel calm?"

Sabina nodded.

"Good. Now…open your eyes and touch the note. It's okay – no one's looking."

Sabina hesitantly did exactly what Faye said. Her breath tightened as she touched the note, but to her relief, nothing happened. She was still there in the canteen holding the note!

"*A treat for my favourite (okay, only) daughter. Sorry I didn't get to meet your new friend, but invite her around on the weekend? Love you infinity!*"

Sabina beamed. "My mum wants to meet you this weekend – I think you'll get on so well!"

"I look forward to it," said Faye seriously. "Now, a couple more questions before I fill you in on what I've learned. How do you feel emotionally? Out of ten? You know, if one is super calm and ten is an extreme emotion."

"Um, two? Three?"

Faye scribbled in her notepad. "Good. And how did you feel the last time you touched a note from your mum?"

Sabina thought back to that morning when she'd woken up and found she had super sight. Her emotions had been off the chart! "At least a ten. I was *not* okay."

Faye's eyes lit up. "And what about before you touched the geography test?"

"A nine for sure. I was panicked I'd fail. I couldn't remember a thing about erosion."

"What about with Mrs Fairweather and the tray?"

"Nine. I thought she was going to tell me off."

"And when the Leeches made you touch their flier?"

"Ten," said Sabina instantly. "I'm pretty much always a ten when I'm around them. They stress me out. Wait." Her eyes shone with sudden understanding. "Are you saying that when I'm really emotional, *that's* when I get visions?"

"I think so," said Faye. "I was trying to work out why only some objects trigger your visions and others don't. I thought it was about the objects' emotional charge, but it's about *yours*! When your emotions are high, you're likely to get visions by touching random things. But when they're low, you're okay!"

Sabina gasped loudly. "Faye, you're a genius! You've worked it out! That makes TOTAL sense!"

Faye flushed awkwardly. "Anyone with a scientific approach would have figured it out."

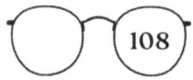

"But...does this mean *any* emotion can trigger a vision?" asked Sabina. "Could I get one when I'm really happy and excited?"

"From what I can tell, it's *any* intense emotion," said Faye. "An unpredictable one. But if you're feeling calm and content, for example, I think you'll be fine."

Sabina stared at her. "But...I can't do that! I'm always happy or sad. I'm never in between!"

"Well, you'll just have to practise. I think if you can stay emotionally balanced, and use your meditation and breathing to help you, then you can avoid random visions. I also think the more you meditate, the more you'll be able to get visions on demand! That's what Diva said about controlling them."

Sabina shook her head adamantly. "No thanks, I don't want MORE visions. I'll just...work on being super chill and avoiding anything stressful! That'll work, right?"

Just then two familiar sing-song voices called out: "Heeee-eeeey!" Sabina and Faye looked up to see the Leeches beaming at them. "Happy Friday!"

"Oh no," whispered Sabina, her heart already starting to race.

Alicia turned to Faye. "*Loved* your FP website. So creative. I even shared it on my socials!"

"Why?" asked Faye suspiciously. "I'm your competition."

Alicia shrugged, smiling. "Oh, you know, generosity. I'm a team player."

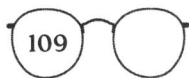

"It's true," added Felicia. "We're not the kind of team who want to take our opponents down. We believe in fairness."

"Yes, I really do," said Alicia. "Anyway, Sabrina, we just wanted to borrow you. Leesh has a question for you."

Sabina paled. "I...can't, sorry. Faye and I are busy."

"It will only take a sec," said Felicia.

"She said no," said Faye firmly. "We're eating."

"But I thought you were going to eat with us today," said Alicia, looking innocently at Sabina. "You accepted our invitation, didn't you?"

Sabina's heart sank; the Leeches had meant their lunch invitation after all! She looked down at the table, avoiding Faye's eyes, her blood pounding. "I'm sorry, I, um, forgot."

"Well then, you owe us, don't you?" said Alicia sweetly. "So, you can just look at something, can't you? Leesh wants to show you a message Alexis sent her so you can do a vision for us!"

"No, no," said Sabina, instinctively backing away as Felicia tried to put her phone into her hands. She couldn't touch a thing right now – not when her emotions were so high! And definitely not for the Leeches – they were acting like she was their personal psychic!

"Leave her alone," said Faye. "We're busy."

But it was too late. Felicia forced her iPhone towards Sabina, and it brushed against her fingers.

Sabina gasped as a jolt shook her body, and everything started to spin. When it finally stopped, she was in the school car park.

It was utter chaos. People were crying, howling with grief, and even *Mr Grant* was sobbing as he leaned against his car. The Leeches were right next to her, with Felicia using her phone to film Alicia.

Sabina had been about to blink, but now she couldn't. She needed to know exactly what had happened.

Alicia was speaking into Felicia's phone.

"It's a tragedy," she sniffed, tucking a stray hair behind her thick red velvet hairband. "Katniss Evermean – the world's most beautiful and sassy cat – has...died. The circumstances are horrific. She was only seven years old. It was way before her time. She 'officially' belonged to Mr Grant, but really, she belonged to all of us. Me and Leesh had a particularly special relationship with her – she was our spirit animal, the way she always had perfectly natural eyeliner, and was *very* clear about her boundaries. She used to sit on my lap during philosophy. But..." Alicia's face set into an angry expression. "She won't be able to do that ever again. Because Mr Grant MURDERED her with his car."

Sabina cried aloud in shock and accidentally blinked. She was back in the canteen, tears pricking her eyelids. Her previous worries about the Leeches trying to force her into doing visions for them were gone. It all paled in comparison with what she'd just seen.

Katniss Evermean was dead.

Chapter 11

"What did you see?" asked Faye.

"Come on!" said Alicia. "We don't have all day!"

"Does Alexis ask me to the Winter Ball?" asked Felicia.

Sabina stared from the Leeches to Faye, confusion and grief flooding her body. Nothing mattered any more – except for making sure Katniss was okay.

She tried to think. The car. Alicia had said Mr Grant murdered Katniss with his car – that was why everyone was outside. But *when* did it happen? She needed to figure it out so she could stop it.

"Tell me!" whined Felicia. "Leesh knows she's going with Dillon, but I don't know who *I'm* going with! How can I pick an outfit when I don't know?"

Sabina frowned at the Leeches in frustration – couldn't they be quiet and let her think? – then she gasped. They were both wearing velvet hairbands – Alicia's was red, and Felicia's was green – just like in her vision!

"Do you wear those headbands every day?" she asked.

The Leeches looked mortally offended.

"As if," said Alicia frostily. "We change headwear daily."

Sabina's eyes shone with sudden hope. "Then it was *today*! I can do something!" She faced Faye. "We need to go to the car park. Now."

Faye didn't even hesitate – she just shoved her notepad in her bag and stood up. But when Sabina followed her, a cold hand curled around her wrist.

"Wait," demanded Alicia. "You need to tell us what you saw first."

Sabina shook her hand off. "There's no time! It's Katniss Evermean – we need to save her from death!"

The Leeches went pale beneath their make-up.

"Katniss!" cried Felicia. "She's basically a third Leesh!"

"The car park!" cried Sabina impatiently, racing out of the canteen, with Faye and the Leeches following her. She didn't stop running until she reached Mr Grant's navy-blue Honda. "Katniss!" she called out, looking around the car park. "Katniss Evermean! Where are you?"

"What is it?" asked Faye breathlessly, the Leeches by her side. "What did you see?"

"I saw Felicia filming a live of Alicia speaking about the tragic death of Katniss Evermean," replied Sabina, too anxious to care about the fact that the Leeches would now have extra proof of her powers. "She said Mr Grant murdered her with his car. And they were out here. The whole school was. Mr Grant was crying. I think it happens later today."

"Noooooooo!" shrieked Alicia, her body convulsing with sobs, as Felicia clung onto her. "Katniss!"

"He must have accidentally run her over," whispered Faye, a look of tight pain on her face. Nobody at MG was immune to loving Katniss Evermean. "Which means we need to find her before that happens and keep her safe."

"We need to find her NOW," said Sabina, upping her pace. "Come on, everyone!"

The Leeches pulled themselves together, determined to save Katniss, and they all disappeared into the car park, looking under cars and up trees. Sabina felt her heart race in panic as they searched to no avail. Why hadn't her vision been more specific? She'd seen the car...she'd seen Mr Grant crying...but she hadn't seen Katniss's body on the ground in front of the car. It must have been underneath it.

Suddenly Sabina paused. What if...Katniss's body had *already* been under the car?

Sabina knew this was unlikely, but she had to try. She dropped to her knees to look under the Honda, but she couldn't see a thing.

"There's nothing there," said Alicia. "We already looked."

Sabina felt her heart sink, but she decided to look one last time just in case. And then she saw something!

A lump on top of the back wheel. Everything was black with the shadows, but Sabina could vaguely make out the outline of a cat, curled in between the car shell and the wheel. She was so tucked away that her fur had blended into the shadow, and it was no surprise the Leeches hadn't spotted her. But Sabina's super sight had.

"Katniss!" she called out, reaching her hands in to try and grab the silky cat. "Come out, baby!"

"Oh my God, Sabina's found her!" called out Felicia.

But Sabina didn't look up – she was too focused on trying to get Katniss out. She stroked the cat awkwardly, her hand practically inside the back of the car. Katniss refused to move, but Sabina kept coaxing her out gently, making little *pspspsps* noises.

Finally, Katniss leaped out onto the gravel.

Sabina picked her up in relief, hugging her tight as she turned to face the others. Faye was smiling at her in evident relief, while the Leeches held out their phones.

"Katniss is safe!" cried Alicia into her phone. "We've rescued her!"

Sabina frowned. "Are you filming this?"

"We're doing a live," explained Felicia. "To celebrate the saving of Katniss Evermean."

"I can't believe Katniss could have died," said Alicia to the phone. "I mean, she actually *did* in the future. Mr Grant murdered her with his car. But Sabrina saw it. Because Sabrina Patel can SEE THE FUTURE! And *we* helped her stop it!"

Sabina froze, her mouth open, as Katniss miaowed and sprang out of her arms. The Leeches were telling everyone her secret!

"It's all because of her psychic powers," added Felicia. "We have loads more examples we can tell you about! Like how she found out Mrs Fairweather got diarr—"

"Enough," snapped Faye. "Stop filming people without their consent. Sabina, we're going." She slid her arm through Sabina's to steer her away. "It's going to be okay. Don't worry."

But Sabina didn't believe her. The Leeches had outed her secret to the whole school – and possibly the whole internet! From now on, her life at MG was going to be a complete and utter nightmare.

"That's her!"

"No way – she looks so *normal*."

Sabina kept her head down, pulling up the lapels of her blazer as though they could make her invisible. Ever since lunch, people had been whispering about her. Two Year Sevens had brazenly asked for a selfie! Sabina had been so shocked that she'd barely protested when they'd snapped a photo with her. She still couldn't believe this was happening. Up until now, nobody at MG had noticed her. But now she couldn't walk down the hallways without someone pointing at her!

The Leeches were shameless. They'd already posted another video explaining more about Sabina's powers as proof for their followers – Alicia had explained how Sabina knew Dillon Vadia would ask her to the Winter Ball, and Felicia had revealed the full diarrhoea story. Sabina had watched the videos in horror. Her secret was out – and *everyone* believed it! There were a few deniers who had commented their doubts on the video, but the Leeches had so much social power that most of MG believed everything they said without even questioning it.

It was awful knowing that everyone knew about her psychic abilities – abilities Sabina still didn't even fully understand. But as much as this was her worst nightmare and she wished she hadn't trusted the Leeches, she couldn't regret saving Katniss. She wouldn't have been able to live with herself if she hadn't. And Katniss was officially safe for now – *and* for the future. The Leeches had gone to Mr Grant's house and made him promise on live video to never get into his car without checking for Katniss Evermean – who was now, incidentally, curled up on his sofa, happily licking her paws. He'd rolled his eyes when they'd spoken about psychic visions – to Sabina's relief he clearly thought they were talking nonsense – but he had agreed to keep Katniss extra safe. And that made everything worth it.

But Sabina wished she could go back to her old life before any of this had happened. Things had been so much better when she was another normal student at Hackney High, hanging out with Harry and Ria. Her new life was a total nightmare. If she was going to have powers, she wished they were the kind that would take her back to the past rather than showing her the future!

"Sabrina, right?" Alexis stood in front of Sabina, blocking the corridor with her strong lacrosse shoulders.

Sabina halted in surprise. The last time she'd seen Alexis, it had been in the future, when she was breaking up with Felicia at the Winter Ball. Alexis couldn't know anything about that, could she?

"I need your help. It's the lacrosse championships and I need to know who'll win in the NFCS vs Granger High game next week, so we know which of them we'll be playing in the final."

"Um...I'm sorry, I don't know anything about lacrosse," said Sabina apologetically.

"Yeah, but you're psychic, aren't you?"

Sabina's eyes widened. "What? No...I mean..." She felt her heart race, and tried to walk past Alexis, but she moved to block Sabina's path.

"You don't want to help MG win the lacrosse championships?!" asked Alexis, her voice rising. A group of Year Nines turned to stare, whispering.

Sabina felt her heart race, unsure what to say. But then a Year Nine came to speak to her.

"Hey, I need a fortune reading. How much do you charge?" she asked.

"Uh, she's already helping *me*," said Alexis.

A brave Year Seven with nails like the Leeches' walked over. "I can pay double whatever they're paying."

Sabina stared helplessly, overwhelmed, as more and more students swarmed around her with requests. She could feel her emotions rising. She quickly dropped her school bag, making sure she wasn't touching anything so she wouldn't get a vision. "Sorry, I can't help," she mumbled, backing into a corner.

"Why not?" whined the Year Seven.

"I need your help," said the Year Nine. "It's urgent!"

Sabina tried to think of something to make everyone go away, but before she could, there was a piercing whistle sound. She whirled around to see the Leeches standing behind her in matching zip-up sports hoodies with sports bands round their heads.

"Leave the psychic alone," said Alicia. "She's ours."

"Sorry, babe," Felicia mouthed to Alexis.

"All requests to speak to her have to go through us," said Alicia loudly.

"What?" cried Alexis. "That's not fair!"

"I'll expedite yours," promised Felicia, her voice trailing off when Alicia glared at her.

Sabina stared open-mouthed. The swarm of students were reluctantly disbanding, clearly aware that they couldn't beat the Leeches. Sabina didn't know whether to be grateful or furious. She didn't *belong* to anyone!

Alicia grinned at her. "Welcome to fame. You'll get used to it, Sabrina."

"Totally," said Felicia. "You're the only psychic at MG. You're going to be so busy doing readings for everyone – well, only the popular people. We'll filter them for you."

"NO!" cried Sabina. "I mean, this isn't what I want! I'm not going to be an on-demand psychic!"

"Of course you are," said Alicia. "They'll pay you, if that's what you're worried about." She stared pointedly at Sabina's scuffed trainers. "You can get new clothes!"

"But I don't want to," said Sabina, feeling a wave of panic rising again. She tried to breathe, and kept her fingers firmly in the air so she wouldn't touch a thing. "Why did you tell everyone? I thought you'd keep it secret."

"We never promised," said Alicia. "And the situation changed. It was life or death."

"But you told everyone once Katniss was already safe," said Sabina. "There was no need!"

Alicia shrugged. "So? Everyone loves psychics. They're in right now."

"Everyone wants you to be their psychic!" said Felicia.

"I don't *want* to be everyone's psychic!"

"You have to!" said Felicia.

"Wait," ordered Alicia, putting a finger to her forehead. "I'm thinking." Felicia fell silent, until Alicia spoke again. "I've got it! This can work in our favour! We'll tell everyone Sabrina's too busy for requests, and we're the only ones she does readings for! That makes us even more exclusive than before."

"You're a genius, Leesh!" declared Felicia.

Alicia smiled smugly. "Exclusivity *is* everything. And who won't want to vote for me for FP when they know I have a psychic?"

The Leeches linked arms and walked off, without even looking back at Sabina, who was standing there with her mouth wide open. She could not *believe* that had just happened. The Leeches had acted like she wasn't even there. They'd told her private news to the whole school and then claimed her as their personal psychic! Sabina had no idea how she was going to get through this...

Chapter 12

The next day, Sabina sleepily answered a three-way video call from Harry and Ria. "Hey! How come you're both calling so early on a Saturday?"

Harry's pixelated face loomed on the screen. "Uh, maybe because we've just heard our best friend has gone viral as a psychic!"

"Viral?" asked Sabina, startled awake.

"Harry, stop freaking her out," chided Ria. "We saw the Leeches' video. We started following them when you told us about them. Their video has had hundreds of views already."

Sabina's head dropped into her hands. "Of course it has."

"Babe, this is the opportunity you were waiting for!" cried Harry. "You felt like nobody noticed you. But now *everyone*'s going to notice you. You've even got a brand – telling the future!"

"I don't want a brand!" wailed Sabina. "Some Year Sevens came up to me yesterday and asked me to *touch* them! They wanted me to have a vision, like I'm some kind of on-demand psychic."

"You kind of are?" said Harry.

"Not yet," corrected Ria. "Didn't you read Faye's latest hypothesis from Sabs? She can't control her visions yet."

"Thank God you have Faye," remarked Harry. "She's the only voice of reason in all this. I mean, other than myself."

Sabina rolled her eyes. "Sure, because telling me to turn my powers into my brand is really reasonable. And can you please stop talking about me like I'm not here!"

"Okay, but this could make you legit famous!" said Harry. "You could be popular!"

Sabina flushed. Harry and Ria didn't know that was what she'd secretly hoped would happen when she'd arrived at MG. But she'd never wanted it to happen like *this*!

"So, when are you going to do our futures?" continued Harry. "I want to know if I end up being an influencer."

"You don't," said Ria. "Even I can tell you that. So you're going to need to pass your GCSEs. Ooh, maybe Sabina can tell us what grades we'll get!"

"Please don't make me do your futures!" cried Sabina, panic rising in her. "What if I see something terrible? Then you'll hate me! And what if they're good, but then something changes and they don't come true? I can't do this! I don't want to risk losing you!" Then she shrieked and almost dropped her phone. "Oh my God, my emotional levels are reaching a nine!"

"BREATHE," shouted Harry. "Quickly!"

"That's not helping," hissed Ria. "Sabina, just chill. Deep breaths. You're all good."

"That's literally what I said!" said Harry.

"Uh, you shouted it," said Ria. "There's a difference."

Sabina burst out laughing. "Wow. Your arguing has taken me down to a six. It's nice to see you haven't changed."

Ria grinned. "If only! And, Sabs, on a serious note, I understand what you were saying about doing our futures. It makes sense."

"Uh, not to me," said Harry tartly. "What's the point in us having a best friend with powers if she doesn't use them to help us?"

"Best friends support each other – remember?" chastised Ria. "So don't worry, Sabs, we've got you."

Sabina exhaled loudly in relief. "Thank you. That takes me down to a three. It's not fun knowing your friends' futures. I already found out something I didn't want to about Faye losing Form Prefect to Alicia. I'd hate to be in a similar situation with either of you two."

"That is hard," agreed Ria. "Have you told her? Because if it was me, I'd way rather know."

"Me too," agreed Harry. "At least then I could prepare to lose."

"No," said Sabina, her chest tightening as she forced herself to stay calm. The thought of telling Faye made her feel sick. "I mean, Faye's going to find out the results next week anyway – is there any point in upsetting her beforehand?"

"Uh, yes," said Harry. "You can warn her!"

Sabina could feel her emotions heightening so she quickly changed the topic. "She's actually coming over this afternoon!"

"Oh my God, Saturday plans with Faye – love that for you!" said Harry. "Now you don't have to be jealous when Ria and I send you selfies from our sleepover."

"Oh, I'll still be jealous. But at least I don't have to make your selfies my screensaver and hang out with my phone all night, pretending you're here with me."

Harry and Ria exchanged a glance.

"That is the most tragic thing ever," declared Harry. "I'm going to pretend you didn't say that."

"Maybe we can meet Faye when we come over in the holidays?" said Ria. "I've been following her socials and she seems so cool. Did you know she's a chess genius?"

"No!" exclaimed Sabina, beaming at the thought of Ria thinking her new friend seemed cool. "But she's the smartest person I know, so I'm not surprised. I love the thought of us all hanging out together – that makes me SO happy! I can't wait for it to happen – I wish the future would hurry up already!"

And then suddenly, she gasped.

"No!" she cried as an electric jolt rushed through her body.

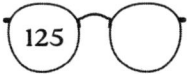

She was having another vision! And she hadn't even been upset or stressed – she'd just been really happy!

Everything spun around until she wasn't in her room any more... Sabina realized that she was at her old school! On the football field! That was weird – she'd never been there before.

She looked around, smiling as she saw some of the boys from her year playing football, including Harry's crush, Zain. And then her mouth dropped in disbelief. Because right there, standing in the goal, was Harry himself!

She blinked just as he did an impressive save that led to everyone cheering, and then ended up back in her room, staring at his and Ria's awestruck faces on her phone.

"Did you have a vision?" whispered Ria. "You looked so... psychic."

Sabina nodded, wiping sweat from her brow. "I didn't expect to. This is so unfair. I hate my powers!"

"What did you see?" cried Harry. "Tell us!"

"You," said Sabina flatly. "Playing football at school. You were goalie. And you saved a goal."

Harry made a face. "Yeah, whatever. What's the truth?"

"No, that's it," said Sabina. "I promise."

"Maybe your visions are broken?" asked Ria uncertainly. "You know Harry doesn't do sport."

"I think he should start," said Sabina sadly. "He's good. And Zain was there."

Harry perked up. "Did he see me save the goal?" Sabina nodded and Harry's eyes lit up. "I love this for me! Thanks, Sabs."

"You're welcome," she said. "At least one of us is allowed to be happy."

"Wow, Faye, that sounds very impressive," said Sabina's mum. She raised her glass of orange juice. "Here's to you winning your chess competition."

"To Faye!" joined in Sabina.

"Thank you," said Faye. "I am four years younger than most of the people in the competition, but statistically, I do have a high chance of winning."

"I know I haven't known you long, b—" said Sabina's mum.

"Forty-five minutes," interjected Faye.

"Exactly," continued Sabina's mum, hiding a smile. "But I would *definitely* put my money on you. And I'm very glad Sabina now gets a new episode at MG." She winked at her daughter.

"Mum!" Sabina gave her an embarrassed look. Before Faye had arrived, she'd been telling her mum about the latest episode of her life at MG: *The Friendship of Sabina Patel and Faye Collins, feat. Katniss Evermean.* She'd missed out any reference to magical powers, instead telling her mum they'd found Katniss stuck in Mr Grant's car just before he drove it.

Her mum had been as relieved as everyone else.

"You'll be glad to know, I'm going to head out to give you both some space," said her mum.

Sabina's face fell in disappointment. "But I thought you could give me and Faye manicures! Like when you used to do them for me, Harry and Ria?"

"Oh, I'm sorry, Sabs," said her mum, genuinely apologetic. "I didn't know that's what you were thinking! How about instead I promise to give you both manicures – in *non*-school-appropriate colours – for the Winter Ball? Any design of your choice!"

Sabina blushed. The Winter Ball was still two weeks away, but she'd been so excited that Faye had wanted to go with her that she'd told her mum. She hoped Faye wouldn't think she was a total loser!

But Faye's eyes lit up. "Do you think you could give me a manicure inspired by the periodic table?"

"That would be a complete first for me." Sabina's mum smiled, wrapping her favourite silk scarf around her neck. "But I don't see why not!"

Sabina frowned. Her mum was wearing make-up – something she rarely did for work. "You look nice. Is that for Beauties?"

Her mum hesitated. "Um, yes. Though I might meet a new friend after too, if that's okay?"

"Of course, have fun!" said Sabina, happy her mum had

finally made a friend in the village. She hoped she was as nice as Faye!

"Thanks, Sabs," said her mum, giving her a hug. "I'll be back in a few hours. Have fun, girls – and don't burn the house down!"

"The garden doesn't count though, right?" replied Sabina.

"Ha ha," said her mum, blowing her a kiss. "Bye!"

"Your mum is *so* cool," sighed Faye as the front door shut.

"I know," said Sabina, quickly grabbing Faye's arm. "But it's actually good she's gone because I *need* to speak to you about my powers. I had another vision when I was on the phone to Harry and Ria this morning!"

Faye grabbed her notebook. "Did you breathe? How were your emotional levels?"

"I breathed *so* much!" said Sabina. "They went up a few times, when we were speaking about them wanting me to do their futures, and, um, about something else… I managed to calm myself down and avoid a vision."

"Well done!"

"But then we were talking about them coming at Christmas and meeting you! And…I got really excited about it. Then when I was happy, I had a vision – of Harry playing football."

Faye looked up. "So you were happy about the future? Not the present moment?"

Sabina nodded.

"Interesting," said Faye, scribbling in her notepad.

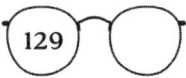

"Interesting? It's a nightmare! How can I stop myself being too happy?"

"We'll work it out," said Faye calmly. "Oh, and I'd love to meet Harry and Ria by the way. They sound wonderful."

"They are. But...what do I do?"

"We need to speak to Diva," said Faye matter-of-factly. "First thing on Monday before our class. Now. How about a chess match?"

"Chess?" asked Sabina. "Now?"

"It's the one thing that always makes me feel calm and balanced," said Faye. "Which I think is *exactly* what you need."

Sabina sighed. "I suppose you're right." She handed Faye the chessboard and frowned as she set up. "Wait, why are you only putting half the black pieces out?"

"I'm playing black," said Faye. "And I need to remove half my pieces, so it's a fair match."

"Is that really necessary? I'm not terrible at chess."

"I think it is," said Faye. "No offence."

Chapter 13

Sabina took a deep breath as she pushed open the school doors on Monday morning. She had no idea what to expect. The notifications on her socials had been buzzing all weekend, but she'd taken Harry and Ria's advice to just ignore everything and delete the apps from her phone. So she had no idea if everyone had gone back to ignoring her – or if she was still the psychic who'd saved Katniss Evermean.

"Oh my God, it's her!" loud-whispered a Year Seven. "But we're not allowed to speak directly to her. We have to go through the Leeshes."

Sabina's stomach sank as she realized nobody had forgotten and the Leeches were *still* trying to manage her.

"Sabina!" Faye waved to her from outside the gymnasium.

Sabina felt her spirits rise. She'd spent the rest of Saturday evening playing chess with Faye (it turned out that even with half her pieces gone, she'd beaten Sabina in twenty minutes) and laughing hysterically. She hadn't had so much fun since her last sleepover with Harry and Ria.

"How are you?" asked Faye. "Emotional levels? Meditating? Fill me in."

"Uh...I *was* a three. But your list of questions is taking me to a four."

Faye made a face at her. "I'm just trying to help."

Sabina grinned. "I know, thanks. And you'll be glad to know I've been meditating every evening. I even did one with my mum after you left on Saturday!"

She smiled at the memory. Her mum had come home just as Sabina was arranging the cushions, and she'd sat right next to Sabina, still in her silk scarf. They'd breathed for so long together that an entire hour passed before either of them realized. It had been so relaxing, and when they'd opened their eyes, they'd both given each other a long hug.

The following evening, her mum had been back at work, so Sabina had meditated alone. She hated that her mum had to work on Saturday *and* Sunday – she'd never worked a full weekend before. But Sabina knew this meant her mum's business was doing well, so she was trying to be happy for her. She loved her job, and if she was starting to make friends with her clients, then that was even better!

"Good," said Faye. "Ready for Diva's class? I thought we could try to speak to her afterwards?"

"Perfect," said Sabina.

"Oh also, I wanted to ask you one quick thing..." said Faye, biting her lip. "Would you be free to come to a Form Prefect rally I'm doing this lunchtime?" Sabina's stomach clenched in pity. She *hated* that Faye didn't win – but more than that, she hated that she knew! "It's going to be outside the science department so I can keep reminding them of my petition."

Just then the Leeches walked by, winking at Sabina. They were *everywhere*! She turned back to Faye, distracted. "Uh, yes, sure."

"Great!" said Faye, her eyes shining. "One-thirty. I'll be there early, preparing. So, you can come early too, if you like!"

"Girls, come inside!" said Diva, ushering them into the gym. "We're starting."

Sabina was in a state of zen as she folded up her mat and put it away. The chakra meditation had left her feeling more relaxed than ever.

"Sabriiiiiiiiiina?"

Her zen disappeared when she saw the Leeches standing next to her. "We have something for you," said Alicia, gesturing to Felicia.

Felicia held out a folded piece of pink paper. It was scented. Sabina stared at it in alarm, reluctant to touch it.

"Go on," said Alicia. "It won't bite."

Sabina remembered her emotional levels were low post-meditation. She reached out for the note, moving her hand slowly as she breathed deeply to stay calm. It worked! Nothing happened at all as she took the note from the Leeches.

They smiled brightly at her, wiggling their fingers at her in a wave. "See you later!" they sang in unison.

"Are you ready?" Sabina turned to see Faye waiting for her.

She quickly pushed the note into her pocket to read later. "Ready!"

They walked over to Diva, who was humming to herself as she folded blankets. "Oh, hello, girls."

"Hello, Diva," said Faye. "We'd like to ask you some more questions, please. About Sabina's powers."

"You can ask away. Though I can't promise I'll be able to answer them."

"It's...about how my visions happen," said Sabina hesitantly. "We realized they're linked to my emotions. So if I'm really stressed or something, I tend to get visions when I touch things. I was using my breathing to avoid them, just like you said. But—"

"That's not exactly what I said," interrupted Diva. "I said breathing will help you *control* them."

"Okay, fine, but the problem is that now I'm getting visions even when I have really good emotions!" said Sabina. "Am I meant to avoid feeling excited about things too?"

Diva smiled. "It isn't about avoiding anything. As I said

before, resistance makes everything harder. You aren't meant to avoid having feelings – whether they're stressful or exciting. The goal is to learn to be with them. To sit with them, breathe through them, and then work with them. But the most important thing is to be in the present moment – not to get caught up in what's already happened or what's happening in the future."

"So...if I do that, then the visions will go?"

Diva shook her head. "Sabina, your powers are here to stay. They're inside of you. Learning to balance your emotions is helping you ensure the powers don't take over. But it won't make you get *rid* of them."

Faye paused her rapid note taking. "Of course! We were going about it the wrong way! It's not about stopping the visions – it's about working *with* them!"

"Exactly," said Diva. "Breathing, meditating and keeping your emotions in check will help you control your visions. The faster you can accept that they're here to stay, the quicker you'll be able to control them."

Sabina's face fell in dismay, but Faye looked excited. "Is the control all just in the breathing? Or is it in the thoughts as well?"

Diva beamed at Faye. "Wonderful question, Faye. You're right. It is in the thoughts. Specifically, the *intention*." With that, she put away the last blanket and walked away.

Sabina turned to Faye with her eyebrows raised. "I seriously hope you know what she was talking about because I have NO idea."

Faye smiled. "I think I might! Do you have any plans tonight?"

Sabina shook her head automatically. Apart from Faye coming over on Saturday, she hadn't had a single social plan since coming to MG, unless waiting for her mum to come home counted.

"Good," said Faye, grabbing her bag. "I'll come over after advanced chem. See you at the rally!"

Sabina smiled happily. It turned out she did have plans after all! She suddenly remembered the note from the Leeches. She pulled it out, the smile dropping off her face as she read their loopy handwriting.

You are cordially invited to lunch with us. One o'clock in the dining room. On the menu: poké bowls. Love, the Leeshes xxx

PS If you want our continued protection, you MUST attend. Otherwise, you can deal with the entire school's psychic requests on your own!

There was no apology at all – it was emotional blackmail! Sabina felt a wave of anger rising in her, then she remembered to breathe deeply. There was no point stressing herself out for nothing. This was clearly how the Leeches said "sorry" –

and unless Sabina was ready to have the entire school hounding her for her visions, she'd better show up.

Sabina walked into the canteen, clutching her Tupperware filled with kidney bean curry and rice. She really didn't want to have lunch with the Leeches, but she couldn't think of a way out of it. She shuddered as she remembered how terrifying it had been when she'd been cornered by all those people straight after the Leeches' video had gone viral. She'd do anything to avoid that again – even eat with the Leeches. She just hoped they wouldn't mind if she ditched the poké. She didn't have enough money for it, and she didn't want to waste her packed lunch from her mum.

"Sabriiiiina!" Alicia and Felicia called to her from their usual table, beaming beneath their respective lilac and yellow berets. Katniss Evermean was sitting next to them on her own chair, licking her paws.

"We saved you a seat next to Katniss *and* we got you a poké bowl," said Alicia.

"Oh, wow, thanks," said Sabina, caught off guard. "Hey, Katniss!" She reached out to stroke the cat, and Katniss purred happily, offering up her neck for a massage. Sabina obliged, glad that she had an ally for her lunch with the Leeches.

"We got you the vegan tofu one," continued Alicia. "With extra cado."

"What's cado?"

"Avocado," said Felicia. "You have eaten it before, right?"

"Yes, but I just normally call it avocado. You really didn't need to get this for me."

"You're sitting with us now," said Alicia. "We *always* treat our guests."

Sabina smiled hesitantly, sliding her lunchbox back into her bag. It would be rude to reject the Leeches' offer. And the colourful bowl, with its bright edamame beans and tofu chunks, did look delicious. Maybe it was their way of apologizing to her for revealing her secret to the school.

"So, we were wondering if you could maybe redo my vision?" asked Felicia. Or maybe it was just their way of persuading her to do more psychic readings for them. "You know, about the Winter Ball? Because last time it ended up being about Katniss, not Alexis." Her eyes lit up. "Oh my God, maybe your vision got confused because their names rhyme?!"

"Let her eat first," chided Alicia, as Sabina obediently took a mouthful. "And *then* we can talk about the future! I'd love to know how things progress with me and Dillon."

Sabina gulped, her appetite already gone. "Look, um, it's just...my visions...they're not very predictable. I don't even know if they're always right. Maybe it's best if we don't do more of them?"

"I totally get that," said Alicia seriously. "But, babe, we're helping protect you from the entire school. Do you know how many DMs we're getting for you? Do you want that many messages in your inbox?"

Sabina shook her head quickly. "No, I don't. But—"

"So, then you have to help us!" said Felicia. "It's only fair!"

Sabina was trying to think of a polite way to tell Felicia that fair would be them not emotionally blackmailing her, when a group of Year Nines came up to their table.

"Hey, Leeshes. Love the berets!"

The Leeches blew them kisses in return.

Sabina waited for the Year Nines to leave, but they didn't. Instead, they turned to *her*.

"Hey, Sabrina," said Leah, the most popular. "Love the psychic stuff – so cool you saved Katniss!"

"Thank you," she whispered. The coolest girls in the year above had spoken to her *and* they knew her name! (Well, kind of – Sabrina was only one letter off.)

"Maybe you can do our fortunes one day?" asked Maria, a super-tall prefect. "Such a cool skill. You should enter the talent show too!" With that, they waved and walked off.

Sabina stared, open-mouthed, as an edamame bean fell off her fork. She couldn't believe that had just happened.

"Oh my God, they're *so* right," cried Felicia. "You should enter the talent show! You know, it's hosted by Lucy Locket. She lives in the village too – the nice side."

Sabina's eyes widened at the name of the famous TV presenter. She knew who she was – but she'd never heard of the talent show. "The village has its own show? Or is this another MG thing?"

Felicia laughed. "No, it's a village thing! Thousands of people watch it. And obviously the whole of MG. Not everyone enters – there's a *very* high standard – but now that we're thirteen, we definitely will!"

"Exactly," said Alicia tightly, shooting Felicia a look. "We've already had our entry confirmed. We're doing a Taylor Swift cover. It's probably not your thing, Sabrina."

"But if she enters, we could be part of her entry and it would give us two chances to win!" said Felicia. "And two spots in the limelight!"

"Huh," said Alicia, her voice more relaxed. "That's true."

Sabina quickly spoke before the Leeches took over any more of her life. "Thanks, but there's *no way* I'd enter a talent show. As I said, I'm not using my powers any more."

"You have to," cried Felicia. "I need to know if Alexis and I go to the dance together! She's so hot and cold, it's hard to tell how much she likes me. We've broken up so many times over the last year, I'm so confused."

"I'm sorry, I can't—"

Alicia interrupted her. "Oh, but you *can*," she said sweetly. "At least, if you want us to continue protecting you. Otherwise, I'm sure the entire canteen has some requests they'd love to share with you."

Sabina's face crumpled as she looked around the room.

Sure enough, dozens of girls were pointing at her and whispering. The interest in her clearly hadn't died down.

But she couldn't do the Leeches' fortunes again! And they'd never leave her alone if she kept refusing – that just made them try even harder. Unless...she gave them what they wanted *without* doing a vision?

She had already seen Felicia and Alexis in her vision of the Winter Ball. They did technically go together – only then Alexis broke up with her. But maybe she could just tell the Leeches the bit they wanted to hear? Then they might *finally* leave her alone!

"Well..." she said slowly, turning to Felicia. "I did see you and Alexis together when I had the vision of Alicia and Dillon. You definitely went together."

"Oh my God, yes!" squealed Felicia. "I'm so happy! Thank you!" She hugged Sabina tight, and Sabina smiled uncomfortably.

But her smile disappeared when she saw the time on Felicia's smart watch. "Oh no! It's one forty-five!"

"Fifteen minutes left to finish your poké," said Alicia. "And maybe do me a quick vision about Dillon? I'd *love* to know if he has plans for the weekend."

"Can't you just ask him?" said Sabina. "I have to go, sorry!" She grabbed her bag.

"*Ask* him?" echoed Alicia in confusion, as Sabina raced off. She couldn't believe she'd spent so long with the Leeches! She *really* hoped Faye wouldn't mind that she was late...

"Where have you been?" cried Faye as Sabina arrived, breathless and sweaty.

"I'm so sorry," gasped Sabina. "I lost track of time." She leaned against the wall to get her breath back, then looked around. "Where is everyone?"

Faye flushed. "There...weren't many people. And they've already gone."

"Oh." Sabina felt her heart melt for Faye. If only she'd been there from the start! "I'm so sorry. People probably didn't know it was happening."

"I put it on the Year Eight WhatsApp thread," said Faye. "Twice."

"I'm really sorry I wasn't here," apologized Sabina. "Maybe we can do it again later this week?"

Faye shrugged. "It's fine. We only have one more day till we vote on Wednesday anyway – it's not like I could change anything drastically now. I'll focus on my digital campaign – I'm obviously not so good at the in-person ones."

"That's not true! Oh, I *wish* I'd been here to help."

"Me too," replied Faye, looking past Sabina at a bunch of students who were pointing at her in awe. "Then people definitely would have turned up. Considering you're the school celebrity."

Sabina made a face. "As if!" Then something struck her.

"Hey, have you had lunch?"

Faye shook her head. "I didn't have time. I was going to get a sandwich."

"How about a kidney bean curry and rice?" asked Sabina, proudly pulling out her lunchbox. "Made by your favourite mum – mine! You can eat this in ten minutes, right?"

Faye's face lit up. "She gave you an extra one for me? That's so nice of her!" She immediately opened it up and began spooning it into her mouth. "Mmm it's so good, I'll be done in five!"

Sabina smiled hesitantly, not wanting to correct Faye. If she told her the truth, Faye would find out she'd had lunch with the Leeches. And she *really* didn't want Faye to feel like she'd deliberately chosen to spend her lunch break with them instead of coming to her rally. She knew Faye would probably understand she didn't have a choice. But it wasn't worth the risk. It would be better if Faye never found out at all.

Chapter 14

"Sabiiiina, Faye's here!"

Sabina hurriedly dropped her maths textbook and sped into the hallway. "Faye, hi!"

"Nice to see you again, Faye." Sabina's mum smiled. "I'm so glad you're keeping Sabs company because I have to head out to work again. Emergency manicures never stop!"

"I had no idea a manicure could be an emergency," said Faye, serious as ever. "Oh, and I'd just like to thank you, Ms Patel, for the delicious curry and rice."

Sabina's eyes widened in panic. "Come on, Faye, let's go upstairs!" She was about to grab Faye's arm, then realized she couldn't risk touching her when her emotions were rising. She forced herself to breathe instead.

"Curry and rice?" said Sabina's mum, confused. "Oh, dinner! You're welcome! I hope you enjoy it! I might stay out a little longer to meet a friend – if you don't mind, Sabs?"

"Uh, yes, fine," said Sabina, distracted, as she gestured for Faye to follow her. "Come on!"

"All right," said Faye, walking towards her. "I'm coming! Bye, Ms Patel!"

"Bye, girls!" said Sabina's mum, grabbing her coat and blowing them kisses as she left. "Make sure you get your homework done!"

"I've already done mine," replied Faye. "I asked Ms Baker what it was going to be last week, then did it over the weekend. More time efficient."

"Right," said Sabina's mum, taken aback. "Perhaps you can take a leaf out of Faye's book, Sabs! I might have a drink after work with my friend again!"

"Okay, bye!" said Sabina impatiently, waiting for the door to close behind her.

"Your mum was being odd," remarked Faye. "Why did she say the curry was dinner not lunch? And she said 'enjoy' in the present tense instead of 'enjoyed'."

"She probably got confused," said Sabina. "She's made curry and rice for dinner tonight as well. Anyway, let's go to my room. I'm ready to hear your idea."

"You might not like it," warned Faye. "But I think you need to learn to control your powers by learning how to have visions. On-demand ones."

Sabina crossed her arms. "No way. Absolutely not. That's

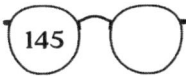

not the plan! You were meant to help me *stop* having visions. Not to get more visions!"

"Didn't you hear what Diva said? You can't get rid of them. All you can do is learn to control them. Which means accepting them and *embracing* them."

"You want me to hug my powers?"

Faye rolled her eyes. "Embracing in the metaphorical sense. You need to work with them. And I'm sorry, Sabina, but if you want to stop having random visions, you need to control them. Which means learning to breathe to calm yourself down to not get unwanted ones, but also learning to have visions."

"But WHY?" cried Sabina. "Can't I just focus on stopping them?"

Faye shook her head. "There's too much energy in you. You have to use your powers sometimes or they'll come out anyway. Like when you were really happy on the phone to Harry and Ria."

Sabina groaned and dropped her head into her hands. "Seriously? These powers won't give me a break?"

Faye shook her head. "Doesn't look like it. You need to learn to use them. Which means practising having visions. Now."

"But...what if I have visions about you?" cried Sabina. "I don't want to hurt you!"

Faye grinned. "I've had an idea that will avoid you having visions about anyone but yourself."

Sabina frowned. "Myself? Is that even possible?"

"We're about to find out!"

Sabina and Faye stood silently in front of the bathroom mirror, looking at their reflections. Faye's eyes met Sabina's in the mirror.

"Are you ready?" she asked.

Sabina had never thought of telling her own future – she'd been focused on avoiding all visions as much as possible. But now there was a chance of it happening, she was nervous. She had no idea what she'd see. What if she ended up having lunches alone for the rest of her time at MG? Or – worse – something happened to her friendship with Harry and Ria?

"It'll be okay," said Faye gently. "And at least this way you won't know things about anyone else. It'll just be about yourself. Which can't be that bad!"

"I hope you're right..."

"I am," said Faye confidently. "Now, we need your emotions to be nice and balanced for you to have a vision, so I'm going to suggest you start with a meditation."

"But...I thought I get visions when my emotions are super high?" asked Sabina, confused.

"Yes, random uncontrolled visions," said Faye. "But we're trying to control your visions and get on-demand ones, which means you need to start with balanced emotions. And then you need to come up with an intention for having a vision."

"Why is that better than just having random visions when I'm emotional?"

"I think this way you might be able to control exactly *what* you have a vision about!" said Faye. "Come on, you'll see what I mean. Just breathe deeply, engage your chakras, and whatever else you do when you meditate."

Sabina reluctantly closed her eyes, and let her breath deepen. She started to imagine the seven bright lights down her spine. After a few breaths, she felt herself sink into her body, aware of it in a way she hadn't been the whole day.

"Are you ready for the next bit?" said Faye quietly. "You need to focus on your intention. You can say something in your head like, 'I want to have a vision about myself.'"

Sabina did what Faye said, repeating the phrase in her head. Twice.

"Okay, now gently reach your hand out to touch your reflection in the mirror. And keep focusing on your intention. There you go, no a bit more to the left, higher…there you go!"

Sabina's left hand landed on the smooth glass of the mirror and she gasped as a sharp jolt ran through her body. The bathroom swirled around her until she wasn't there any more. She was in…a swimming pool! Only it didn't look anything like the local pool her mum had taken her to when they first arrived in the village. This one was indoors, wooden and super luxurious. There was loud music playing, and the whole of Year Eight was there!

Sabina saw three girls lying on inflatable beds in the pool, wearing sparkling bikinis, taking a selfie together, even though they could easily drop the phone into the pool. The Leeches, obviously. Alicia was in a bright fuchsia bikini, Felicia was next to her in a blue sequinned one, and on their right was a girl in a green shimmery bikini. Sabina frowned – this girl had brown skin, long dark hair and looked kind of like Sabina without glasses.

That was when Sabina cried out loud – it *was* her! Hanging out with the Leeches!

She blinked and the next thing she knew she was back in the bathroom, with Faye looking excitedly at her.

"What did you see?" asked Faye. "It worked, didn't it?"

Sabina swallowed anxiously. Everyone knew the Leeches were throwing a pool party for their Form Prefect victory. She couldn't bear for Faye to know she'd seen that happen in the future. Let alone the fact that she, Sabina Patel, had been there, wearing a bikini and taking a selfie with the Leeches! She didn't even *own* a bikini!

"Well?!"

"Um...I...saw myself with the Leeches," said Sabina eventually, trying to think of a way to minimize what she'd seen so she wouldn't hurt Faye. "I...took a selfie with them."

"Okay," said Faye, jotting it down in her notebook, completely unperturbed.

"That's...it? You don't think it's weird?"

"You're the school celebrity. Of *course* the Leeches want a selfie with you!"

Sabina laughed nervously. "I'm not really. The Leeches just..."

"Like any attention, including the attention you're providing them," said Faye matter-of-factly. "Now...do you want to try the next part of the experiment?"

"There's a next part?"

"Yep," said Faye, her eyes shining in excitement. "And I think you'll like this part more. It involves having an intention *not* to get a vision!"

"But isn't that what I've been doing lately anyway? Breathing to control my emotions so I don't get a vision?"

"Yes, but I think adding in the intention will make it even stronger!" said Faye. "If it works, you'll be able to control when you do and don't get a vision – just by breathing and having intentions! Won't that be good?"

"It would definitely be better than now," agreed Sabina.

"Okay, so, eyes closed. Breathe again. Get nice and relaxed. Then when you're ready, focus on your intention to *not* have a vision, and touch the mirror. Okay?"

Sabina took her time, allowing her mind to clear as she breathed in and out a few times. When she felt fully relaxed, she slowly reached out to touch the mirror, with the sentence "I do not want a vision" repeating in her mind.

Her fingers touched the cool glass and…nothing!

She opened her eyes delightedly. "It worked!"

Faye beamed back at her. "Celebratory curry and rice?"

"Yes, please!"

Chapter 15

The next morning, Sabina padded down to the kitchen to find her mum simultaneously heating up a saucepan of chai and a pan of scrambled eggs. "Mum, you're still here!" she said in excitement. "I thought you'd be at work!"

"I don't have any clients till ten so I thought I'd treat us to a proper breakfast. One piece of toast or two?"

"Two, obviously," said Sabina, sliding onto a stool. "How was the emergency manicure last night?"

"Oh, you know, the same as always! It turned into a facial, and then a therapy session. I wish I'd trained in therapy – then I could charge for that too!"

"Why don't you?" asked Sabina. "Everyone needs a side hustle."

Her mum laughed. "I don't think it's very common for beauty therapists to have a side business as real therapists."

"The clue's in the name, Mum." Sabina slurped her milky chai. "But I guess you're already living your dream by owning Beauties, right?"

Her mum smiled softly. "I am definitely doing what I've always wanted to do. It's just not exactly how I thought it would be."

"At least you're doing it!" said Sabina. "So, was it your client you hung out with after last night? Is she nice?"

Her mum hesitated. "Uh...very nice. Plate, please - eggs are ready!"

Sabina handed over her plate, wondering why her mum was being so vague. "Thanks. Are you going to be home this evening? Maybe we could watch a movie?"

"Oh, Sabs, I'm sorry. I'd love to - but I'm going to be at the salon till late. I have to do some bookkeeping."

Sabina sighed. "Of course. I should have guessed." Then her eyes lit up. "Wait, what if I come and sit at Beauties to do my homework while you do your book stuff? We could order in?"

Her mum's face fell. "Oh...I would have loved that...but I...can't."

"Why not?"

"I just don't think it's a good idea, when I have so much to do tonight," said her mum. She grabbed a slice of bread and shoved it in her mouth. "Mmm, bread!"

Sabina scrutinized her mum. She was a terrible liar, and it

was clear she was hiding something. What was it? Why didn't she want Sabina to come to the salon that night? Was something wrong?

Sabina felt her mind start to whir with possible disasters her mum could be hiding from her. It would be exactly like her to keep something a secret, thinking she was "protecting" Sabina, when Sabina could *definitely* handle the truth.

She realized her emotional levels were rising, and she forced herself to breathe deeply so she wouldn't have a vision. Then she paused. What if she *tried* to have a vision about her mum? It could tell her exactly what her mum was hiding from her!

Before she could change her mind, Sabina closed her eyes and breathed deeply. She channelled all her energy into relaxing and focusing on her intention: "I want a vision about something my mum's hiding from me."

"Here's your food," said her mum, putting a plate down in front of her.

Sabina reached out to touch her mum's hand. The jolt hit her instantly. She inhaled deeply as the kitchen whirled around, until she wasn't in it at all. She was back on the street outside Beauties. Except this time, there was no car or parking ticket. There was just her mum standing outside the salon, and a big *FOR LEASE* sign next to her. Sabina didn't understand – was this from the *past*? She remembered the sign from when they'd first gone to see the shop.

But then she noticed her mum was locking the door and crying. And Beauties was completely empty. There were boxes next to her mum, filled with all *her* stuff from the salon. The pretty nail polishes Sabina had helped her select. The soft white towels. And a framed photo of her and Sabina that had sat on the reception desk. Her mum sobbed harder, and with total horror, Sabina suddenly understood. Her mum was closing the salon. After all her hard work, her business had failed!

Sabina blinked as she found herself back in the kitchen. No wonder her mum didn't want her to come to the salon – she was trying to protect Sabina from seeing that the salon was failing. No wonder she was working weekends and spending more time at Beauties than ever. Sabina had thought it was a good thing her mum was so busy – that the salon was becoming super popular – but all along, her mum had been trying to save the salon.

"Sabina?" Her mum was looking at her strangely. "Are you all right? What were you doing with your eyes closed like that?"

Sabina plastered a bright smile on her face. "Nothing! Just...an early morning meditation. Diva's idea."

Her mum held her gaze for another moment, then shrugged. "You really are into meditating these days, aren't you? Well, bon appetit!"

Sabina felt her smile fade as she watched her mum spoon

eggs into her mouth. Her poor mum. She was going to lose her dream. And the only person who knew was Sabina. She *had* to do something to stop it.

Sabina slid onto the lab bench next to Faye ten minutes before their chemistry lesson officially began. "Faye! I've been looking everywhere for you. Where have you been all day?"

"Working," said Faye, leaning over her Bunsen burner, goggles on. "This *is* a school, not a social club."

"Are you still mad I missed the rally yesterday?" asked Sabina. "Please don't be. I'm really sorry – and I need your help! There's been a development."

Faye paused mid-Bunsen burner inspection. "One that could affect my thesis?"

"It's about my mum."

Faye sat up straight. "Go on, then."

"Okay, so...I used what we learned last night and deliberately had a vision this morning."

Faye's eyes widened. "It worked?"

Sabina nodded. "I was worried about my mum. So I managed to channel my energy into wanting to have a vision about her and...I did. She was closing Beauties, Faye! *For ever.* There was a For Lease sign outside."

"Oh, your poor mum. She'll be devastated."

"I know! I can't bear the thought of her failing – and I know it's going to be because of money. Money ruins everything."

"Do you know when this happens? Can we build a timeline? Any identifying details? Her clothes?" Faye's notepad and pen were already out.

Sabina bit her lip, thinking. "She was wearing her puffer. So...any time between now and the next three months? Unless it's a cold British summer like we had that year where it rained the whole time."

Faye sighed. "Fine, time unknown. Which means we need to try to save Beauties ASAP."

Sabina's eyes shone. "Really? Faye, do you mean it? You'll help me?"

"It's technically helping your mum," pointed out Faye, with a small smile. "And I'd definitely do that."

Sabina hugged her tight. "Yay, thank you. So where do we start?"

"We're going to need some money. We could campaign, but my Form Prefect campaign is showing that tends to be more successful for popular people. Which is not me. So, we could try other methods. Like..." Her eyes lit up. "I know! There's a five-hundred-pounds cash prize for my chess competition, and I bet I'll win!"

"I can't accept that," replied Sabina immediately. "That's your money, Faye."

"But I don't need it. My parents already have a university fund for me, and that's the only thing I'd need it for."

Sabina shook her head. "It wouldn't feel right, Faye. I can't."

"Well, I could just spend it directly in the salon? I'll pay for as many manicures and facials as I can afford."

Sabina laughed. "Five hundred pounds would definitely get you a *lot* of manicures."

"*Faye Collins* is getting manicures?" Alicia's clear voice cut through their conversation. Sabina and Faye whirled around to see the Leeches looking at them, eyebrows raised. They both wore their hair teased into loose buns with tiny diamantés dotted around them. "Five hundred pounds' worth of them? Where?"

"At my mum's salon," said Sabina, quickly letting go of the pen she was holding. She wasn't going to risk having another vision while the Leeches were in the vicinity. "It's in the village."

"Oh my God, Beauties?" cried Felicia. "I got the best shellac there!"

Sabina nodded, trying not to think about how weird it was that her mum did her classmate's nails.

"You're so lucky," sighed Felicia. "I wish I had a mum who could give me free manicures!"

There was an awkward pause when all of them looked down at Sabina's unpolished, plain nails. She slid her hands into her pockets wishing her mum had been able to paint her nails like she'd been promising for weeks.

"She lets me use her products whenever I want," said Sabina, hoping this would make her seem cooler in the Leeches' eyes. "She has the best face masks."

Alicia frowned as she examined Sabina's skin. "Really? You should check you're using the right ones for your skin."

Sabina flushed. Of course, the Leeches didn't think she was cool.

"Anyway," said Alicia, turning to Faye. "Why would *you* want five hundred pounds' worth of manicures? And where are you even going to get five hundred pounds *from*?"

"I'll win it when I become the under-sixteen chess champion of Greater London. The only real competition is *Hvar*." Faye practically spat out his name. "He's sixteen, but I know I can beat him."

"The prize money is just five hundred pounds? That's nothing," said Alicia dismissively. "Sabina's going to win five thousand pounds in the talent show."

Sabina choked on air. "Wait, what?!"

"You know," said Felicia. "The village talent show the girls mentioned yesterday at lu—"

"Yep!" interrupted Sabina. "I know – with Lucy Locket. But I'm not actually going to enter! I'm not a standing-on-stage kind of girl. Plus, I'd never win."

"Not without us, obviously," said Alicia. "But we'd help you with the stage, set, costume and lighting. Then you could tell Lucy Locket's fortune and we'd all win. We don't need the money – we have loads – so you could have it. We just want to go on Lucy Locket's TikTok with her."

"She always invites the winners to do reels with her," said Felicia excitedly. "It's our dream."

Sabina shook her head. "Sorry, but that's not for me."

"Five thousand pounds is a lot better than five hundred pounds," said Alicia, looking pointedly at Sabina. "You could get ten times more manicures. I'm sure your mum's business would appreciate it."

Sabina's eyes widened. Had Alicia guessed the truth? She was about to say no again, but then she paused. Five thousand pounds was a *lot* of money. She bet it would be enough to help save her mum's business – or at least pay the salon rent for a few months. And she knew she couldn't take Faye's money. "I guess…I could think about it?" she said, deliberately not looking at Faye.

The Leeches cheered simultaneously.

"Yay!" said Felicia. "We'll sign you up at lunch."

"But I'm still not fully sure!" protested Sabina.

Alicia shrugged. "You will be. And the spaces fill up so it's better to be safe than sorry. Remember – five *thousand* pounds, Sabrina!" The Leeches walked off in sync, leaving Sabina and Faye alone.

"What…do you think of that?" asked Sabina.

"It's your life, Sabina," said Faye pointedly. "But I do have to warn you that doing this would open you up to a lot of public scrutiny. Are you sure you want that? I thought you didn't like the whole school treating you like a celebrity?"

Sabina sighed. Faye was right – she couldn't think of anything worse than standing on a stage and revealing her powers to Lucy Locket and a whole audience. But it wasn't like they had another plan. She knew how important her mum's business was to her. "Maybe…I could do this as a backup plan? And if we come up with something else, I can ditch it?"

Faye shrugged. "It's your choice. But these are the Leeches we're talking about."

"It'll be fine," said Sabina, hoping she was right. "They want to help me. And I bet we'll think of something else in the meantime – I probably won't even need to do it."

Chapter 16

Sabina stood in the makeshift wooden booth with her ballot sheet and pencil. It turned out that voting for Form Prefect was yet another event that MG took very seriously. A private wooden booth had been erected in the main assembly hall, and the whole of Year Eight had to queue up so they could go in one at a time and make their choice. It was meant to be their chance to "experience democracy", according to Mr Grant. Sabina couldn't wait to tell Harry and Ria – the one time they'd had to vote in Hackney High, the teacher had asked them to close their eyes and raise a hand.

Sabina's sheet told her to *mark an X in the box beside Alicia Johnson or Faye Collins.* Her pencil hovered above the box by Faye's name. Of course she wanted to vote for her friend. But was there any point when she wasn't going to win anyway? And what if the Leeches found out she hadn't voted for them?

She shook her head. They'd never find out who she voted for. And even if they did, it didn't matter. Faye was her friend; of course she was getting her vote.

Sabina firmly marked an X in the box by Faye's name and left the booth so the next student could go in. She pushed her folded-up paper into a giant wooden box, feeling a tingle of excitement. Perhaps her vision was wrong, and Faye would win after all!

"Sabriiiiiina!"

Sabina looked up as she left the hall – she was starting to forget Sabrina wasn't *actually* her name – to see the Leeches waving at her.

"Isn't this *so* exciting?" cried Alicia. "My populace are voting for me right now! I can't believe I'm going to win!"

Sabina quickly scanned the hallway to see if anyone was listening. They were safe. "Um, yeah," she said weakly. "Good luck."

"They're going to announce the votes on Friday!" squealed Felicia. "And our party will be on Saturday. Though obvs we're going to wait till Friday to *officially* announce it – it would be bad taste otherwise."

Sabina sighed in relief. "That sounds like a good idea."

"Of course it is – it's ours," said Alicia. The diamantés from the day before were gone. Today, she and Felicia each had their hair twisted into two little buns at the top of their heads. "We're grateful for your advance warning though – it means

we've been able to plan everything."

"Uh huh," agreed Felicia eagerly. "The caterers are sorted – and the DJ!"

"All you need to do is sort your outfit," said Alicia. "Dresses for the after-party and bikinis for the pre-party!"

Sabina didn't say anything. She had no intention of going to the Leeches' party. Even if Faye lost, Sabina would rather hang out with her than go to the Leeches' victory celebrations. They could even do a self-care night at hers, with her mum's face masks and creams.

"Oh and are you free at lunch today?" asked Felicia. "We can start practising for your competition entry."

"I'm still not one hundred per cent sure about doing it..." Sabina's voice trailed off at the expression on the Leeches' faces.

"Sabrina, this is a once in a lifetime opportunity," said Alicia firmly. "The competition is happening in just over *two* weeks. We have the Winter Ball in ten days, and then the talent show is the week after! Time is of the essence here. There's a lot going on right now!"

Sabina couldn't agree more.

"And we need to practise all the logistics," said Felicia. "Outfits, delivery, places onstage. Leesh and I are going to be your glamorous assistants."

"Muses," corrected Alicia. "There's loads to discuss, like playlists, scent ambience and general vibes. We'll need every lunchtime up till the competition."

"*Every* lunchtime?" cried Sabina.

"Exactly," said Felicia. "Leesh and I have been practising our routine for weeks already. Time's running out."

"Think about the prize money," reminded Alicia. "And you can repay us for our help in visions. I'd love to know if Dillon's going to come to my pool party this weekend. Oh my God, maybe we'll kiss, then we can celebrate our kiss-iversary at the Winter Ball the following weekend!"

"I LOVE that for you," squealed Felicia. "Sabrina, you can let us know at lunch!"

The Leeches turned in sync and walked off towards the classroom, leaving Sabina reeling from everything they'd said. Thank goodness they'd left when they had – she'd felt her emotions starting to rise scarily high.

Sabina hadn't realized that by making the talent show her backup plan, the Leeches would expect her to practise *every* lunchtime until then! She really hoped Faye would come up with another way to help her mum, but in the meantime, she had no choice but to work with the Leeches.

Which meant that she needed to keep practising to balance her emotions so she could control her visions. So far, it seemed to be working. She'd managed to avoid having a vision in English when Mrs Fairweather had picked her to do her spontaneous soliloquy first. Sabina had felt her palms go sweaty as she'd walked to the front of the classroom, panicking as she remembered the last vision she'd had around Mrs

Fairweather. Luckily, she'd caught Faye's eye, and everything came back to her. She forced herself to breathe deeply until she calmed down. When she had to pick up Macbeth's crown, she'd inwardly repeated her intention – "I do not want to have a vision" – and it had worked. She'd put on the crown, recited the soliloquy she'd practised after Mrs Fairweather had warned her it wasn't so spontaneous after all, and not humiliated herself once.

Sabina was grateful she was managing to control her powers, but she also knew it could change at any moment. It was why she was still doing her nightly meditations. Last night, her mum had been stuck at the salon till late *again*. Sabina had felt terrible knowing that she was trying so hard to save Beauties when her vision showed it wouldn't work. It made Sabina even more determined to try and change the future. So she'd pushed her worries to the side, and spent an hour on her cushion with her crystal doing her chakra meditation. It had been as relaxing as usual, and it meant her emotional levels felt very balanced today. Plus, she was starting to get used to her super sight. It would be weird to *not* see every detail of Mr Grant's face (he was starting to get a new spot, millimetres from where the old one was. Sabina was predicting a whitehead).

"What did they want?" Faye appeared by Sabina's side, gesturing towards the retreating Leeches.

"Oh, to talk about the show. They want me to practise

every day. Please tell me you've thought of another way to help my mum?"

"Well, we could invest my chess money once I've won it and try to make a profit?"

"Faye, you know I can't take your money," said Sabina, trying to hide her disappointment that Faye hadn't come up with a genius idea. "My mum wouldn't like it."

"Would she like you telling futures on a stage?"

Sabina hesitated. She had no idea what her mum would think of her doing the talent show. It was yet another thing she was keeping from her... She wasn't used to hiding so much – before the move, they'd always shared everything. Even the two-day crush she'd had on Harry in Year Six, before he came out as gay. The only reason she was even managing to keep all this from her mum was because she was so busy at work that they hardly saw each other any more. But Sabina knew it was better this way – her mum had enough problems of her own, and she'd freak out if she discovered her daughter was psychic.

"I'm going to have to hope she'll be fine with it, because right now it's my only option."

"There must be another way," said Faye. "We can try to find one at lunch?"

"The Leeches want me to practise with them at lunch."

Faye gave her a look that Sabina couldn't decipher. "Right. Well, we'd better go to geography. Ms Baker hates it when people are late."

"Which makes her a total hypocrite," pointed out Sabina. "Seeing as she spends most of class looking at cat memes on her phone."

Faye's eyes widened. "She does? How do you know?

"Super sight," said Sabina. "Wait till you hear what Mrs Fairweather's screensaver is…"

"Silence everyone, it's time for another surprise test," said Ms Baker.

The entire class erupted in protest.

"But we just HAD one," cried Alicia. "That's not fair!"

"Yes, and apart from Faye and Sabina, everybody else failed," pointed out Ms Baker. "So, we're doing another one. And if the whole class doesn't pass, then we'll be doing surprise tests *weekly* for the rest of term."

They all turned to look at each other in alarm. This was awful news! Even Faye looked mildly stricken.

"Right, here they are," said Ms Baker, pulling out a stack of sheets. Then she frowned. "Oh, I forgot to print the rest! Grace, will you – oh no, it's a test, I can't ask you to photocopy it." She stood up reluctantly. "Right, I'll be back in ten minutes, girls. You can use this time to do some much-needed revision. One clue, volcanoes."

There was a loud rustling as everyone opened their textbooks to the chapter on volcanoes. Everyone except the Leeches.

Alicia – who hadn't even taken her textbook out of her bag – walked towards Sabina with a funny smile on her face. "Sabrina. I've just had an idea."

"What...is it?"

"I need you to do what you did last time we had a geography test. Look into the future for the answers. Except this time, you can do it for all of us."

Sabina paled. "But...I can't...that's *cheating*! It was an accident last time, I swear!"

Alicia turned to face the class, clapping for attention. "Who here thinks Sabrina should use her psychic powers to tell us the answers for the test?"

Everyone – except Faye – shot their hands up immediately.

"That's not ethical, Alicia," said Faye. "We could all get in trouble. Especially Sabina."

"Says the class geek," said Alicia. "This is the only way the rest of us can avoid getting weekly quizzes."

"Look, there's even a test here you can touch, Sabrina!" said Felicia, standing by Ms Baker's desk, holding up a sheet of paper.

"Leave her alone," said Faye. "If you want to cheat, can't you at least do it the old-fashioned way and use your textbook to find out the answers? It isn't fair to get Sabina in trouble."

"That'll take way too long," dismissed Alicia. "And no one will get in trouble. It's not like it's a national exam. It's just a pointless surprise quiz made up by a bored old woman."

"I think she's only in her thirties," said Sabina. "But...it *is* pointless."

"Exactly! So, help us pass!"

Felicia walked over to Sabina's desk with the test, placing it in front of her. "Here you go."

Sabina bit her lip, feeling her emotions rise. She didn't know what to do. The whole class was now chorusing their requests for her to use her powers and save them – except Faye, who shook her head wordlessly. So many things could go wrong if she cheated – she could get caught, maybe even *expelled*, and her mum would be furious if she found out. But if she didn't, then the whole class would hate her, the Leeches might stop helping her with the talent show, which would leave her without a single plan to save Beauties, *and* she'd fail her geography test, which would still mean her mum would be furious.

Besides, Sabina *really* didn't want a surprise quiz every week. And maybe it wasn't that unethical if she helped the entire class? Last time she'd felt guilty because she'd been the only one to get top marks when she didn't deserve them – but at least this way, everyone would. And it wasn't like it was deliberate cheating. She wasn't googling the answers or anything – she was just touching a piece of paper!

Sabina glanced at Faye, and mouthed, "Sorry." Before she could change her mind – or see Faye's reaction – she closed her eyes, took a deep breath, and focused all her energy on

what she was about to do. She reached out to touch the paper with her intention: "I want a vision of the corrected answers." Her eyes shot open as she felt a jolt run through her body and everything spun around her.

Just like the last time, she found herself back in the geography classroom, looking at the sheet in front of her. And exactly like before, she could now see all the answers on the sheet written in pen, after being corrected by Ms Baker. She scanned them quickly – magma, lava, plate margins... She read them one more time, and when she was sure she knew them all, she blinked.

"Whoaaah, you were so out of it," gasped Felicia, as Sabina came back to reality. "That was wild!"

"Did you get the answers?" asked Alicia, as the rest of the class stared in awed silence.

Sabina nodded.

"Quick, write them down!"

Felicia handed Sabina a piece of paper, and Sabina followed Alicia's command, studiously avoiding looking at Faye. "There, that's all of them."

Felicia held up the piece of paper and Alicia took a photo of it on her phone. She tapped her screen a few times, and within seconds, it was sent to the entire form.

"Done!" she said. "Quick, Leesh, get rid of Sabina's sheet. And put the test back!"

Felicia followed Alicia's orders while the rest of the class

silently studied the answers on their phone screens. Sabina stole a quick glance at Faye to see if she was doing the same, but she was the only one reading her textbook. She felt a lump of guilt in her throat, then swallowed it away. This wasn't a big deal. It was only a surprise quiz and Faye could do whatever she wanted. And so could Sabina. Just because she took Faye's advice on her powers didn't mean she had to do *everything* she said.

By the time Ms Baker walked back into the classroom, everyone's phones were away and they had memorized the answers. "Right. Textbooks away. Felicia, hand the tests out. Fifteen minutes. Go!"

Chapter 17

The next day, Sabina walked into the form room and halted in surprise. There were two huge boxes of cupcakes in the middle of the room – gorgeous, vanilla-smelling cupcakes with pastel-coloured buttercream icing on top. She was so blindsided by the unexpected sight that it took her a moment to notice that the Leeches were standing by them, matching pastel-coloured headbands in their hair.

"Sabrina, *finally*," cried Felicia. "We've been waiting for you to hand out the cupcakes!"

"What, why? Is it your birthday?"

Alicia rolled her eyes. "Uh, were you not in geography this morning? We all passed with full marks because of YOU. Well, almost all of us. So, we ordered in celebratory cupcakes for the form!"

Sabina's smile faltered. Ms Baker had returned their tests

that morning, telling the class she was amazed by their results. All of them had got full marks – except for Faye, the only one who hadn't cheated. She'd still got 95%, but Sabina felt bad about it. Especially when Faye had slipped out of the lesson as soon as the bell went, meaning they hadn't even been able to talk afterwards. It wasn't that Sabina *regretted* using her powers to help everyone – Ms Baker had confirmed their unexpected results meant she would honour her promise and the rest of term would be test-free. It was more that she felt guilty about doing something Faye hadn't approved of.

"Come on," said Alicia impatiently, clapping her hands for attention. "Listen up, everyone! We've ordered you these delicious cupcakes – from the vegan bakery in the village – to celebrate our *incredible* geography scores!" The class cheered. "As we all know, we would never have got full marks if it wasn't for Sabrina and her magic powers – so, Brina, do you want to do the honours and hand them out?"

Sabina flushed as the whole class fell silent to watch her walk over to the cupcake boxes. She lifted one up with a nervous smile, and the room erupted in loud applause. Sabina couldn't help but grin.

"Please do *not* take photos of Sabrina," called out Alicia, as some of their classmates reluctantly lowered their phones. "She's not available for selfies or psychic readings. Cupcakes only."

Sabina had already handed out a whole box to her

classmates – all of whom had gushed over how incredible her powers were – when Faye walked into the room. Sabina rushed over to her. "Faye! I have a cupcake for you!"

Faye took the pink cupcake from Sabina's outstretched hand, pleased. "Thanks. What's the occasion?"

"Our geography results, of course!" said Alicia, sidling up behind Sabina. "Also, Brina, Leesh and I came up with the PERFECT name for your talent-show act! Wait for it…Sabrina the Teenage Witch!"

"But…I'm not a witch," replied Sabina, confused.

"Nor is your name Sabrina," muttered Faye, but the Leeches acted like she hadn't spoken.

"It's the name of an old TV show our mums watched when they were our age," explained Felicia. "Isn't it retro? I love it!"

"The judges will totally have heard of it because they're old too," said Alicia. "So, it's perfect!"

"I'll think about it." The Leeches' faces fell so Sabina quickly added: "I mean, it's great. It's just I don't really… identify as a witch."

"You've got to think about the branding," said Alicia, sounding just like Harry. "Witch sounds way better than psychic. It's more intriguing!"

Faye put her cupcake down without taking a bite. "I have some chemistry revision to do."

"Maybe we can have lunch together?" suggested Sabina.

"You can't," said Alicia. "Practice, remember? We need at

least half an hour at lunch today to discuss costumes and set design – as well as the big plan we need to tell you!"

Faye shook her head. "It looks like you don't need me for any more plans."

"Wait!" cried Sabina. "I do!"

But it was too late. Faye had already walked out of the classroom door.

Felicia stared after her in amazement. "I can't believe she didn't want a cupcake! She knew they were vegan, right?"

Sabina glanced at the clock. The Leeches had been talking non-stop for twenty minutes about costumes, set design and what aesthetic would work best for their act. Sabina had given up trying to join in because she didn't understand what they were talking about, and she couldn't wait for them to finish. They had meditation straight after lunch, and she was hoping to get there early so she could speak to Diva before class. She wanted to update her. But she also had questions. Mainly about whether she'd definitely be able to get on-demand visions for Lucy Locket in front of a huge audience.

Because that was the Leeches' big plan for her. They wanted her to touch Lucy Locket's famous locket – a gold, mysterious-looking antique necklace she wore around her neck. There had been endless tabloid articles speculating about what was inside the locket. What was in it? A parent? A pet? Her best friend? Or even a boyfriend? Nobody knew and Lucy hadn't told a soul. But the Leeches wanted Sabina to use her powers to find out and tell the whole world. Or at least the village audience at the talent show.

Sabina was terrified. She knew she'd improved when it came to on-demand visions, and the intentions were helping. But she wasn't sure she'd be able to get a vision about who was inside Lucy's locket. It was so specific. And did that count as looking into the future? She had no idea, and the only person she could speak to about it was Diva. Normally, it would be Faye. But Sabina knew she didn't approve of the talent show plan. And even though it had started as a backup, right now, it felt like the *only* way to help her mum save Beauties.

"So, Sabrina, we've already emailed the show organizers and they've confirmed Lucy is okay with us touching her locket," said Alicia. "All you need to do is make sure you can see what's inside!"

Sabina gulped. "You've heard back from them already?"

"Obvs," said Felicia. "We're super efficient!"

"And we need to make sure *nothing* goes wrong," added Alicia. "This isn't just about you – it's our rep on the line. We're the ones introducing you. And bringing you the locket. And explaining to the audience what's happening when you have your vision. We're kind of the main part of the act."

"Okay," whispered Sabina nervously. She was surprisingly glad that the Leeches would be onstage with her – she was

terrible at public speaking but it was clearly the Leeches' forte. "Thanks."

"You're welcome," said Alicia graciously. "We'll manage everything – winning the audience over, the logistics, the outfits. You just need to make sure you can control your powers."

"Do you want to practise now?" offered Felicia. "You can try touching my jewellery?"

Sabina shook her head quickly. She was too nervous to risk a vision – who knew what would come up? – and she was scared of it going wrong. Because she knew that if there was the slightest chance of her failing, the Leeches would instantly rescind their offer to help, and she'd be back to square one. If Sabina was going to save Beauties, she *needed* their help.

"Diva, please can I speak to you?" said Sabina. The rest of the class were coming in and settling on their mats, while Sabina had joined Diva as she put on relaxing music. "I want to ask you something."

Diva raised an eyebrow. "No Faye today?"

Sabina flushed. "No. Um, she's been helping me. With the breathing and intentions, and we've worked out how to control the visions a bit more. But...there's something she can't help me with."

"Go on," said Diva, glancing at her watch. "You have precisely two minutes before we start."

"I need to do a talent show," burst out Sabina. "To help my mum save her dream. So I'm going to use my powers. Onstage. I have to touch Lucy Locket's locket and see what's inside, but does that count as seeing the future? And what if it doesn't work? And I don't know if it's the right thing to do!"

Diva held up a hand. "Breathe," she commanded. "Sabina, I can't tell you what to do. Your powers are yours and you're the only one who can truly understand them. But the powers *are* linked to integrity – to being true to yourself. So, what I will suggest is that you think deeply about your intention. Why are you doing this? Does it feel right to you on a deeper level? And does it feel honest?"

Sabina frowned. Her intention was obvious – it was to help her mum. Wasn't that honest? And the right thing to do? Diva's answer made her feel even more confused. She opened her mouth to reply but Diva was busy clapping her hands for attention. The sound reverberated around the gym, causing everyone to fall silent.

Sabina's two minutes were up.

"Welcome," said Diva. "I hope you have all managed to practise your yoga and meditation since we saw each other at the beginning of the week." There was an awkward silence, as everyone avoided eye contact with her. "Or maybe not," said Diva drily. "Either way, we're going to do more today. We'll start with a few stretches and then go into our meditation.

Now – hands on shoulders and make circles with your elbows."

Sabina obeyed, frustration flooding her body. She didn't understand why Diva had to be so cryptic all the time. What did she mean about integrity? It was like she was suggesting Sabina's intention was wrong – but how could it be when it was so selfless?

She wished Faye had been there to translate for her. She glanced at Faye, who was on her left, stretching with the same amount of focus she used to solve algebra equations. Sabina missed telling Faye everything. Maybe she could try again? She knew she'd disappointed Faye by cheating on the geography quiz, but they were still friends. Maybe they just needed to spend more time together?

"Faye," she whispered suddenly. "Do you want to come over this weekend?"

"Shh, you need to focus," Faye whispered back. "Meditation helps keep your powers balanced, remember?"

"Please," begged Sabina. "If you say no, my emotional levels might rise to a nine..."

Faye suppressed a smile. "Oh, fine. I'll come after chess on Saturday."

Sabina grinned. "Yay! I'll ask my mum if we can have a sleepover."

"Excuse me." Diva cleared her throat and looked directly at Sabina. "I'm sure whatever you're talking about is of the utmost importance, but I do expect full concentration in my class. Otherwise, I'll have to ask you to leave. So, do I have your attention?"

There was silence then Diva spoke again. "That was not a rhetorical question. Sabina?"

Sabina felt her cheeks flush. She rarely got called out in class and she really didn't like it. "Yes. Sorry."

Diva nodded. "Glad to hear it. Right, now let's begin our meditation. Get comfortable, eyes closed, and...let's connect to our chakras."

Sabina fidgeted as Diva guided them through the familiar chakra meditation. She hated that she'd just embarrassed her in front of everyone – especially when Diva knew what she was going through! She was the star pupil when it came to meditation – so why was Diva being so un-understanding? A wave of resentment washed over Sabina as Diva told them to imagine a bright red light at the root of their spines. It wasn't fair – the Leeches had been whispering throughout the stretches too; she'd heard them!

Nothing was fair at the moment. Sabina kept upsetting people without meaning to. But did nobody understand that it wasn't easy to suddenly develop psychic powers and super sight? She felt the anger grow hot inside her, and then a rush of electricity tingled through her fingers. She opened her eyes in alarm. She'd almost felt the familiar jolt that happened before having a vision – but she wasn't touching anything!

Sabina forced herself to breathe. She didn't want to have a random vision in the middle of meditation class – that did not suggest she was on her way to controlling her powers. She turned to Faye, about to tell her that she was reaching a nine.

But just as Sabina opened her mouth to whisper to Faye, she caught Diva's eye. Her teacher stared directly at her, then beckoned Sabina with her finger. Sabina hesitated, unsure what to do. Did Diva really want her to stand up in the middle of the meditation? But her teacher's repeated gestures suggested that was exactly what she wanted.

Slowly, Sabina walked over to her.

"Sabina," said Diva quietly. "You're not present today. I don't want your energy affecting the other students, so I'm going to ask you to leave."

Sabina's mouth dropped open. "But I—"

Diva raised a hand. "We can talk about it another time – let's not disturb the others."

Sabina shook her head as she walked towards the door, frustration rising in her. She couldn't *believe* Diva had done that! She turned around one last time to see if the teacher had changed her mind, but Diva's back was facing her. Sabina noticed the Leeches peering at her with one eye open each. Great. Now *everyone* would know she'd been kicked out of class.

Sabina stormed off to the changing rooms and slumped down on a bench, furious, her emotions still rising. She'd only been trying to get help for the powers that Diva and her mystic chakras had given her. And now she was sitting out here all alone. She didn't know what to do – but then it hit her.

Harry and Ria – of *course*! She rummaged around in her bag for her phone, and quickly called her friends. But they didn't answer. A moment later, her phone vibrated with a message.

> Ria: In maths! All okay?

> Sabina: NO! Can we chat?

> Harry: Soz babe, but you're going to have to chat to Faye instead.
> Mr Carter is in a major mood.

> Ria: ...

Sabina could see Ria typing out a message – but then it stopped before she hit send. Clearly Mr Carter had got in the way of their communication. She sighed loudly, feeling a wave of longing. She really missed her friends. She'd managed to keep them updated on all the major things going on lately, with messages and voice notes, but they hadn't had a proper chat in *ages*. It felt like the more time passed, the harder it was to keep in touch.

She opened her phone to the lock screen so she could look at the selfie of her, Harry and Ria. She desperately wished she was with them right now, even if it meant being bored to death by Mr Carter. She reached out to rub a speck of dirt from her screen – it was on Ria's forehead and made it look like she had a spot – and then gasped as her whole body jerked with the now-familiar signal that she was, whether she liked it or not, about to have another vision.

Sabina clutched onto the phone tight as everything around her whirled. When it stopped, she saw herself on a video call with Harry and Ria.

Harry's pixelated face looked serious. "That's not cool, Sabina," he said finally. "I'm going to need some space from you."

"Me too," said Ria. "I know you're going through a lot, but you're not the Sabina you used to be. We should go."

Sabina gasped at exactly the same time as her future self did. "I am!" cried Future Sabina. "Look, I didn't mean what I said. You'll still come to watch my show, won't you? Please, I—"

But the call ended and their faces disappeared from the screen.

Present Sabina blinked in pained shock and found herself back in the changing room. Had she really seen Harry and Ria saying they needed SPACE from her?! They'd never had an argument in their lives – well, apart from silly squabbles over snack choices and what constituted a good movie – but this was totally different. Sabina had done something "not cool" and her best friends were upset with her.

She swallowed sharply at the severity of what she'd seen, trying to piece it together. There was no real information about when her vision took place, but it had to be sometime between now and the talent show. She had no idea what she'd said that had upset Harry and Ria so much, only that she regretted it. And she didn't even know where she'd been when she'd video called them – all she could see was a white wall behind her, which could be *anywhere*!

With so little information, how could she avoid this coming true? There was no way she could cope if that conversation actually happened. She'd *die* without Harry and Ria.

She needed to do something! But what?

Suddenly, Sabina understood. There was only one way to avoid saying something to upset Harry and Ria. She had to stop speaking to them – or at least video calling them – until the talent show was over and she was sure the vision couldn't come true.

The thought of not speaking to her best friends made her want to cry. But it was the only way she could think of to save their friendship.

Chapter 18

The next morning, Sabina walked to school feeling grateful that it was finally Friday. The week had felt never-ending – she couldn't believe how much had happened, from turning up at school on Monday as some kind of celebrity, to upsetting Faye by missing her rally, cheating on the geography exam, having a vision about her mum's business closing, practising for the talent show with the Leeches, getting sent out of Diva's class, not to *mention* her vision of Harry and Ria not speaking to her...

They'd tried to video call her last night, but she hadn't picked up. Even though she'd been sitting in her bedroom with zero plans, she'd messaged them back instead.

Sorry, homework!! But don't worry, all good! Catch up soon, followed by a string of their favourite emoji. It had hurt, but she knew she was doing the right thing to make sure her vision didn't come true.

Sabina was so ready for the weekend – she deserved it after the week she'd had – especially because Faye was coming over on Saturday and her mum had agreed to Faye sleeping over *and* using her Deliveroo to order whatever they wanted!

Sabina hoped Faye would be just as excited as her – they could stay up till midnight watching movies on her iPad, eating pizza or poké bowls, *and* her mum had promised to buy ingredients so they could make their famous quadruple chocolate brownies for Faye. Sabina wasn't entirely sure if they'd be consolation brownies once the Form Prefect results were out and Faye knew she'd lost – or if her vision wouldn't come true and they'd be celebratory brownies instead!

She gulped as she glanced at the clock and saw that assembly was about to start. Which meant that the Form Prefect results were about to be announced...

Sabina crept into the main hall, taking a seat at the back, just as Mr Grant walked onto the stage to get everyone's attention. His spot had *finally* faded, leaving behind a dark red scar. Although Sabina could see that he'd tried – and failed – to cover it with concealer. She made a grossed-out face as she noticed little bits of make-up flake off into the air. Then she breathed in sharply as she realized she'd seen this exact sight before, in her vision.

It was about to happen. On cue, Mr Grant started reading out the FP results for Year Seven. Sabina gripped the edge of her seat tight, her stomach churning in anticipation.

After what seemed like for ever, Mr Grant moved on to the results for Year Eight. "It was a very close race, but we do have a winner for Form Prefect." There was a major pause of suspense, as everyone looked around the room in hushed excitement. Then he spoke: "And so, please welcome to the stage, the new Year Eight Form Prefect...Alicia Johnson!"

The entire hall erupted into applause and, with a feeling of total déjà vu, Sabina turned her head to see Alicia beaming, striding down the aisle, waving as she made her way to the stage. That was where her vision had ended, but in real life, Sabina kept her head swivelling until she saw Faye. She was clapping for Alicia, but her eyes looked sad. Sabina felt her heart sink when she saw how disappointed her friend was. Poor Faye.

The second the assembly ended, Sabina rushed over to her. But the Leeches beat her to it.

"Faye, I just wanted to say no hard feelings," said Alicia, rearranging her sparkly hairclip with her left hand as she stretched out her right hand towards Faye.

Faye shook her hand, then withdrew it sharply. "Wait, is Felicia taking a photo of us?"

Felicia poked her head out from behind her phone to reveal her own sparkly hairclip. "You don't mind, do you? It's for our socials."

Faye scowled. "I do mind and I have to go to maths."

Sabina stepped forward. "Wait, I just wanted to say I'm

so sorry, Faye! Oh, but, uh, congrats, Alicia."

"Thanks, babe," said Alicia. "Though of course, thanks to you it wasn't exactly a surprise."

Sabina's eyes widened. Oh no. Alicia needed to stop talking! She took Faye's elbow quickly. "Let's walk to maths together?"

But Faye stayed put. "What do you mean, Alicia?"

"Well, Sabrina told me this would happen, of course!" Alicia giggled. "She had a vision!"

Faye's face went rigid. "Sabina, you *knew*?"

"I'm so sorry," cried Sabina. "I didn't *want* to know. I wish I hadn't seen it!"

Faye exhaled slowly, but then she nodded sharply. "Okay. This is hard for me to process, but I can understand how that would have put you in a difficult position."

Sabina felt a rush of gratitude towards her friend. "Oh, thank you, Faye. You're the best. And I *wish* I hadn't had that vision!"

"Uh, your visions are everything," cried Felicia. "Things have been *so* good with me and Alexis ever since you told me I'd go to the Winter Ball with her when we had poké on Monday."

"You had lunch together on Monday?" repeated Faye. "When...I had my rally?" Her face cleared. "The lunch you said your mum made for me. That was meant to be yours, wasn't it?"

Alicia's eyes sparkled. "Oh my God. Drama! We should leave you both to chat alone." But neither she nor Felicia made any effort to move.

"It's not what you think," said Sabina, flushing. "I'm really sorry. My mum would have loved you to eat it! And I didn't mean to not come to the rally. I lost track of time, just like I told you. I'm sorry."

Faye shrugged coolly. "It's fine." She turned on her heels and walked away.

Sabina ran after her, leaving the Leeches straining to hear what was going on. "Faye, wait! Please listen. It's not what you think."

"You *lied* to me," said Faye. "Twice. About having lunch with the Leeches on Monday, and your vision about Alicia winning."

"I didn't lie, I just...omitted telling you," said Sabina, feeling a rising wave of panic inside her. She didn't want to upset Faye like this – it was what she'd been trying to avoid this whole time. "But either way, I'm so sorry! Please can I make it up to you on Saturday? My mum said we can have a sleepover and order in."

"I don't think that's a good idea. It's best if I have a bit of space from you this weekend."

Sabina's face fell, tears threatening to spill from her eyes. "Please, Faye, I'm so sorry!"

"Me too," said Faye, turning to leave.

Sabina reached out in desperation to grab Faye's arm to

stop her from leaving, but as her fingers grazed her blazer, Sabina jerked in shock. Oh no. She was having an uncontrolled vision!

Everything around her swirled, until she wasn't in the corridor any more. She was...standing on a stage! And everyone was clapping! There were bright lights and a huge audience. But more than that – Faye was standing right by her and they were hugging! The lights were so bright that Sabina blinked before she wanted to – and then she was back in the school corridor, alone.

Faye had gone.

Sabina stood still, uncertain about what to do. She hated that Faye was upset – she hated it SO much. But...her vision had been so lovely. It must have been the talent show, and if everyone was clapping, that meant she'd *won*. She'd saved Beauties. And Faye had forgiven her and was hugging her!

There were just over two weeks until the show, which meant she and Faye would be fine by then. Maybe she needed to trust that all Faye needed was a bit of space? It was frustrating though. Sabina felt like all she was doing lately was giving her friends space so they wouldn't be mad at her.

"You okay, babe?"

Sabina whirled around to see the Leeches. "Uh...I think so."

"We got you an almond croissant from the dining hall in case you needed cheering up," said Alicia, holding it out. "Eat it on the way to maths?"

Sabina hesitated, then reached for the croissant. It wasn't like she had anyone else to speak to right now – she may as well spend time with the Leeches while she waited for her friends to be her friends again.

The Leeches linked arms with her, and Sabina munched into the sweet pastry as they walked down the corridor, a trail of warm buttery flakes floating to the ground in her wake.

Chapter 19

"So what time is Faye coming over?" asked Sabina's mum as she stirred something suspiciously green on the hob. "I've bought all the brownie ingredients so we can make them together before I go out."

Sabina looked up from her juice in surprise. "You're working on a Saturday night *again*?"

Her mum looked sheepish. "Well, no...I'm actually going to have dinner with my friend. I didn't think you and Faye would want me hovering around during your big sleepover."

Sabina turned back to her juice, dejected. She hadn't told her mum that her sleepover with Faye was off, but she'd been hoping they could hang out instead. It had been ages since they'd had a night in together and Sabina really missed it. She wished they could watch funny movies, eat pizza and do their breathing ritual together. Things hadn't been going so well when she'd tried to do it alone...

She'd started to meditate the night before, but her mind had been full of worries about Faye being upset with her that day, Harry and Ria being upset with her in the *future,* and general panic that she would upset someone else soon. So, she'd ditched her meditation halfway through, not even getting to the heart chakra, hoping she could do it with her mum instead. But now that wouldn't be happening, and what if she couldn't meditate alone any more and her visions started becoming uncontrolled again? Then it would be impossible to get a vision about Lucy Locket's locket and save Beauties.

"Sabs, what is it?" asked her mum. "I thought you'd be super excited about tonight."

Sabina felt tears prick her eyelids. Maybe she should tell her mum everything – she felt so lonely keeping it all to herself. And if her mum understood, she'd definitely cancel her plans to be with Sabina.

But her mum was working so hard to save Beauties and she deserved a break to hang out with her new friend. Sabina didn't want to be selfish and stop her from having fun.

"It's just..." Sabina felt her voice break as a tear slid down her cheek. Oh no. She quickly let go of her juice so she wouldn't get a vision. "I..." She tried to control her breath whilst thinking of something she could share with her mum. "I miss Harry and Ria." She really *did* miss them – everything would be so simple if she still lived around the corner from them.

"Oh, baby." Her mum abandoned her green stew and came to sit next to Sabina. "I'm sorry. I know it must be hard. But they're coming over in the holidays, remember? It won't be long now – there's only a couple of weeks left till the end of term!"

Sabina really hoped they would still be coming in the holidays to watch her show. She just needed to make it until then without saying something to make them hate her.

"Making new friends can sometimes bring up grief and fears about losing old ones," said her mum gently. "But you've got to trust it will all work out the way it's meant to."

"I guess," sniffed Sabina, feeling slightly better.

"And at least you've got Faye!"

Sabina felt slightly worse again.

Her phone beeped with a message from the Leeches – they'd created a group chat with just her.

> Don't forget, 3 p.m. today! Swimwear AND dresses! Party of the YEAR.

Sabina bit her lip. She'd never thought she'd actually go to the Leeches' party. Even though she'd seen it in her vision, she hadn't believed she'd end up there. It would have felt like she was choosing the Leeches over Faye.

But...now that Faye wanted space from her, and she didn't have any Saturday plans at all, maybe she *could* go?

"Actually, Mum, Faye's not coming over any more," said Sabina suddenly. "There's a big party happening at Alicia's house."

"But...I thought you two didn't get on with the Leeches. Unless there's been an episode I've missed? *Sabina and Faye befriend the Leeches?*"

Sabina shifted uncomfortably. "Not exactly. But they aren't so bad. And everyone's going to be there. It's to celebrate Alicia being Form Prefect."

"Oh, Faye lost," cried her mum. "What a shame! But I'm impressed she's magnanimous enough to go to Alicia's victory party."

Sabina very much doubted that Faye would go. But she didn't want to tell her mum, because then she'd find out that she and Faye had fallen out, and she'd be worried about Sabina. Or worse, disappointed in her...

"Well, a party does sound fun," agreed her mum. "You can take the brownies. I can do your nails too, if you'd like?"

Sabina's eyes shone with excitement, her spirits finally lifting. She'd been waiting *weeks* for her mum to have the time to do her nails. "I'd love that, thanks, Mum!"

"What colour would you like? I've got a new purple or a fun orange you might like."

Sabina thought back to her vision and what she'd been wearing at the Leeches' pool party. "How about a sparkly green?"

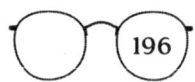

Sabina's eyes widened as she approached the driveway of Alicia's house through two iron gates. The house was ENORMOUS. It looked like something out of the period dramas her mum watched on TV and there were several shiny sports cars outside. Sabina didn't care about cars but even she knew these ones were expensive. She adjusted the foil on the tray of brownies she'd brought, then lifted the gold lion-head knocker.

The door opened instantly. Sabina blinked at the sudden glare of bright light and colour. It took her a few seconds to make out the Leeches, standing there in sparkly, floaty dresses.

"Sabina's here!" cried one. "And she brought brownies. I hope they're vegan." Sabina was still too dazzled by the amount of sequins and sparkle to realize which Leesh was speaking.

"Come in! Leave those...brown things. The caterers will deal with them."

Sabina put down her brownies, then gasped as she took in the giant chandelier in the hallway, the ornate gold photo frames and plush velvet armchairs. "This is *so* nice, Alicia."

"Thanks, babe. Come upstairs and we can finish getting ready."

Sabina followed Alicia up the winding staircase – she could

now see that Alicia was in fuchsia and Felicia was in electric blue – until they were in a giant lavender bedroom. There was a four-poster bed in the middle, and pale-pink chiffon hanging from it.

"Wow," said Sabina, speechless. "Your bedroom is amazing. But, uh...where is everyone?"

"They're all coming later," said Felicia. "We invited you early!"

"Oh. Why?"

"To coordinate, silly!" said Alicia. "Now we're doing an act at the show together, people associate us as a trio. So everything you do and, most importantly, everything you wear, reflects on us." She paused. "Which means you can't wear...*that*. Not while we're wearing this!"

Sabina looked at all their reflections in Alicia's giant mirror. She'd thought she looked quite nice in her denim skirt and black crop top. But next to the Leeches, she looked like she was going to the library.

"Put this on," instructed Alicia.

Sabina was instantly distracted by the mass of soft, sparkly green fabric that Alicia had shoved into her arms. "A dress? I... don't know. It looks expensive."

"It is," confirmed Felicia. "But it's actually a kaftan. And it totally matches your nails, which are amazing!"

"Thanks," said Sabina, proudly admiring them. "My mum did them for me."

"Obsessed," declared Alicia. "Now put on the kaftan. And you'll need swimwear to go underneath."

"I've got my swimming costume in my bag," said Sabina. "I can—"

But the Leeches began snorting with laughter so loud that Sabina couldn't finish her sentence.

"A swimming costume?" shrieked Alicia. "This is a bikini party! Come on, Sabrina! You're going to look SO cute in the green – I specifically chose it to match your colouring. I googled what looks best on Indian skin!"

Sabina wasn't sure whether to be offended or flattered. But she knew there was no point resisting the Leeches – especially when she'd already seen the future in her vision. "Okay," she agreed. "Let's do it."

"Yay!" squealed Alicia. "Also, your glasses are super cute and all, but they're going to have to go."

"I need them to see!"

But Alicia was already prising them off Sabina's face. "You'll be fine."

"Oh my God, you look better already!" said Felicia.

"Does that mean I don't look good in them?" asked Sabina hesitantly. The first thing the Leeches had ever said to her had been a compliment about her glasses. Had they been lying?

"This is just more party appropriate," said Alicia. "Super glam!"

Sabina squinted at her reflection. She supposed she did

look quite glam – albeit slightly blurry. "I guess I *could* survive without them. I don't normally wear them for swimming anyway."

"Perfect!" said Alicia. "And here's your bikini."

The bikini was made of shimmery green fabric, covered in gold sequins. It was the exact bikini from her vision. It was all coming true. Sabina was hanging with the Leeshes.

Sabina laughed loudly as the Year Nine girls jumped into the deep end of the pool, splashing everyone around them. She couldn't believe how much fun she was having! But it would be impossible not to have fun. The Leeshes had hired a burger truck and they'd all spent ages stuffing themselves with vegan burgers and truffle fries. They were unbelievably delicious, so Sabina had eaten two portions of everything.

Alexis was DJing and she was incredible. The swimming pool was the coolest thing Sabina had ever seen – everything was made of wood, and it was so luxurious she felt like she was in a movie. She'd also drunk so many fizzy drinks that she was high on sugar, and all her problems felt very far away.

Plus, for the first time since coming to MG, Sabina had actually spoken to the boys from the school next door – even Dillon. He'd only said "hey" and "cool powers", but he knew who she was, which was *major*. The wildest part had been when Dillon's friend Jason had asked Sabina to tell his fortune.

Sabina had been tempted to say yes – it felt so good to have a boy, especially a popular boy, talk to her. But then all the boys had crowded around wanting their fortunes read as well, and Sabina had felt her emotional levels getting out of control.

Just when she was about to panic, the Leeshes had intervened. Felicia had turned the music off while Alicia had used her fingers to whistle loudly. It was so piercing that it cut through every conversation. The party fell silent, and Alicia sweetly announced that Sabina was NOT available for visions, but if they wanted to see how amazing her powers were, they could all come to the village talent show. In the meantime, Sabina would be conserving her energy.

Sabina was still grinning about it as she drank her lychee boba (there was also an unlimited boba bar). Not only had the whole school wanted to speak to her, but the Leeshes had stood up for her. For a moment, it had felt like being part of a trio with Harry and Ria again. She hadn't had to deal with everything alone – she'd had two people by her side, supporting her.

"Sabrina!" cried the Leeshes, interrupting her thoughts. "Take off your kaftan and get in the pool with us!"

Sabina looked down, self-conscious. There were *boys* at this party.

"Come on!" said Alicia impatiently. "We saved you a lilo." She tapped the inflatable bed next to her.

Sabina knew that this was the moment from her vision.

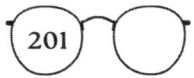

It was destined to happen, so why was she resisting it? Without thinking, she shrugged off her kaftan to reveal her green bikini and jumped into the middle of the pool, right on top of the lilo. Everyone cheered as she landed perfectly.

Sabina turned to face the Leeshes. They were grinning at her, resplendent in their sequins.

"Selfie?" she suggested.

"Uh, *obviously*," said Alicia. "Leesh, get your phone."

Felicia held her phone out in front of them. "One...two...three...smile!"

Chapter 20

Sabina yawned loudly, feeling extremely relaxed. She reached for her phone and realized why: it was midday. Oops. But she'd needed the lie-in after the best Saturday night *ever*.

The pool party had only been the beginning. After that, there'd been a huge *FORM PREFECT ALICIA* cake (life-size in the shape of her entire body) with giant sparklers, then they'd moved upstairs where a professional DJ had taken over from Alexis and turned the living room into a proper club with disco balls, where they'd danced for hours. Sabina had been having so much fun that she'd missed three calls before she'd realized it was past 10 p.m. and her mum was waiting outside.

> OMG, LAST NIGHT AM I RIIIIGHT!!!

Sabina's phone started vibrating with messages from the

Leeshes. She giggled as she opened the photos they sent. The selfies they'd taken in the pool were amazing. She looked so glamorous and cool. Not to mention the ones they'd taken on the dance floor in their matching dresses. Because obviously the Leeshes had changed outfits again and they'd taken Sabina upstairs to put on a green version of their strappy dresses. She'd always thought twinning – or even tripleting – was kind of silly, but when she was doing it with the Leeshes, it felt completely different. She couldn't resist sending the photos to Harry and Ria.

A second after pressing send, her phone vibrated. Clearly, Harry and Ria thought the photos worthy of a call. Sabina hesitated. She knew she shouldn't do a video call with them, because it could risk her vision of them having an argument coming true. But she missed her friends so much, and if she kept avoiding calls with them, then *that* might cause an argument!

Sabina answered the call before she could change her mind. She was *desperate* to hear what they thought of the photos!

"I have no words," said Harry, before immediately contradicting himself. "Are we in a parallel teen movie where you just had a makeover? Are you even still Sabina Patel?"

"Yes!" laughed Sabina, delighted by his reaction. "It was only one night. I'm still me."

"You looked *unreal*," cried Ria. "I'm obsessed with your dress! Where did you get the clothes from?"

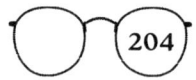

"The Leeshes," said Sabina. "We were tripleting."

"The Leeches? Since when have you ditched your name for them?" asked Harry.

"They're not so bad once you get to know them. Besides, they *really* know how to throw a party. There was a burger van. With truffle fries."

"Wow," said Ria, then she paused. "Wait, there's something different about you today. Oh my God, your glasses! Where are they?"

"Oh, probably still in my bag somewhere," replied Sabina. "I took them off for the party. I was thinking of trying out contact lenses instead."

"You can't do that," cried Ria. "You always wear glasses!"

"And you look great in them," said Harry. "They're part of your look. They make you into a total queen."

"You're just saying that because you chose them," pointed out Sabina, slightly annoyed. "Are you saying I'm not a queen without them?"

"I guess we're just not used to seeing you without them," said Ria.

"Contact lenses!" spat out Harry. "I mean, we always knew MG would change you. I just didn't expect it to take you in a new stylistic direction, after the hours I spent helping you curate your look."

"MG hasn't *changed* me," replied Sabina. "It's...given me magic powers!" She suddenly remembered her vision and realized this conversation was getting into dangerous territory – she needed to avoid any conflict. So, she smiled brightly. "Anyway, guess what? It's only two weeks till term ends and you both come visit. Which means you can watch me in the talent show!"

"Yes, girl!" said Harry. "About time you showed that village what you can do."

"How's the prep going?" asked Ria. "Do you think you'll be able to see what's inside Lucy's locket?"

Sabina's smile faded. She'd forgotten to meditate last night in the excitement of the party. She hadn't practised her visions much either – but she'd avoided loads of unwanted visions by controlling her breathing. So maybe that was enough?

"It'll be fine," she said confidently. "The Leeshes have ordered some amazing outfits for us – velvet cloaks with sparkles on them. We look very official."

"Sounds it," remarked Ria. "I still can't believe you decided to definitely do it. Aren't they live streaming it for socials? Are you okay with everyone seeing your powers?"

Sabina shrugged. "It's worth it to help my mum. And it's not like anyone will watch it! There's way better stuff on the internet than a village talent show."

"Well, I can't *wait* to come," declared Harry. "I need to show these village people what a real London outfit is."

"Me too." Ria grinned. "And I'm super excited to meet Faye!"

Sabina grinned right back at her as she remembered her vision of the talent show. Things with Faye weren't great right now, but they'd be better in no time at all.

Sabina wandered around the house, bored. Her mum was out at work – Sundays were her busiest day in the salon – and there was nothing to do. She'd watched TV, finished her homework, scrolled through all the photos from last night on her socials, and messaged the Leeshes about how fun it had been. She'd even made herself scrambled eggs on toast for a 4 p.m. brunch. But now it was almost evening and she had nothing to do. She knew what she SHOULD do – meditate. It was just that it had been so *hard* lately. Before, when she'd been doing it with her mum, it had been fun and relaxing. And even when she'd been doing it alone in the last couple of weeks, it had taken away all her worries and allowed her to focus on her chakras. But in the last few days, something had changed, and now, every time she breathed, her mind wandered.

Sabina decided to try one more time. Faye's research had proved that she needed to keep meditating to control her powers, and seeing as the show was in two weeks' time, she *really* needed her powers under control!

So, Sabina made a nest for herself on the floor of her room, piling up cushions and getting her crystal ready. She even lit a candle to set the mood. Then she sat down, cross-legged, eyes closed, trying to focus on her breath.

She wondered what the Leeshes were up to? She bet they never had boring Sunday evenings like this. Oh no, wait, the chakras. Sabina tried to bring her attention to the red light at the base of her spine. She wished her mum was there – it was so much easier to meditate with her by her side. But she wouldn't be around that evening because she was going out with her new friend again.

Sabina was starting to get curious about her mum's new friend. When she'd come to pick her up from the Leeshes' party, she'd been wearing lipstick and heels. Her mum *never* wore high heels, and she hardly bothered with lipstick because it always smudged. She was making a lot of effort for her new friend. Maybe she was a client from the nice side of the village, so her mum had to make an extra effort to fit in with her, like Sabina was with the Leeshes.

Sabina had tried to ask her mum more about her mystery friend, but she'd hardly said anything. A doubt flashed through Sabina's mind – what if they *weren't* a client of her mum's? What if they were a *male* friend? Like a boyfriend? But that couldn't be. Her mum had never dated before – she'd always said Sabina was enough for her. Oh no, what if her mum had befriended someone super embarrassing, like one of Sabina's teachers? That was just the kind of awful thing Sabina had worried would happen in a tiny village!

She opened her eyes, officially giving up on her meditation. She was way too curious about her mum's mystery friend to concentrate on her breathing. She needed to know who it was. Asking her mum hadn't worked. She could snoop around the house to see if she could find any clues that pointed to this friend's identity? Or...she could use her powers!

Trying to ignore the guilt rising in her chest, Sabina wandered into her mum's room. She picked up the silk scarf her mum had worn on some of her recent outings, then prepared for a vision. She closed her eyes, breathing deeply, and began channelling all her powers into her intention: "I want to have a vision about my mum and her new friend." Then she gently reached out to touch the scarf. There was a little fizzle of electricity – but that was it. Nothing else happened.

Sabina opened her eyes in surprise. That was weird. It always worked! She tried one more time, focusing as hard as she could, but this time, the fizzle was even *less* pronounced. Maybe Faye was right, and her powers wouldn't work on demand if she didn't meditate? Sabina groaned at her predicament. The only way to have a vision about her mum's mystery friend was to meditate – but she couldn't meditate because she kept getting distracted by thinking about her mum's mystery friend!

Then she had an idea. What if she used her crystal for an extra boost? Diva had given it to her to take her meditating to a new level, and she'd said it would help unlock her third eye. Maybe it could help now?

Sabina ran up to her room for the crystal, eventually finding it underneath her French vocab. She tried again, clutching her right hand around the crystal, placing the silk scarf on her bed. She breathed deeply, trying to calm her emotions and channel everything into what she was doing. She focused on her intention and reached out her left hand to touch the scarf.

There was an instant jolt, and everything started spinning. It was working!

Sabina found herself standing onstage in front of a packed auditorium.

She recognized this – it was the same vision she'd had when she'd touched Faye! Right on cue, she saw herself hugging Faye onstage while everyone clapped. But this time, the vision didn't stop there. Sabina kept her eyes wide open, trying hard not to blink, as she looked around the audience until she saw her mum, sitting next to Harry and Ria, who were both cheering loudly. Sabina beamed at the sight, then noticed that her mum was sitting next to a man. A tall Indian man with a moustache, who Sabina instantly recognised. In that moment, her mum leaned over to KISS him.

Sabina blinked in shock, finding herself back in her mum's bedroom. She couldn't *believe* what she'd seen. She didn't just win the talent show with Faye by her side, and Harry and Ria cheering her on. Her mum was right there too, kissing her dad.

Chapter 21

"Hey, girl, love your hair today! Did you use your powers on it?"

"Oh my God, Sabrina, HOW much fun was Saturday?!"

"I saw Katniss earlier – thanks to you and your powers!"

Sabina laughed as she waved and chatted to what felt like the entirety of MG on her way to the dining hall. Everyone remembered her from the Leeshes' party and they were all being so *nice*. It was a million miles away from her first few weeks at MG where she'd felt like a ghost in the corridors. Now *everyone* knew who Sab(r)ina Patel was. For the first time in her life, she was popular!

But Sabina's happiness faded momentarily when she walked past the cabinet of chess trophies. She hated that her popularity had meant Faye falling out with her. Hopefully the space over the weekend had helped Faye forgive her for lying.

And if not, well, it didn't matter. Because her vision had proved that they'd be friends again at the talent show.

Besides, Sabina couldn't help feeling happy. It wasn't just the party and her newfound popularity – it was the vision she'd had of her mum kissing her *dad*. The one thing she'd wanted her whole life was going to come true. She'd seen it. Her dad was coming back into their lives. They'd finally be a family of three. Her mum would have a partner, and Sabina would have a father who loved her.

Just thinking about it made Sabina want to cry with relief. If her dad came back, it meant there was nothing wrong with her – she was enough the way she was. A tear slid down her cheek, and Sabina quickly wiped it away, remembering to breathe deeply. Now wasn't the time for a vision. She was too busy enjoying her last one. She still had no idea how it had happened – had her dad called her mum? Had he found her at the salon? Her mum hadn't said a thing! But she *had* been acting weirdly lately. Sabina had assumed that it was because of her struggle to keep Beauties afloat, and that every time she was out, she was seeing her new friend. But all along, she'd been seeing her dad.

In normal circumstances, Sabina would have been furious at being lied to – and part of her was still a bit hurt that her mum had kept this from her – but she'd forgiven her the second she'd confirmed that the man in her vision was her dad. The proof was in the Drawer of Important Things where her mum kept their passports, boring paperwork and the only photo they had of her dad. Sabina had spent hours scrutinizing his image last night, until she was one thousand per cent positive that he was the man her mum had been kissing. They were both the same height, with the same skin colour, thick moustache and smiling eyes. Their faces did look a *little* different, but that was bound to happen in thirteen years.

There was no doubt about it. Sabina had seen her mum kissing her dad at the talent show. Which meant that in just under two weeks, she'd get to finally meet him.

"Sabrina! I *love* your look today!" Felicia blew her a kiss from the other side of the corridor, her perfectly curled hair bouncing cheerfully.

"Your hair still looks great from Saturday," said Alicia, micro-adjusting her own curls with her pink nails. "But you need to find some contact lenses soon. You look way better without glasses."

Sabina's smile faltered. After speaking to Harry and Ria, she was no longer sure she wanted to ditch her identity as a glasses-wearer. But if the Leeshes thought she looked so much better without them, maybe she *could* get some contacts – even if they were just for special occasions.

"So, you're ready to practise for the competition today?" asked Felicia. "With some visions?"

Sabina nodded confidently. She'd been avoiding practising on-demand visions with the Leeshes out of fear that she'd fail and they'd stop helping her, but now she had the crystal, she had nothing to be scared of. She hadn't even bothered to meditate before bed last night. There was no point now she knew the crystal was the key to controlling her powers.

"I've got my crystal," she said proudly, pulling it out of her pocket so the girls could see its purple shimmer. "It helps me with my visions."

"Oh my God, obsessed," cried Alicia. "Let's go into the empty music room and do it now."

"Okay," said Sabina, following her in. "What do you want me to do the visions on?"

"Us, obvs!" said Felicia. "I need to know what Alexis is getting me for our one-month anniversary on Friday."

"Haven't you been together way longer than that?" asked Sabina, confused. Felicia had shown her cute selfies of her and Alexis from way back in the summer.

"We're on-off," explained Felicia. "But we're counting our anniversaries from our fresh start!"

"Go on," instructed Alicia. "Then you can do me and Dillon."

Sabina hesitated, realizing she was suddenly nervous. But there was no need to panic – all she had to do was breathe, use the crystal to have a vision, and tell the Leeshes what she saw. Everything would be fine.

Sabina gripped the crystal in her right hand, breathing deeply while she focused on her intention – "I want to have a vision about Felicia and Alexis's one-month anniversary." Then she gently reached out her left hand to touch Felicia. Her hand barely grazed Felicia's shellac when everything started spinning. It was working!

This time, Sabina found herself in an unfamiliar bedroom. Everything was white and gold, but there were bright pops of colour coming from the photos of the Leeshes on the wall and the clothes scattered everywhere. Sabina turned to see Felicia and Alexis sitting on what was clearly Felicia's bed.

"Happy anniversary!" beamed Felicia, pulling out a little turquoise box.

Alexis's eyes widened in surprise. "Oh...uh, thanks." She took out a pretty silver chain with the letters A and F on it. "It's...lovely. I can't believe it's already our, uh, one year anniversary?"

"It's our one month!" cried Felicia, crestfallen. "You didn't remember?"

"I...didn't know when we were counting from, sorry."

"Our big reunion last month, *obviously*," said Felicia, tears streaming down her cheeks. "I can't believe you forgot."

"I'm sorry," said Alexis awkwardly. "I'll make it up to you with—"

But before she could hear the rest of Alexis's sentence, Sabina blinked and found herself back in the music room with both Leeshes staring at her expectantly.

"Well?" asked Felicia. "What did she get me?! I want to

know so I can practise faking a smile in case I hate it."

Sabina gulped. She hadn't expected to see something *bad*. She didn't know what to do. It had been horrible enough to see Felicia sobbing in her Winter Ball vision – she didn't want to tell her the truth and have her start crying right now. Unless…she could find Alexis, tell her about the anniversary, and make sure she bought an amazing present? That way she'd avoid Felicia being upset in the first place!

"Um, I didn't see," said Sabina, thinking quickly. "But she *definitely* remembered it. You guys were super cute!"

Felicia beamed happily. "Yay! I knew she'd remember."

Sabina exhaled in relief, making a mental note to find Alexis IMMEDIATELY.

"Me now," announced Alicia. "I want to see if Dillon and I will finally kiss at the Winter Ball on Saturday."

Sabina froze. She wasn't sure she wanted to do another vision – not after what she'd seen for Felicia. "I don't think that's a good idea," she said haltingly. "I should rest my powers, and I'm feeling a bit—"

But Alicia didn't let her finish her sentence. "Sabrina Patel, you cannot just do Leesh's future! That is NOT fair, and if you want me to help you win this talent show, you NEED to do mine. The Winter Ball is happening in FIVE DAYS! I need to be prepared! OKAY?"

Sabina was too taken aback to speak. She nodded, trying to calm herself down so she'd be vision ready. She squeezed the crystal tight, breathed deeply and closed her eyes, inwardly repeating her intention to have a vision about Dillon, Alicia and a kiss, before slowly reaching out to touch Alicia's soft hand. Her body jerked as the shock came and everything whirled.

Sabina found herself standing outside the school gymnasium where the Winter Ball was happening. But Alicia was nowhere to be seen. Sabina sighed in frustration – her vision had gone wrong. Alicia must be inside dancing. But then Sabina noticed someone in the darkness. It was Dillon. He was in the car park and he was kissing somebody!

Sabina gasped happily – Alicia would be thrilled! Then she noticed that the girl he was kissing was *not* wearing the gold sparkly dress she'd seen Alicia wear to the dance in her last vision. This girl was wearing bright purple...

Sabina blinked and she was back in the music room.

"Well?" cried Alicia. "Tell me!"

Oh no. Sabina couldn't tell Alicia she'd seen her boyfriend kissing someone else. But then again...was Sabina even *sure* it had been somebody else? Alicia had worn three different outfits for her pool party. Who was to say she didn't have two dresses for the Winter Ball?

"You kissed," blurted out Sabina. "In the car park."

"Oh my God, yaaaaay," squealed Alicia. "I knew it!"

Sabina was lost in her thoughts as she walked to geography. The Leeshes were still in the music room riding high from her visions – or at least, the bits she'd told them about. But she didn't feel so great. It had never occurred to her that she'd see *negative* things in the Leeshes' futures – their lives always looked so perfect. And now she'd lied to them.

But it was fine; they'd never find out. Sabina just needed to tell Alexis about her anniversary with Felicia, and make sure Alicia wore purple to the dance. She'd changed the outcome of her visions before – like with saving Katniss – and she was definitely going to do it for her mum with Beauties, and now she'd do it for the Leeshes too.

"Sabina, hi."

Sabina's eyes lit up. "Faye! It's so good to see you! How are you?"

"Better, thanks, said Faye. "I've realized that not being Form Prefect doesn't mean I have to stop helping the school. I'm coming up with a new petition to improve the history curriculum so we can learn about all the things Britain did WRONG."

Sabina laughed happily; the space had worked and Faye wasn't mad at her any more. "I can't wait to sign it! And I can help you with the title if you want?"

"I've already done it."

Sabina's face fell. Or maybe the space *hadn't* worked. "Okay."

"But…I do need someone to practise my victory speech with for the chess competition."

"You've already won?"

Faye shook her head. "No, it's happening the weekend after next. But I'm just preparing in advance."

"Of course you are. I'd love to help you."

"Thank you. Tomorrow lunch?"

Sabina nodded eagerly. "I'll be there. Though I'll have to leave at half past if that's okay…"

Faye's face tensed up. "Talent show practice?"

"Yes," said Sabina, trying to shake off the feeling of guilt that was creeping into her belly. She didn't need to feel bad about what she was doing – they were her powers, and it was her life.

"So, it's not just your backup any more?"

Sabina shook her head. "I couldn't think of a better plan. And the Leeshes are really helping."

"The Leeshes," echoed Faye softly. "Right. And…are you still meditating?"

"Kind of. But it doesn't matter. Because guess what? I came up with a scientific discovery of my own!"

Faye waited expectantly.

"When I hold the crystal, I can automatically control my visions!" cried Sabina, her voice full of pride. "Isn't that cool?"

The expression on Faye's face did not suggest she found

it cool. "So...you're not controlling your powers – the crystal is?"

"It's still me! The crystal is helping me stay balanced so I can control the visions. I still breathe when I'm doing them, and I do my intentions. But the crystal helps even when I don't meditate. I don't know why we never tried to use it in the first place."

"So you're not meditating at *all*?" asked Faye. "Sabina, that does not sound good to me. Remember what Diva said – it could be dangerous to stop meditating. And relying on the crystal means an extra variable that could go wrong."

"Nothing's going to go wrong," said Sabina, annoyed. "The crystal works perfectly. Diva's the one who gave it to me, remember? Besides, it helped me work out that my mum is dating my dad."

Faye's eyes widened. "What? Your mum and your dad are together? I thought you'd never met him and he was in India!"

"He's back! My mum's been dating him but hasn't told me yet. Probably because she's waiting till she's definitely sure about him. She'll tell me any day now, I know it."

"So...this is all conjecture?"

"No, I saw it in my vision! They kiss when I win the talent show."

"You win the talent show?"

Sabina nodded. "Yup! It must be down to the crystal."

"Are you sure your visions are as accurate as they used

to be?" asked Faye. "The crystal could be affecting things. Your powers came from meditation – so maybe they only work accurately when you meditate?"

Sabina shook her head, irritated. "No, I saw everything just like I always do. Unless you think I'm not capable of winning?"

"Of course you are. I'm just being cautious. Science is about not jumping to conclusions."

"Can't we save that for when we're older?" replied Sabina. "I'm too young to be cautious! Especially when I have so many amazing things to look forward to – like saving my mum's business and meeting my dad!" She did an involuntary dance at the thought.

Faye couldn't help but smile at Sabina's unconcealed joy. "All right. Just…keep meditating anyway. I'd better go to advanced chem – but I'll see you tomorrow to practise my speech?"

"One thousand per cent," promised Sabina. "It'll be the highlight of my Tuesday!"

Chapter 22

"Mum, I'm hooooome," Sabina called out as she raced up the stairs towards the spicy smell coming from the kitchen. She'd been waiting all day to see her mum now she knew the truth about her and her dad. She wasn't going to specifically ask her about it – she was scared to do anything that would ruin her vision – but she was hoping her mum would drop some hints.

"In the kitchen! I've made a vegan bean lasagne without the lasagne," called out her mum.

Sabina made a face as she poked her head round the kitchen. "So...just beans?"

"Bean lasagne," corrected her mum proudly. "With sweet potato instead of pasta."

"No offence, but I think I would have preferred the pasta."

"Wait till you try it before you judge it," said her mum, pulling a tray out of the oven with a flourish. "Ta-da!"

Sabina raised an eyebrow at the steaming pile of orange. Her mum looked at it defensively, then burst out laughing. "Okay, fine, I admit it doesn't look great. Next time, I'll make normal pasta."

"I'm going to hold you to that," said Sabina, setting the table. "What's the special occasion anyway?"

"To celebrate us finally having an evening together," said her mum, pulling up a seat in front of her. "I thought we could even do our breathing – sorry, *meditating* – later if you want?"

Sabina's smile faltered. She'd been wanting to meditate with her mum for days, but now that she finally had the chance, she wasn't so keen. She wasn't even sure she'd be able to now she had so much going on in her mind. "Maybe. Or we could have a beauty night instead? Facials and massages?"

"If you're offering to give me a massage, then yes please!"

"You're the expert," replied Sabina. "I think it's best if we leave the massages to you."

Her mum laughed. "Oh, all right. I do owe you some 'us' time. And I have it booked in my diary that I'll be giving you and Faye full manicures before the Winter Dance on Saturday."

"Winter Ball," corrected Sabina. "They take linguistics very seriously at MG. Also, I wanted to tell you about the latest episode in *Sabina Survives MG*. It's called *The Talent Show*."

"Ooh I'm intrigued," said her mum, as she served them both her "lasagne".

Sabina took a deep breath as she began stage one of her plan. It was simple, but flawless. All she needed to do was get her mum to come and watch the talent show, not knowing about Sabina's powers. She'd find out about them during Sabina's performance onstage, and she wouldn't be upset her daughter had psychic powers she knew nothing about, because Sabina's dad would be right there by her side, ready to cheer her up.

"So, it's this big live-streamed show in the village with Lucy Locket presenting it," said Sabina, as her mum's eyes widened in recognition. "And the Leeshes asked me to enter with them. They're doing a dance routine to Taylor Swift." That was true – but the entry they wanted to do with Sabina was about her being a teenage psychic. But Sabina's mum didn't need to know that. Not yet.

"Wow, I didn't even know you liked dancing," replied her mum.

"It's...new. But please tell me you'll come. I've already told Harry and Ria, and because it's the weekend after term ends, they can come too."

Her mum laughed at Sabina's excitement. "Of course, I'll be there. As if I'd miss a live instalment of *Sabina Dances with The Leeshes!*"

Sabina's heart soared. Everything was working out. Her mum was going to come *and* she'd bring her dad. Then Sabina would win and get enough money to save Beauties. Her mum wouldn't be mad when she saw the ginormous prize money. And when this was over, they'd be the family that Sabina had always dreamed of. She wouldn't have one parent who loved her – she'd have two.

"Also, Sabs, there's something I wanted to share with you," said her mum nervously. "I've...been meaning to tell you for the last few weeks, I just...wasn't sure how."

Sabina bolted upright. This was it. Her mum was going to reveal she was dating her dad. "Great! Yes! I'm SO here for whatever you want to share."

Her mum gave her a watery smile. "So, um, you know I've been spending a lot of time with my new friend?"

"Yep. And wearing lipstick and perfume and going out late," said Sabina, ticking each thing off on her fingers.

"Oh." Her mum looked taken aback. "I suppose I have been doing those things... Well, um, I wanted to tell you..."

"Go on," urged Sabina. "You're..."

"Well...I'm actually...dating—"

"My dad!" blurted out Sabina.

But at the exact same moment her mum finished her sentence: "—a man called Manish."

Sabina frowned. "My dad's name is Manish? I thought it was Rohan."

Her mum didn't reply. Her mouth was wide open, and she was staring at Sabina in shock. "What...but...honey, why would I be dating your *dad*?!"

"I saw you together," said Sabina, before realizing what she'd said. "I mean, uh...in real life somewhere. But wait – are you NOT dating my dad? I don't understand."

Her mum shook her head. "Baby, I haven't seen your dad since before you were born. You know that. He's still in India for all I know. I'm dating Manish. He's very nice, he's an accountant and—"

"No!" cried Sabina, disappointment flooding her veins. Did that mean it hadn't been her dad in her vision – it had been Manish? "What about Dad? I thought...who even IS this *Manish*?"

"That's what I was trying to tell you," said her mum in a small voice. "I know it's only ever been us two, so this might be hard for you to adjust to, but—"

"It wouldn't be hard for me to adjust to you dating Dad!"

"He's really nice, Sabina," pleaded her mum. "He's been helping me with Beauties. I couldn't have got through these last few weeks without him."

Sabina gasped in horror as it all became clear. "Oh my God. All those late nights where I thought you were working – you were with him? That night I wanted to come to the salon to do my homework with you, HE was there, wasn't he?"

Her mum had the decency to bow her head in shame. "I'm so sorry, Sabina. He was...but he was helping me with the accounts. We only started dating recently. I didn't mean to keep it from you."

Hot tears started to pool in Sabina's eyes, and she shook her head angrily. "You *lied* to me!"

Her mum looked dejected. "I'm sorry. Could I at least introduce you to Manish? He's looking forward to meeting you."

"Oh, so Manish knew I existed?" cried Sabina. "But you didn't tell me about him? Sounds like you're already putting him first."

"Sabina, that's not fair! I didn't want you to know about him until it was serious."

"It's serious?" Sabina's heart was pounding and she wanted to simultaneously scream and cry. Just then she felt a jolt of electricity run through her veins, and she gasped aloud. Was she about to have a vision? She wasn't even touching anything! But the jolt faded without anything spinning, and Sabina was still right there in the kitchen with her mum, as her heart shattered.

She forced herself to breathe. The last thing she needed right now was an uncontrolled vision. She'd been wrong. It wasn't her dad. Her mum had some horrid new boyfriend instead. "I'm not hungry any more. Have fun with Manish and his MOUSTACHE!"

"He doesn't have a moustache," said her mum, confused. "Look, baby, please stay and talk. Come on—"

But it was too late. Sabina was already running up the stairs to her room.

She collapsed onto her bed, hot tears streaming down her face. She couldn't believe this. She'd been convinced her parents were getting back together and she'd FINALLY have a dad. But things couldn't be further from the truth. Her mum was with some random man called *Manish*. What a ridiculous name. Man-ish. He sounded like a made-up person. But he wasn't. Because he was the reason her mum was wearing lipstick.

Suddenly, Sabina sat up straight. Her mum had just said that Manish didn't have a moustache. But the man in her vision had definitely had a moustache. And Sabina had known it was her dad – she'd recognize him anywhere! So...what if it *was* her dad who kissed her mum in her vision, and Manish was simply a distraction? Perhaps her mum and Manish would break up soon? And her dad would arrive in time for her competition?

That must be why her powers had given her this vision – so that *she* could make it happen. All she had to do was find her dad and invite him to the talent show. Then he'd come to see her win and would kiss her mum! Everything would happen the way it needed to. Manish was obviously an inconvenience, but Sabina doubted it would be hard to get rid of him. She'd make up an accounting emergency or something and he'd be gone in no time.

She felt her breath slow down again. This was it. She had a plan. And first things first, she needed to ask Faye for help. If anyone could track down her dad, it was the smartest girl at MG.

Chapter 23

"... So, in conclusion, I need your help to make my vision come true!" announced Sabina, breathless after her speech.

Faye pushed her fork around her spag bol. "So...you want me to help you find your dad?"

"Exactly!" Sabina beamed. "I'm sure you'll find him in no time. We could even start now? Maybe on Facebook, where old people hang out."

"But...what about my speech?" asked Faye. "I thought the plan was for you to listen to me practise it?"

"Oh, definitely," replied Sabina. "But we might have more time if we do it after school instead? Or on the weekend, before the Winter Ball? You'll be at mine anyway."

"I'd rather not wait. I get nervous doing speeches, and if I know it's prepared, then I can focus on my chess."

"I promise I'll help later," vowed Sabina. "But can we *please* find my dad first? He might need time to sort his flights to come to my competition. I'm scared we're running out of time!"

"What if he doesn't *want* to be found?" asked Faye. "Or what if you were mistaken and your mum was kissing Manish, not your dad?"

"No way," cried Sabina. "I've seen that photo of my dad a million times – it was definitely him. Manish doesn't look like that – trust me, I can sense it with my super intuition. And my mum confirmed he doesn't even have a moustache."

"Well, maybe your mum doesn't want to be with your dad," suggested Faye. "She might prefer Manish."

Sabina's mouth dropped open in disbelief. There was no way her mum would pick someone else over her dad. "Faye, this is my dad we're talking about. Of course, my mum would prefer him! He's the only man she's ever loved – she told me that when I was little. Besides, I saw them in my vision and they were happy. He came back for us. Like I always knew he would."

"But he left her alone with a baby."

"Yes, me," said Sabina hotly. Suddenly a frisson of electricity jerked through her body and she quickly dropped her fork. But the spark didn't lead to a vision. She breathed deeply and turned back to Faye.

Faye was looking at her curiously. "Did you just have a vision?"

"No," said Sabina abruptly. She didn't want Faye to know this wasn't the first time she'd *almost* had a vision when her emotions were high or Faye would give her another lecture

on meditating. But Sabina was fine. She wasn't even getting full uncontrolled visions – there were just these little jolts. Besides, she had the crystal, and she'd meditate as soon as she got the chance – maybe even that very evening.

"Look," said Sabina. "The most important thing here is that I saw my dad come to my show. I've never met him, Faye, not once. I didn't try to find him before because I didn't want to hurt my mum. But now I've seen her with him, which means she wants it too. So, all I need to do is find him. This is proof that he regrets leaving me – he's ready to come back!"

Faye bit her lip. "I don't know… What about Manish?"

"Oh, we'll get rid of him."

"We?"

"I need your help," said Sabina, looking right into her friend's eyes. "I can't do any of this without you!" She glanced at her watch and groaned loudly. "Oh no, I need to go practise with the Leeshes. I'd skip it, but now my dad's coming to the competition, it's even more important that I win. Then I'll save Mum's dream *and* get my parents back together!"

"So, I'll just stay here and google your dad?"

"Thank you, that would be amazing!" said Sabina, grabbing her bag.

"Are you serious?" cried Faye. "That was *sarcasm*. You really think it's okay for me to sit here and spend more time helping you, when you've completely reneged on our plan to practise my speech?"

"I don't know what that r-word means but, Faye, this is my dad! He's more important than a speech."

Faye shook her head, her braids swinging. "I can't *believe* how selfish you've become lately, Sabina. I've tried to look past you keeping things from me, to understand your side. I know it's not been easy for you with your powers. But that doesn't excuse this. I mean, I've spent hours helping you with your visions – but you can't even give me one lunch break for my speech?"

"I said we could do it tonight instead," said Sabina. "Or on the weekend. My show is in less than two weeks – I'm running out of time."

"And I'm not? Do you even know when my competition is?"

Sabina's mind went blank. "Um...next month?"

Faye shook her head. "It's the day *after* your talent show, Sabina. The fact you've forgotten is proof you don't care."

Sabina's stomach sank. She should have remembered Faye's competition. But it didn't mean she didn't care. "Of course I do! You're one of my closest friends."

"The evidence suggests otherwise," said Faye primly. "You didn't tell me about not winning Form Prefect. You're always busy with the Leeches when I need you. You missed my rally to be with them. And...you went to their celebration party on the weekend. I saw the photos."

Sabina felt a sharp twist of guilt in her stomach, but she

ignored it. This wasn't her fault – it was a misunderstanding. "Only because you cancelled on our sleepover," she said, defensive. "I had nothing else to do!"

"I did that because you hadn't been a good friend to me. You'd kept so much from me that I was hurt."

"But I only did that because I didn't *want* to hurt you!" protested Sabina. "I was trying to be a good friend."

"You only come to me when you need help," pointed out Faye. "That's not friendship. It should be equal – not transactional."

"Please, Faye!" cried Sabina, a wave of panic washing over her at the thought of losing Faye. "You are my friend. I need you!"

"I'm sorry, Sabina," said Faye, closing her lunchbox. "But...I don't need you. Not the way you are now, anyway." She picked up her bag and walked away, leaving Sabina standing there, open-mouthed and crestfallen.

"Hellooo? Sabrina?"

Sabina jumped. "Sorry, what?"

"Oh my God, you are so distracted today," complained Alicia.

"Sorry," said Sabina automatically. "I'll...practise at home."

"Maybe we should end practice early today?" suggested Felicia. "We could go get vegan ice cream instead?"

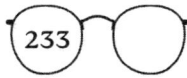

"Fine," agreed Alicia. "At least your visions showed me I'll pass geography. I guess I can wait till tomorrow to find out if Dillon and I get married."

"Can you IMAGINE?!" cried Felicia. "I'm thrilled my parents are going to take me to Barbados in the holidays! I knew they were lying when they said we'd be going hiking in Scotland!"

Sabina slumped down deep into the hard wooden chair. She'd lied to the Leeshes again about their visions... The truth was she'd seen Alicia getting a D in geography. And she'd seen Felicia howling in dismay when her parents told her they weren't going to Barbados this year. But she couldn't bring herself to tell them the truth. She knew they'd be upset and would take it out on her, which she couldn't risk when she needed their help to win the competition. Too much was riding on it for her to do anything that could jeopardize winning.

"Are you coming?" asked Felicia. "They have salted caramel."

Sabina shook her head. "I'm going to stay here. I'll see you in English."

Alicia shrugged. "Your loss. Ciao!"

Sabina exhaled loudly as the Leeshes left the music room that they'd been hijacking for their practices. She still felt awful about her fight with Faye earlier, on top of the awfulness she was already feeling about her mum and the Manish situation. She wished she could speak to someone about it, but there was nobody left. The Leeshes wouldn't understand, and she had to avoid Harry and Ria so they wouldn't end up hating her too.

But she missed them *so* much. And she knew Harry and Ria would make her feel better – they always did. Perhaps one little phone call would be okay? She couldn't imagine them being mad at her – not when she was so sad…

Quickly, Sabina pulled out her phone and pressed "call" in their group chat. Her heart raced in anticipation as she looked at her pixelated face and the white walls behind her, waiting for them to answer.

"Look who it is," said Harry, his face looming on her screen. "Finally, she has time for us."

"It's only been two days since we last spoke," objected Sabina, smiling at the sight of her two best friends.

"Exactly – do you not remember when you were calling every ten minutes?" asked Harry.

"It's good to see you anyway," said Ria. "How are you?"

Sabina sighed loudly, relieved to finally be speaking to people she didn't have to pretend with. "Not good. Everything is such a mess right now."

"We have…fifteen minutes till maths," said Ria, checking the time. "Spill."

Sabina launched into an explanation of the events of the last few days: her vision about her dad, her mum telling her about Manish, and then everything that was going on with

Faye. How she was mad at Sabina for missing her rally, not telling her about the FP winner, asking her to help her find her dad instead of practising her chess speech with her, and for going to the Leeshes' celebration party.

"And now I don't even know if she's still going to come to the Winter Ball with me!" finished Sabina.

There was silence.

"Helloooo? Is the signal okay?" asked Sabina. "Can you hear me?"

"The signal's fine, but we're not," said Harry, glancing at Ria, who nodded in agreement. "Sabina, I can't believe all of this about Faye. And you didn't even *tell* us. How come you kept it to yourself? Also, we specifically told you to tell Faye about your vision of her not winning FP. If you'd done that last week, none of this would have happened."

"I couldn't," protested Sabina. "It was too hard!"

"And then you completely bailed on her," continued Harry. "You chose the Leeches – girls you don't even *like* – over her!"

"I didn't mean to! I just wanted them to help me win the talent show. You know I need to win the money to help my mum and make sure my vision of her kissing my dad comes true."

"You literally went to the party they had to celebrate beating Faye," pointed out Harry.

Sabina looked helplessly at Ria, waiting for her friend to support her against Harry's harshness, like she always did.

But Ria just shook her head silently. "I don't get it, Sabina. Why didn't you *tell* us the Leeches' party was for Alicia becoming Form Prefect? We spoke to you the morning after and you didn't mention it. I presumed it was Alicia's birthday or something."

"I...didn't think it was a big deal."

"Of course it is!" said Ria. "No wonder Faye was hurt. Imagine if you went to a party that celebrated me losing my next Bollywood competition!"

Sabina paused. "Okay, when you say it like that, I kind of get it. But I never *meant* to hurt Faye. Doesn't that count for something?"

"Not when you've been using her," said Harry. "First, as your personal scientist to help you with your powers. Then you need her to be your personal detective to find your dad. But when *she* needs *you*, you're AWOL every time."

"You could have asked us to help you out if you were struggling," said Ria. "We're your best friends. But you've barely kept us in the loop. It feels like lately you only ever come to us when you need to...what's the phrase?"

"Emotionally dump," finished Harry. "I'm with Faye: you *are* more selfish lately, Sabina. You haven't even asked me about my crush on Zain in WEEKS."

"That's because I've had loads going on," cried Sabina. "You're not the one who had to move house and schools and deal with magical powers!"

"I may as well have, considering I've listened to you complain about all of it," retorted Harry. "And are you saying my stuff isn't important? Because Zain asked me to pass him the ball last week, when I was goalie. But you don't even care about my blossoming football career!"

"It was my vision that inspired you to do football in the first place," said Sabina. "And I'm not saying your stuff isn't important. It's just that mine is really intense right now. I'm trying to find my long-lost dad and save my mum's business."

"Nobody's denying that, but it's not an excuse for the way you treated Faye," said Ria. "And I don't know why you're just using your powers on the Leeches to talk about prom and being popular. You could change people's lives with them, Sabina. Look how you saved Katniss."

"I'm in Year Eight," cried Sabina. "I'm too busy trying to change my own life!"

She felt a fizzle in her fingertips, but it disappeared as quickly as it came. She tried to force herself to breathe deeply as she remembered her vision of Harry and Ria getting angry with her. She needed to do everything in her power to make sure it wouldn't come true.

"Maybe that's the problem," said Ria softly. "You're changing."

"True that," agreed Harry. "I barely even recognize you any more. You're not even wearing your glasses in your profile picture."

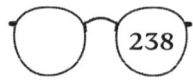

Sabina's shoulders raised defensively. Her new picture was of her in the green dress at the Leeshes' pool party. She thought she looked nice – but clearly her friends didn't agree. She felt a rush of anger. "Well, maybe you both aren't changing *enough*!" she countered. "Maybe I'm growing up and you're not!"

Both her friends' faces fell and Sabina instantly regretted her words. She should have tried harder to stay calm. What was wrong with her? She was risking her vision coming true! "Sorry, I—"

But Harry interrupted her. "That's not cool, Sabina. I… think I'm going to need some space from you."

Sabina's heart stopped. It was happening.

"Me too," said Ria. "I know you're going through a lot, but you're not the Sabina you used to be. We should go."

"I am!" cried Sabina, desperate to try to repair the damage she'd caused. "Look, I didn't mean what I said. You'll still come to watch my show, won't you? Please, I—"

But her friends had already ended the call, and she was left staring at her phone screen with a sick feeling of déjà vu. After *everything* that she'd done to avoid the worst thing she could ever imagine, her vision had come true anyway. Her best friends weren't speaking to her. And she had no idea what to do about it.

Chapter 24

Sabina stared listlessly at the contents of her poké bowl while the Leeshes had an impassioned conversation about whether or not they should get fringes for the Winter Ball tomorrow. She wasn't really listening; she was too busy feeling sorry for herself, just as she had been since that fateful Tuesday when all her friends had decided to stop speaking to her.

It was Friday now, and nothing had changed. Harry and Ria hadn't replied to her messages asking to talk (apart from Ria clarifying they still needed space) and Faye was completely ignoring her. Sabina had asked if they were still going to the Winter Ball together on Saturday, but Faye hadn't even replied. It had hurt more than Sabina could have predicted. She'd tried to sit next to her in Diva's meditation class the day before, but Faye had simply got up and swapped yoga mats. The rejection had burned so deeply that Sabina hadn't been able to focus for the rest of the lesson. And then after class, Diva had asked her to stay behind again. Sabina had thought she was in trouble for not focusing, but Diva had simply asked her how things were going. Sabina had thought about admitting everything, but in the end, she'd pretended things were fine. She didn't want her teacher to give her more cryptic advice – but Diva had done it anyway. "Don't lose yourself, Sabina," she'd said. "Stay *with* yourself. Stay in the present – not the future."

Sabina had no idea what that meant. How could she lose herself? She *was* herself! And of course she was staying with herself – where else would she go? She'd left the class feeling confused, but also grateful, because Diva hadn't asked if Sabina was meditating regularly. She wasn't. She hadn't been able to all week because it was impossible to stay focused on her breathing when she was so sad. She hadn't even been able to do it with Diva guiding them through the chakras – her mind was too busy. And she kept getting weird almost-visions with little shocks every time her emotional levels went too high. Sabina didn't know what it meant, but it couldn't be a big deal because her visions still worked when she used her crystal. She'd been practising for the talent show with the Leeshes, and the crystal had shown her their futures perfectly. Of course, she hadn't always told them *exactly* what she'd seen – neither of the Leeshes ended up at Harvard, for example – but university was years away, so it wasn't like she'd be found out any time soon.

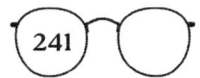

What Sabina was most frustrated by was how hard it was to find her dad. She'd spent hours searching for Rohan Patel online, but there were thousands of them. She had no idea which one was her dad, and the whole thing felt hopeless. Especially because there was only a week left until the talent show and her mum was *still* seeing Manish – they'd gone out for dinner on Wednesday, and even though they'd invited Sabina to join them, she'd declined on principle. She'd had to eat freezer dhal instead of going to the yummy Chinese in the village, but it was worth it. She couldn't betray her dad by supporting Manish.

Sabina just wished she wasn't so alone in it all. None of her friends were there to help her. She knew she'd hurt them, but she also didn't think it was fully her fault. It wasn't her fault she'd got magic powers that had changed her. And it wasn't like she was choosing the Leeshes over her friends – they'd chosen *her.* All she was trying to do was save her mum's salon and get her dad back. But somehow, she'd lost all her friends in the process.

Except the Leeshes.

"Leesh, I have the bone structure for a fringe," said Alicia. "It would be a total waste of my face to not get one."

"But I don't have cheekbones like yours!" wailed Felicia. "And we need to twin for the Winter Ball!"

Just then Alicia narrowed her eyes at Sabina. "What do *you* think? Are you even listening to us?"

Sabina realized that if she didn't join in their conversation, she was in danger of losing the only people who weren't mad at her. "Um...of course I am! I think you'd both look great with fringes!"

"Even with my cheekbones?" asked Felicia doubtfully.

"Totally!" said Sabina.

"Did we have them in your vision of the Ball?" asked Alicia. "Are fringes in our destiny?"

Sabina shook her head.

Alicia sighed. "Fine, let's hold off. We don't want to risk your visions not coming true."

"I still can't believe the Winter Ball is happening in almost twenty-four hours!" cried Felicia.

Neither could Sabina – she'd been so wrapped up in everyone hating her that she'd barely thought about the dance. It didn't seem to matter now that she and Faye wouldn't be going together.

"Are we getting ready at mine or yours, Leesh?" asked Felicia. "My mum said she'd make us snacks if we do it at mine."

"It's easier at mine," said Alicia authoritatively. "Come for 4 p.m. I'll order vegan sushi. Sabrina, make sure you bring your dress and we'll get the hair and make-up artist to steam it."

Sabina's eyes widened. "A hair and make-up artist?"

"As if we'd go to a dance without one!" Alicia laughed. "Don't worry – she can do you too. What dress are you wearing?"

"I haven't really thought about it," admitted Sabina. "I'll

probably wear a strappy black dress I wore to my school disco last year."

"You want to re-wear it?" echoed Felicia.

"Leesh is right," said Alicia. "That's *not* going to work. And, no offence, but your dress sounds boring. You can borrow something from my wardrobe instead."

"It's fine," said Sabina. "I don't mind looking—"

"Sabrina, you're hanging with us now," interrupted Alicia. "You need to look the part." She paused, taking in Sabina's sad eyes and split ends. "Maybe you should come at 2 p.m. The hair and make-up artist might need more time with you."

Sabina drifted out of the Leeshes' conversation again. Hackney High's disco last year had been SO fun. She'd gone with Harry and Ria, and they'd spent the whole time dancing madly while the year aboves gave them weird looks. But they hadn't cared because they'd had each other.

Sabina prayed that her vision of the talent show would come true next week. As hard as it was to find her dad, she couldn't lose hope now. Somehow, things would work out the way she'd seen them. Her dad would come back for the daughter he'd always loved, she'd save her mum's business and her friends would finally forgive her. It all had to come true – otherwise she'd be stuck talking about fringes with the Leeshes for the rest of her life.

The next day, Sabina was getting ready to meet the Leeshes when her mum walked into her room. "Hey, Sabs. What time is Faye coming over?"

Sabina busied herself with her clothes. "She's not, actually. I'm going to get ready with the Leeshes instead."

Her mum frowned. "What? Why? I've got everything ready downstairs to give you both manicures! I even brought stencils from the salon. Has something happened with Faye?"

"It's...a long story."

"I've got the time," said her mum. "I can...still do your nails while we talk? And you can tell me about the latest episode of *Sabina Survives MG*?"

Sabina wasn't sure she *was* surviving MG any more. "I can't. I have to be at Alicia's house at 2 p.m."

"We could invite them over here instead? I could give you all manicures?" suggested her mum.

Sabina tried to imagine the Leeshes at her house, but it was impossible. They belonged in a world of mansions and four-poster beds – not tiny flats with only one bathroom. "They've already got a hair and make-up artist coming."

"Of course they do," sighed her mum. "Sabs, are you okay? Can we talk?"

For a second, Sabina felt herself melting. She really did miss her mum. But then she remembered how betrayed she'd felt when she'd figured out that her mum had been with Manish the night she'd wanted to go to the salon – and her mum hadn't even *told* her. She'd lied to her for weeks.

"I have to go, Mum," she said. "Or I'll be late."

Her mum looked sad for a second, but then she stood up straight. "Fine. I'm taking you."

"I'm not a baby! I can go on my own."

"But I am still your mother and if I say I'm taking you, then I'm taking you," replied her mum determinedly. "Come on. Maybe I can even say hello to Alicia's parents. It doesn't feel right you spending so much time at her house without me meeting her parents."

Sabina followed her mum out to the car, knowing this was a battle she'd lost.

"So, I was speaking to Harry and Ria's parents," said her mum as she started up her red Ford Fiesta. "And you know they were meant to come up next weekend, in time for your talent show? Well unfortunately, something's come up, a school project or something, so they won't be able to make it. I'm sorry to be the bearer of bad news. But hopefully they'll still be able to come up later in the holidays."

Sabina stayed silent, her brow furrowed. She knew that "something's come up" was code for "we're still mad at you". She knew she'd upset them but she hadn't thought they'd be so angry that they'd cancel their trip to see her.

They had to change their minds again though, because she'd seen them in her vision at the talent show. They were probably just being dramatic – she bet Harry had told his parents to cancel in a flurry of emotion and would take it back soon. All Sabina had to do was wait things out, and her friends would forgive her. They had to.

"Sabina, has something happened with Harry and Ria?" asked her mum. "And what about with Faye? I really like her."

Me too, thought Sabina.

"Sabina?" asked her mum. "What's going on?"

Sabina thought of telling her the truth – that she was doing it all for her, to win the show, save Beauties and reunite her with her dad. But the last time they'd spoken about her dad, her mum had gone on about *Manish.* Sabina couldn't bear to hear about him again. So instead, she lied: "Everything's fine."

Her mum sighed as they pulled up to Alicia's mansion. "I know you're upset about Manish, but you can still speak to me, Sabina."

Sabina's phone beeped. "Alicia says her parents are in Mexico. So, unless you want to meet the housekeeper, there's no point getting out the car."

Her mum shook her head in resignation. "The girls at MG really are different to the kids at your old school, aren't they?"

"*Everything*'s different here," said Sabina emphatically. And it was true. It wasn't just the school and her new friends. It was the fact her mum had a boyfriend. That she had third eye chakra powers. And that Harry and Ria weren't speaking to her.

"Well, sometimes different can be a good thing," said her mum hopefully. "Change is healthy."

Sabina raised an eyebrow. She wasn't so sure.

Her mum waited for a response, but when none came, she gave up. "All right, go have fun. I'll collect you from the dance later."

"You don't need to – Alicia's driver is dropping me off home after, she already said."

"A driver?! All right, I'll let Manish know – we'll be able to go and watch a movie after all. Sabina, don't make that face! I'm allowed to talk about him!"

But Sabina had already slammed the car door and was walking through the wrought-iron gates to Alicia's mansion.

Chapter 25

Sabina banged the giant lion door knocker, but nobody answered. She peered through the side window and saw the hallway was empty. She pounded the lion again, checking her phone to make sure she'd got the right time. 2.10 p.m.

The door opened.

"Oh my God, FINALLY," cried Alicia. "Could you be any later?!"

There was a high-pitched screech in the background and they both winced. "What is that?" asked Sabina. "It sounds like a fox is being attacked!"

Alicia grabbed her arm and dragged her into the house. "It's Leesh. I've been dealing with her for hours. It's your turn now."

They raced up the stairs to Alicia's bedroom. Sabina heard the sobs before she saw her. Felicia was lying on Alicia's bed, face down, crying loudly into a pillow. "Leesh?" she asked. "What is it?"

Felicia rolled over, revealing her hot red cheeks and mascara tears. "Sabriiiiiiiina! You…were…wrong!" she choked out. "Alexis didn't get me an anniversary present at all – she forgot!"

Oh no. Sabina's face paled as she realized she'd completely forgotten to warn Alexis about her one-month anniversary with Felicia. She'd been so caught up in her misery after her fights with Faye, Harry and Ria that it had totally slipped her mind!

"It's not the first time Alexis has forgotten something," said Alicia, rubbing moisturizer onto her face as though Felicia wasn't sobbing on her bed. "Anniversaries, birthdays…you name it. These two are the definition of an on-off relationship."

"I LOVE HER," wailed Felicia. "And she doesn't even CARE!"

"I'm sure she does," said Sabina, sitting next to Felicia to pat her sweaty hair. "She just has her own way of showing it." She thought back desperately to what she'd seen in her vision. "Didn't she…try and make it up to you?"

"By offering to order us a pizza!" spat out Felicia. "Like that's an anniversary-appropriate dinner!"

Sabina didn't see what was wrong with pizza, but she nodded knowingly. "I'm sorry. But it doesn't mean she doesn't care about you."

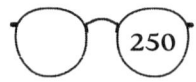

"And you acting like this isn't exactly going to make her more into you," said Alicia tartly. "So have a shower, get changed and let Hanna work her magic so you look hot for the dance."

Felicia sniffed. "I suppose I can talk to Alexis there..." She whirled her head round to look at Sabina. "But why did you *tell* me she remembered? If I'd known she wouldn't get me anything, I would have prepared myself. Or at least not spent my whole month's allowance on that necklace!"

Sabina gulped. She couldn't tell the Leeshes she'd lied; they'd be furious. "I'm...sorry – maybe my vision was wrong? Or...I misinterpreted it?"

"You probably saw their next one-month anniversary instead," said Alicia, tweezing her eyebrows in the mirror. "They've already had five."

Felicia's eyes lit up. "Oh my God, do you think so? That we start from scratch again, and next month she remembers?!"

Sabina hesitated. Felicia and Alexis's relationship sounded a bit toxic. But it wasn't her place to say anything. And Alicia had just given her the *perfect* excuse. So, she nodded. "That makes sense. I must have seen further into the future."

Felicia rubbed her face, cheered. "And you said you saw me and her at the dance together, so maybe everything will be okay!"

Sabina's face fell as she remembered her vision of Felicia and Alexis breaking up *and* Dillon kissing a girl in a purple dress. She'd need to do everything in her power tonight to make sure that Alicia was the girl Dillon kissed, and that Felicia and Alexis made up.

Sabina's heart raced as she scanned the blurry dance hall. Dillon and Alicia were by the drinks, looking like a celebrity power couple with Dillon in his tux and Alicia in the gold shimmery dress from Sabina's vision. *Not* a purple dress... She hadn't even brought one with her, despite Sabina's serious protestations. Which was why Sabina was now on the lookout for a girl in a purple dress whilst simultaneously hunting for Alexis, so she could convince her not to break up with Felicia.

But Sabina was not having any success, mainly because she'd let the Leeshes convince her to ditch her glasses. She could hardly see a thing! How was she ever going to find Alexis when everything was a giant blur? She wished she'd worn her glasses, then she would have had her super sight and could have found Alexis in seconds. Instead, she had to do it the longest way possible, walking carefully in her tight red dress and Alicia's gold chunky platforms, searching the gym person by person.

It took for ever, but when Sabina's feet were on the verge of giving out, she finally found her. Alexis was sitting in the corner, behind the stage, munching on cheese sticks with her friend Phoebe.

"Alexis!" cried Sabina. "Can we speak? It's about Felicia."

"Of course it is," sighed Alexis, as Phoebe gave her an understanding smile and walked away. "Now what?"

"It's just...I was...wondering how you feel about her?" Sabina cringed. Alexis was going to think she was a total weirdo.

Alexis shrugged. "Who knows? She changes all the time. Sometimes, she's the chilled-out girl I fell for. But then she gets so needy I can't cope."

"She *is* chilled out! I mean, I know she freaked out about the anniversary thing, but she didn't mean it. She's not needy – she just really likes you!"

"I don't know...I was thinking of ending it with her tonight."

"Please don't!" burst out Sabina. "I mean, it would break her heart!"

Suddenly Alexis's eyes narrowed. "Oh my God, did she *ask* you to speak to me?"

Sabina shook her head. "No, she doesn't know I'm here."

"She did, didn't she?" Alexis gasped, backing away from Sabina. "Oh my God, I get it now. She wants you to do a vision for me! To see if we end up together! I can't believe it – she's sooo intense. I can't be with someone like that."

"No!" Sabina protested in horror. "That's not it at ALL. I'd never do that. Nor would Felicia."

But it was too late. Alexis stood up to leave. "I don't care if

your visions say that me and her are destined to be together. I can't do this any more. I'm ending things."

"Wait!" cried Sabina, but Alexis melted away into the crowd of people.

Sabina raced after her but was blocked by Maria, the prefect from the year above. "Sabrina, there you are! LOVE the red dress, so cute!"

"Thanks," said Sabina, distracted as she tried to look behind Maria. She knew most Year Eights would be thrilled to get a compliment from her, but right now, Sabina didn't care. She had bigger things to deal with.

"I was wondering, can you do a vision for me?"

"I can't – I need to find Alexis!"

"But this is important. I need to find out if our house wins the MG tournament."

Sabina exhaled in frustration, trying to slip past Maria. She wished she was in her black dress and trainers – it would have been so much easier if she could actually walk. Instead, it took her for ever to edge her way through the crowd of people gushing over her dress and heels, begging her to do their fortunes and trying to dance with her.

By the time she found Alexis, it was too late.

Her vision was happening in real-time. Felicia was sobbing loudly, clutching onto her former girlfriend's arm, while Alexis looked for an escape route.

Alicia and Dillon were standing on the side. Sabina heard

Dillon asking: "What about your friend? Is she...okay?"

Alicia shrugged casually. "They're always breaking up and getting back together again. Let's go dance!"

They walked past Felicia, who was begging Alexis to stay. "Please, don't do this!"

Alexis shook her head. "Sorry, Leesh, but it's best for both of us. And...it's for ever this time."

She walked off, leaving Felicia crying into her plate of hummus and crackers. Sabina ran over to her. "Oh, Leesh, it's going to be okay. Don't worry!"

"But you said we went to the dance together," wailed Felicia, pushing Sabina's arm off her. "You're wrong! Your visions are all wrong!"

"I...didn't see the full picture," said Sabina desperately. "I'm sorry! So sorry! But it's all going to be okay, I promise. Let me get you some cake. Or shall we go to the chocolate fountain?"

Felicia wiped her eyes. "Chocolate fountain. This is an emergency."

Sabina nodded for the millionth time as Felicia complained about Alexis, pausing only to devour more chocolate strawberries.

"Totally," she murmured, squinting as she scanned the room for Dillon and Alicia. They were still on the dance floor. Phew.

And...so was Faye. She was wearing a bright yellow dress with trainers, dancing in the middle of the room with people from advanced chem. Unlike Alicia and Dillon, who were barely moving, Faye and her friends were making faces, singing loudly to the lyrics, and dancing just like Sabina used to with Harry and Ria. She looked on in longing, wishing she was there with them in her trainers. But when Faye saw her, she turned away as though she was deliberately avoiding Sabina.

"Leesh, I brought you a marshmallow stick to cheer you up!" It was Alicia.

Sabina's eyes shot open as she realized there was no Dillon by Alicia's side.

"Thanks, Leesh," replied Felicia. "Honestly I—"

"Where's Dillon?" interrupted Sabina.

Alicia giggled. "Oh, he's gone outside to find his friends. He's *so* cute, I can't even—"

But Sabina was gone before Alicia reached the end of her sentence. She needed to find Dillon *now*. She raced into the car park, panting as she searched for him, hoping it wasn't too late.

And then she saw him. With a flash of purple by his side.

Sabina's stomach clenched in anxiety. This was a disaster. Everything was going wrong – and it was all on her to stop it. She raced over to Dillon, but her ridiculous heels tripped her up. She threw them off in annoyance and ran the rest of the way barefoot. But she froze when she realized it was too late

– her vision had already come true. Dillon was kissing the girl in purple.

"Stop!" cried Sabina.

They both turned to face her in surprise, and Sabina's eyes widened as she saw who it was. Leah. The most popular girl in Year Nine. Alicia would be *furious*.

"WHAT. IS. THIS?!"

Sabina spun round in horror, praying she was wrong about who that voice belonged to. But no. Alicia was standing right there, shimmering in her gold sparkles, blazing with fury like a Greek goddess scorned. Felicia was behind her, hands on her hips, ready to back up her best friend.

"This...is not good," exhaled Dillon, in what was clearly the understatement of the year.

The Greek gods had *nothing* on the Leeshes, and Sabina had a sinking feeling they'd be unleashing their wrath on her straight after Dillon...

Chapter 26

Sabina woke with a yawn as her alarm beeped. She reached for her phone to see she had a message from the Leeshes.

> We need to talk.

Sabina paled as it all came back to her. The dance, Alexis dumping Felicia, Dillon kissing Leah...

After Alicia had appeared in the car park, she had eviscerated Dillon and Leah. She'd told Dillon he only had 900,000 followers because people liked the way he looked, but if they knew what his personality was like, he'd be lucky to have nine. Then she told Leah – a year *above* – that her dress was five years out of season, and she was welcome to such a shallow, pathetic excuse of a boy.

When Dillon and Leah had run off in tears, Alicia had

turned to Sabina. She wanted to know why her visions had been so far off the truth. *She* was meant to be the one kissing Dillon in the car park – not Leah. Felicia had joined in too, and they'd both shouted at Sabina, demanding to know exactly WHAT was going on – why had she told them everything would work out when the opposite had happened?!

Sabina hadn't known what to say. She couldn't tell them she'd lied, because they'd be absolutely furious with her. And she didn't want to make it seem like she felt sorry for the Leeshes; she had a feeling that wouldn't go down well. But she also didn't want them to think her visions were untrustworthy, because then they'd pull out of the talent show, and she'd never save Beauties.

So, in the end, she'd burst into tears of frustration. She'd paused for a second when she'd felt a fizzle of a shock in her fingers, but it had quickly faded without turning into a vision. And it had given her an idea of what to tell the Leeshes.

"My emotions are all over the place," she'd said. "Which is why my visions are unreliable right now. It wasn't my fault – it was the visions. I thought I saw you and Dillon kissing – but it must have been Dillon and Leah."

The Leeshes had wanted to know more, and had quick-fired questions at her, until Sabina had broken down with real tears and told them a half-truth. "It's my dad. I've been trying to find him so I can invite him to the talent show, but it's *impossible.* I can't find him anywhere on the internet and it's so stressful it must be affecting my visions. I'm sorry!"

The Leeshes had still been annoyed, but her answer had appeased them. Felicia had suggested Sabina speak to her therapist so she could heal her family wounds. While Alicia had scowled, saying Sabina should have told them earlier; this could easily be solved by getting her family's lawyers on the case. They'd find her dad in no time!

Sabina had been so taken aback by Alicia's generosity and Felicia's understanding that she'd spontaneously hugged them both. The Leeshes had rolled their eyes and warned Sabina they weren't ready to forgive her yet.

And now it was Sunday morning and Sabina had a "we need to talk" message on her phone. She had no idea what it meant. Had the Leeshes changed their minds? Were they still upset with her? What would they say?

Her phone rang and Sabina knew she was about to find out.

"Heee-eeeey," she said, her voice high-pitched with nerves, as the Leeshes' faces filled her screen.

"Sabrina," said Alicia. It was 9 a.m. and she already had a full face of make-up and freshly washed hair. "We've fixed everything. Tell her, Leesh."

Felicia, who was also made-up and dressed – unlike Sabina who was still in her pyjamas with kirby grips from last night's hairdo poking into her scalp – nodded. "So, to avoid any more situations like last night, we've solved your emotional crisis.

Leesh's lawyers found your dad online, and we sent him a message from you saying you'd love to meet him and would he like to come to the talent show?"

Sabina's mouth fell open. "Whaaaaat?"

"It wasn't hard," said Alicia dismissively. "So, you just need to look out for a reply from him. And in the meantime, you need to use this week to *practise your visions*. Because there is no way you are messing up the show for us. Our reputations are on the line."

"You found my dad?" repeated Sabina.

"I'll send you the link after the call," said Felicia. "We made an account for you on the business site he uses, so we'll give you the login details. I really don't know why you didn't tell us earlier – we're good at this stuff."

Sabina gaped, numb. She couldn't believe the Leeshes had done it – they'd found her dad *and* contacted him. After thirteen years, she was finally going to meet him! Maybe her dad had been waiting for this as long as Sabina had? For all she knew, he might have lost her mum's contact details and spent years dreaming of his daughter getting in touch. This was the miracle that would bring her dad back into her life.

"Thank you," she said at last, her voice thick with emotion. "Thank you SO much. I thought you'd hate me after last night, but...you've just changed my life. This is one of the most amazing things anyone has ever done for me."

"We're still mad," corrected Alicia. "You messed up and almost caused us total humiliation. But...we watched some reels on break-ups last night and they made us realize we're better off without Alexis and Dillon. They weren't good enough for us."

"I don't think I was even *happy* with Alexis," added Felicia. "We didn't really get each other – not like Leesh and I do. I just didn't want to be dumped."

"And Dillon is kind of dull," said Alicia. "He's hot. But his personality is *not*. If it wasn't for me, we would have been in silence the whole time. Leah's welcome to him."

"You deserve better, Leesh," said Felicia.

"Thanks, babe, you too," replied Alicia.

"I'm...so happy for you both," said Sabina, still dazed from the news about her dad. "You're right – you deserve *way* better than Dillon and Alexis."

"We know," said Alicia serenely. "We'll see you at school tomorrow. And make sure your powers are working properly again in time for next Saturday. We need to slay at that show – it's our chance for global, or at least national, fame. Because if not," her voice darkened, "we'll be blaming you."

Sabina nodded fervently. "Don't worry, I'll be the best psychic that this talent show has ever seen!"

The Leeshes hung up the call, and Sabina collapsed onto her bed with joy. The Leeshes were incredible. They'd recovered from heartbreak in less than twenty-four hours *and* they'd found her dad. How had she ever thought they weren't good friends? They were the most amazing friends ever! She was so lucky to have them.

"Sabina?" Her bedroom door creaked open to reveal her mum, eyes narrowed and arms crossed. "What's that I just heard about you being a *psychic* and having powers?!"

Sabina's stomach sank. Her secret was out.

"So let me get this straight," said her mum, looking at Sabina from across the kitchen table. "You somehow developed psychic abilities THREE WEEKS AGO and you're only just telling me now? Not to mention, you're planning on revealing them at the talent show in front of the entire village and the internet?!"

"Yes, but—"

Her mum stood up, running a hand through her bouncing curls. "No, no, no. Do not try and talk your way out of this, Sabina. How could you not have *told* me what was going on?"

Sabina looked down at the familiar stains on the oak table, wishing her mum hadn't found out like this. It was supposed to happen when her dad was there to calm her mum down. "I don't know."

"You don't *know*?! Sabina, we tell each other everything! Why wasn't there an episode of *Sabina Gets Magical Powers* or *Sabina Becomes Psychic and Everyone But Her Mum Knows*?"

"I told you about saving Katniss," said Sabina in a small voice. "I just…missed out the bit where it happened because of my powers."

"That's the most important bit!" cried her mum. "I could have helped you! But instead, you lied to me."

"You lied to me too! About Manish!"

"That was different," said her mum. "And I'm sorry about that. Did you not think I'd believe you?"

Sabina shook her head. She'd never doubted that. "I knew you'd trust me – you've always told me that. But I didn't want to worry you or add to your stress. I was being considerate."

"I'm your mother – it's my job to worry about you." Her mum sighed in frustration. "I could have helped you! I can't believe you've been going through all this alone. Were you planning on ever telling me?"

"I was waiting for the talent show. Then you'd see me win and everything would be fine."

Her mum frowned, confused. "But why do you want to win this talent show so badly? And why are you even entering? Surely you don't want to draw more attention to your powers? You're only thirteen, Sabina – you need to focus on school, not gain a worldwide reputation as a psychic."

"I'm not doing it for the attention! How could you even think that?" cried Sabina, stung. She was doing all this to save her mum's business, but her mum thought she was fame-hungry like the Leeshes.

"Because I don't *know* you any more! The Sabina I knew would have shared all of this with me. But ever since you got to MG…" Her mum's words trailed off but Sabina knew what she'd wanted to say.

"I've changed," said Sabina flatly. "You think I'm different."

"I didn't say that. And it's normal to change, especially when you're getting older."

"It's not puberty – it's my third eye chakra!" said Sabina, as a flash of electricity tingled her fingertips. But she barely noticed because she was too caught up in what she was saying. "It's not my FAULT I'm changing. And…maybe you've changed, too. The old you never had a boyfriend, but now we live in this horrible village and you've found horrible Manish to go with it!"

"Sabina Patel, do *not* speak to me like that," shouted her mum. "Go to your room!"

"Gladly!" Sabina shouted back, hot tears pooling in her eyes. "As if I want to be here!"

Chapter 27

Four days on from her argument with her mum, Sabina still felt terrible, but her anger and sadness had dulled into a hard rock in her stomach – much like the sedimentary rock formation Ms Baker was teaching them about right now. Not that Sabina was paying attention to geography. She was too busy thinking about the natural disaster that was her life.

She'd felt like this all week, deliberately avoiding Diva's classes so she didn't have to sit in her feelings. Everyone else had been in a good mood because it was the last week before the holidays – they were finishing today, a Thursday, which meant it was a shorter week than usual – but Sabina hadn't felt celebratory. She couldn't bring herself to look forward to the talent show that was happening in two days' time, because she still wasn't certain that Harry and Ria would be there. She couldn't even enjoy the fact that she'd be off school for the next few weeks and could spend time with her mum, because she'd be hanging out with *Manish*.

Then there was her dad. He still hadn't replied to the message that the Leeshes had sent him. The worst part was that he'd read it on Monday. But it was Thursday now, and he hadn't said a word in response. Sabina surreptitiously glanced around the room to make sure Ms Baker was still busy – she was droning on about igneous and metamorphic rocks – and slid her phone out of her pocket to check it for the hundredth time that day. She refreshed the app, but there was nothing new. Her dad still hadn't responded.

Sabina didn't understand. Why was her dad keeping her on read? Was he hoping to turn up in person and surprise her? That would be fun – but she wished he'd at least send a few sentences to confirm beforehand. She clicked on his profile again. Rohan Patel. Thirty-five. It was *definitely* him. He looked exactly like the picture she had of him with her mum, complete with a moustache, only he now also had wrinkles on his forehead. But he was still handsome and Sabina knew he was the man in her vision. She smiled to herself, comforted by the thought of what she'd seen. In two more days, *everything* would be okay. It had to be.

"Sabina! What are the main examples of sedimentary rock?" barked Ms Baker.

"Uh..." Sabina hesitated, trying desperately to think of an answer. She looked at the Leeshes but they shrugged helplessly.

Then she heard a voice whisper behind her: "Chalk, clay, limestone, sandstone and shale."

Sabina smiled – she'd know that voice anywhere. Faye. "Chalk, clay, limestone, sandstone and shale," she repeated quickly.

Ms Baker frowned. "Yes. Well done. Now, page ninety-four of your textbooks, everyone."

Sabina turned around gratefully, but Faye was studiously engrossed in her textbook. She tried to catch her gaze to thank her, but Faye avoided all eye contact. Still, she'd helped Sabina when she didn't need to. This was *definitely* a good sign. Faye must be softening just in time for the show on Saturday, when she'd be onstage to hug Sabina when she won!

"Three charcoal pizzas, all vegan," said Alicia, snapping her menu shut.

Sabina had been about to order something different, but she stayed silent. She was in a cute pizzeria on the nice side of the village with the Leeshes, which was apparently their end of term tradition. Sabina was so grateful to be invited after everything that had gone down at the dance that she didn't want to make a fuss over pizza. She was sure charcoal tasted better than it sounded.

"So, how are we all feeling about the talent show?" asked Alicia. "Leesh and I are *killing* it with our dance."

"Yep," said Felicia. "We'll show Alexis and Dillon that we don't need them! We're the Leeshes, and after this, we're going to be *famous*."

"Sabrina?" asked Alicia. "Are you on track? You can't let us down."

"I...think so," said Sabina. She assumed she was still on track. She hadn't had a single uncontrolled vision in weeks – just the little jolts whenever her emotions were too high. Although she hadn't had a controlled vision either... She hadn't felt like practising. Her visions reminded her of when everything started to go wrong – with Harry, Ria, Faye, her mum. But she knew that with the crystal, it would all be fine.

"You think?!" repeated Alicia. "Losing is not an option. You need to WIN."

"I will," said Sabina more confidently this time. Because of course she'd win – she'd already seen it in her vision.

"Can you do one for us now?" asked Felicia eagerly. "I want to know how jealous Alexis will be when I win."

"I can't, sorry. I left my crystal at home."

"But you didn't need your crystal when you did your visions for us at the start," pointed out Alicia. "Can't you try one now? You owe us."

"I...don't know if I *can* still do them without my crystal," admitted Sabina. "But...I can try?"

Felicia put her hand out in the middle of the table, waiting. Sabina closed her eyes, focusing on her breath like always.

She created an intention: "I want to have a vision about Alexis and the talent show." Slowly, she reached out to touch Felicia's hand, waiting for the jolt.

But nothing happened.

"Sorry," said Sabina, blinking open her eyes. She hadn't expected a proper vision, but she'd thought she'd at least feel that familiar spark of electricity. "It...didn't work."

"Try me," said Alicia authoritatively. She placed her hand in front of Sabina.

Again, Sabina breathed deeply. She tried to do what Faye had always told her – to channel her emotions into her intention. Then she reached out to touch Alicia's hand, waiting for the spark.

It didn't come.

Sabina waited for a few more deep breaths. Maybe it was delayed?

"The pizza's here," said Alicia.

Sabina opened her eyes to see three steaming hot pizzas on the table. "Sorry," she apologized, flushing as she realized how drastically her powers had been affected by her lack of meditation. "It will work when I have the crystal, I promise."

"It had better," warned Alicia. "Otherwise, you'll have us to answer to." She gave Sabina a steely gaze, then looked down at her food and broke into a smile. "Yay, pizza! Let's do a selfie! Smile and say 'fauxmage'!"

Chapter 28

It was Saturday, the day of the talent show. Sabina had woken up feeling her palms slick with nerves. She'd messaged Harry and Ria the night before, reminding them the show was later that day. She'd sent them the address and told them their names were still on the guest list in case they wanted to come. But they hadn't replied.

Sabina was starting to lose faith in her vision. She didn't understand how it could work out as planned. Harry and Ria still weren't speaking to her. Nor was Faye. Her dad hadn't replied. She was no longer ever sure her powers would work onstage and that she'd win the five-thousand-pound prize!

But she'd put so much hope into this talent show fixing everything that Sabina knew she had to try and stay positive. There was still time for things to change and for her vision to come true.

She checked her reflection in the mirror one last time. She'd tied her hair into a ponytail and put on her favourite sparkly green earrings, which she was wearing with her jeans and a black top – the Leeshes were bringing her cloak. She had her glasses on too – even though the Leeshes had given her strict instructions not to wear them onstage.

And finally, it was time for the most important thing of all. Her crystal. Sabina picked it up carefully, wrapping it in a tissue, then slipping it into the zip-up compartment of her bag so it would be extra safe. There was *no way* she'd be able to win the contest without it.

"Mum?" called Sabina, thundering down the stairs with her bag. "I'm ready!"

She pushed open the kitchen door to see her mum sitting there in her dressing gown with a cup of chai.

"You're not ready?" cried Sabina. "We have to go soon!"

Her mum looked up at her with tired eyes. "I'm sorry, Sabina, but I'm not coming."

Sabina's jaw fell slack. "What?! Why?"

"I've been thinking about it all night, and...it doesn't feel right to me that you're profiting from using your powers on a stage. Your powers are a gift, Sabina. They come from our culture, our traditions. I don't think it's right to showcase them in front of Lucy Locket and her fans, for five minutes of fame."

Sabina's face hardened, disappointment solidifying in her

veins, but she stayed silent as her mum spoke.

"I've been reading about the chakras, and they're all about integrity, and living in alignment with your values. I don't think using your powers for a live-streamed talent show is in line with that."

"Are you kidding me?" Sabina finally burst out, angry and upset. She was doing all this for her mum, but it didn't even occur to her that Sabina might have a decent reason for being in the show. For a second, Sabina thought about telling her the truth. But there was no point. Her mind was clearly made up. So instead, she said: "They're *my* powers! I get to do what I want with them."

"I know," agreed her mum. "It's your choice. But, Sabs, if you do go ahead with this, I can't be there to watch you. I'm sorry. I love you, but it just doesn't feel right to me."

Sabina felt hot tears pool in her eyes, and she tried to breathe deeply. She didn't understand why her mum was making things so hard for her! She rubbed her eyes angrily and grabbed her jacket.

"Fine, whatever. I'll see you later."

Sabina's heart was racing. She was in the dressing room of the huge venue where the talent show was taking place. There were dozens of contestants, all getting dressed in elaborate costumes. But none as elaborate as the Leeshes, who were preparing for their dance. They'd both found blond Taylor Swift wigs and looked identical to their heroine. Sabina had no idea how they'd done it.

"Leesh, have you put your perfume on?" asked Alicia. "Because this look is not complete without the full sensory experience!"

"Um, Leeshes, I'm going to go to the loo," said Sabina, who could feel her chest tightening with anxiety. "I'll be right back."

The Leeshes were so focused on their costumes that they barely looked at her.

Sabina felt her breath return when she left the dressing room for the quiet stillness of the hallway. She'd looked inside the venue earlier and hadn't spotted a single familiar face – not even Faye's. But there was still at least an hour till her event. Her dad could turn up. With her mum. And Faye, Harry and Ria.

She opened up her socials to see if any of them had posted anything. There was a story from Harry. It was from half an hour ago, and it showed him and Ria...in their local skate park. Which meant they *weren't* on the way to the competition at all.

Her stomach sank in disappointment. It didn't make sense – they were meant to be there. She'd seen it in her vision!

Sabina scrunched her face tight, then realized there was still time for them to get there from London. She just needed to give them a helping hand. And there was only one way to do that.

It was time for her to call in a FRIENDSHIP SOS.

She, Harry and Ria had come up with the concept five years ago, after watching a movie about three best friends who grew apart when they became adults. It had hit them that when they got older, terrible things could happen, like one of them marrying someone the others hated, or moving abroad to the other side of the world.

So, they'd decided to create a pact – the FRIENDSHIP SOS. No matter where they were, or how long it had been since they'd last spoken, if someone called a FRIENDSHIP SOS, the others all needed to get there as soon as possible. Even if they were living in Australia and had three dogs to look after. They were only allowed one FRIENDSHIP SOS each, and once used, it could never be used again.

Sabina knew this was the one time in her life she'd need it most. So, she picked up her phone and tapped out the letters *FRIENDSHIP SOS*. Then she pressed a button to record her friends an accompanying voice message.

"Hey, I miss you both so much. I know it's dramatic to use my one SOS right now but...I'm doing it. I'm at the village talent show and I don't know if I can get through it without you. Nobody is speaking to me right now – not just you two, but also Faye and my mum. The only people who are still my friends are the Leeshes, but they'd stop speaking to me too if they found out that I lied to them about their visions… I told Felicia that Alexis would get her an anniversary gift, and I told Alicia she'd kiss Dillon at the dance. Even though I saw Alexis breaking up with Felicia, and Dillon kissing someone else. I know it was wrong, but I didn't want to upset them, and I needed their help. I wish I hadn't lied to them though, especially when they helped me invite my dad to the show today. I really hope he comes… And that I'll win and Faye will forgive me. I hope you both do too. I know I can't use my FRIENDSHIP SOS to do that – but I'm using it to try. So *please* come. And give me a chance to make everything up to you both."

"You were INCREDIBLE," cried Sabina, beaming as the Leeshes came offstage. And it was true. The Leeshes' dance had been mind-blowing. It wasn't even just a dance – they'd choreographed a five-minute mash-up of all Taylor's best songs. It was a work of art and Taylor herself would have been impressed. "The audience *loved* you!"

"We know," said Alicia coolly, adjusting her wig.

"Are you going to get changed now?" asked Sabina. "Into your sparkly cloaks for our act?"

Felicia glanced at Alicia. "Totally. We…just need some time to process our success. Did you see how much everyone was clapping?"

"Yes, but..." Sabina hesitated, uncertain. She'd draped the shimmery cloak around her shoulders and put on Alicia's sparkly eyeshadow. But she felt silly without the Leeshes wearing their cloaks.

"We'll meet you at curtain call when it's time," promised Alicia. "Five minutes."

Sabina nodded and made her way over to side of the stage. The event organizers were gesturing for her to be there, talking to each other through their headsets. It was all so efficient and official. She'd expected something small, but this was *huge.*

Once Sabina had been miked up, she peered through the curtains into the audience. She *still* couldn't see anyone she knew. But she was sure she'd see them once she was on the stage.

"Sabrina the Teenage Witch?"

Sabina looked up. "Uh...yes. That's me."

"You're on. Now."

"But I can't! I'm waiting for my friends. They're meant to be here too."

"Alicia Johnson and Felicia James? They've removed their names from the list. Go on up."

Sabina gaped at the organizer in horror. She didn't understand. Where were the Leeshes?! She looked around the room desperately, and then...there they were. Still in their Taylor outfits. Standing together, arms crossed, faces defiant.

"We overheard your voice note," said Alicia. "To your *friends*."

"Which means we know you deliberately lied to us about your visions," said Felicia. "You never saw Alexis get me a gift at all!"

The blood drained out of Sabina's face. "I'm so sorry! Really, really sorry. I didn't mean to lie."

Alicia held up a hand to silence her. "Leave it. You're on your own, Sabrina. We don't hang with liars."

"We thought we were friends," said Felicia. "But...you were just using us."

"I wasn't! I didn't mean to. Please. I'm sorry!"

"Whatever," said Alicia, glancing down at something in her fist. "Good luck up there!" She spun on her heels, Felicia following her.

"Sabrina, it's time," said the organizer, directing her to the steps leading up to the stage.

"I...can't," she said, the words catching in her throat. She couldn't go up alone. She needed the Leeshes. They were the ones who were going to introduce her, explain everything to the audience, and give her the moral support she needed to win.

"I'm afraid you don't have a choice," said the organizer, as Sabina heard Lucy Locket saying her name up onstage.

In that moment, Sabina realized the organizer was right. She didn't have a choice. But it was okay. Because she'd already seen this in her vision. She was going to win. She could do this.

She took a deep breath, then opened up her bag to find her crystal. She unzipped her special compartment, then let out a panicked cry. It wasn't there! She rummaged around the bag in desperation, but her crystal was gone.

"Sabrina the Teenage Witch, we need you *now*," said the organizer, gently nudging her up onto the stage. "Come on!"

Sabrina grabbed her glasses from her bag. If the Leeshes weren't going to be there to help her, she could at least use her super sight.

And that was how Sabrina found herself walking onto the stage alone, in front of hundreds of people, blinking at the bright lights, expected to reveal what was inside Lucy Locket's locket – all without her crystal.

Chapter 29

"So, Sabrina the Teenage Witch is going to use her psychic powers to reveal the unknown," said Lucy into her microphone. "She's going to find out what's inside my locket – without opening it!"

The audience gasped and the rumbling sounded like an earthquake. Sabina forced herself to smile, but really, she was busy scanning the audience for her parents, Faye, Harry and Ria. Even with her super sight, it took a while. Sabina's remaining hope fizzled out as she realized that not one of them was there. She was on her own.

"Right then," said Lucy, slowly removing her famous locket from around her neck, holding it up in front of the audience and cameras, before gently putting it on a purple velvet cushion that the Leeshes had ordered for the act. "Ready when you are, Sabrina!"

Sabina's blood was pounding in her veins. Even though she didn't have the crystal, her emotions were a solid ten right now, which meant there had to be a chance she'd get a vision – even if it was a small chance...

"Oooh, she's looking very serious!" said Lucy. "And so she should be – my locket is serious business!" She beckoned for Sabina to approach the locket.

Sabina slowly obeyed, walking over until she was standing right by the locket.

"So, do you just...go ahead and get a vision?" asked Lucy. "Or do you need to do something woo woo first?"

"I...need to touch the locket," whispered Sabina. "If that's okay?"

"So long as you don't prise it open and cheat!" said Lucy with a loud laugh.

Sabina stood over the locket, trying to focus her energy. There was a low whistle, and she glanced across to the side of the stage, behind the curtain. The Leeshes were standing there, waving her crystal at her. Of course they'd taken it. And now they were waiting for her to crash and burn.

But she couldn't give them that satisfaction. She needed to win and save Beauties for her mum.

"Whenever you're ready!" trilled Lucy, a layer of urgency in her voice.

Sabina took a deep breath. She closed her eyes, trying to channel her panicked emotions into a vision. For the first

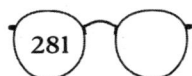

time in weeks, she wished she'd kept up her meditation. Because right now, she was struggling to steady her breath. Her thoughts were all over the place too – why wasn't her dad there? Would her mum come? And where was Faye?!

She needed to calm down and trust in her powers. She'd already seen herself win. And there was still time. Maybe everyone came too late to see her act, but arrived in time to watch her collect her prize. Sabina straightened her spine, feeling more confident. She could do this.

She focused on her intention: "I want a vision that shows me what's in Lucy's locket." And then she reached out a hand to touch the cool metal of the locket. Her breath tightened, but...that was it.

Nothing else happened.

Sabina blinked open her eyes uncertainly, to see the blur of faces in the audience watching her. That was weird. She'd been able to see them properly before. Her super sight had meant she could make out every detail of everyone's face. But now, they weren't so visible.

That was when it hit Sabina. Her super sight had gone. Her eyesight was back to what it used to be. And her visions had gone too. She'd lost her powers.

"Sabrina? Go on – what's in my locket? An ex, a pet, a friend? I want specifics, please!"

"It didn't work," whispered Sabina.

Lucy laughed into the mic. "Who knew psychics got

technical problems?" But to Sabina, she hissed: "Make something up! Fast!"

Sabina didn't know what to do! She wished there was someone to help her. The Leeshes – they'd know exactly what to say. Or Faye. She'd helped her in geography with the sedimentary rocks, and Sabina knew she could have helped her now. But of course, she wouldn't. And nor would the Leeshes. Because she'd hurt them all.

Suddenly, Sabina realized that the common denominator in all of these problems was HER. It wasn't that Faye, Harry, Ria, Alicia, Felicia and her mum were all being unfair – it was that *she*'d been acting unfairly. She'd lied to all of them. She'd expected them to be there for her the whole time – but she hadn't been there for them. She'd missed Faye's rally, she hadn't helped her with her victory speech, and she'd hidden the truth from her. Just like she'd done to the Leeshes.

She was alone, up on a stage in front of hundreds of people, and it was all her fault. She'd alienated anyone who could have helped her. She *had* changed. But it wasn't just because of her powers. It was because of how she was choosing to use them.

"Come on!" hissed Lucy, her voice barely audible. "Your time's running out! Just say something – anything!"

But Sabina didn't care any more. Her vision wasn't coming true. She didn't understand why – but she knew that she couldn't change it.

"I'm sorry," she blurted out. "I have to go."

Sabina sat in the toilet stall, head buried in her hands. Everything had fallen apart and she didn't know what to do. She sobbed out loud, wishing she'd never received those awful powers. Diva, Faye and her mum had been wrong – they weren't a gift. They were a complete *nightmare*!

"It depends how you see things," said a voice from outside her toilet cubicle.

Sabina jerked upright. There was somebody there. And it sounded like they'd replied to what Sabina had said in her *head*. "Hello?" she whispered, trembling. "Who's there?"

There was no reply, and Sabina wondered if she'd imagined the voice. She stood up, slid open the door, and gasped when she saw her yoga teacher.

"Diva! Are you…real?"

Diva laughed. "I am. But good question. You never know these days."

Slowly, Sabina crept out of her cubicle. Diva was wearing her normal leggings with a hoody, her long hair spread out in loose waves, smiling.

"I came to check on you," said Diva. "I had a feeling things might not work out as you'd hoped today."

"Are you psychic too?" asked Sabina, her eyes wide.

Diva smiled mysteriously. "Let's focus on *you*, Sabina. Tell me what's going on."

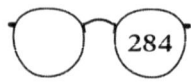

"Everything went wrong," said Sabina flatly. "I didn't win the show. I failed. And it was because I didn't have my crystal."

"It was never about the crystal, Sabina. That just helped to channel what was already inside you."

"Well, clearly what was inside me has gone. Because I've lost all my powers. Even my super sight."

"Your powers are always inside you, they're just maybe not so accessible right now," said Diva gently. "We all have the potential to have powers – but only some people can reach them. People who can connect to themselves on a deeper level through meditation."

Sabina bit her lip. "So I lost them because I stopped meditating so much?"

"Partly. You see, meditation helps keep us balanced," explained Diva. "It keeps the chakras aligned and our emotions steady, which allowed you to connect with your powers. But more than anything, it keeps us in the present moment. And...perhaps you haven't been living in the present moment so much? Maybe you got caught up in the future?"

Sabina frowned. "Yes, but that's because of my powers! They literally *made* me see my future! I saw my mum losing her business, and that's why I wanted to win so badly, to stop it happening. And I wanted to make sure my other vision came true – of Faye hugging me onstage, and my dad kissing my mum. But my dad isn't here. He didn't even reply to the Leeshes' message. The future was all a lie!"

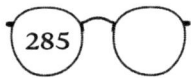

Diva nodded thoughtfully. "It sounds like you've been living so deeply in the future that you've forgotten about the present. And, Sabina, our gifts can only work in the present. If we lose ourselves and become imbalanced, the gifts fade, and we can struggle to see things clearly."

"But it's the powers' fault that I've been in the future!" cried Sabina. "They kept showing it to me!"

"I know, it's not easy. But the real gift lies in seeing the future and knowing it's only the present that matters. Otherwise, you can end up only seeing what you want to see."

"Whaa-aaat?"

Diva laughed at the expression on Sabina's face. "I know. It sounds complicated. But it's simple, really. We can think about the future – but we can't obsess about it. It's best to hold it loosely, not clutch tightly to it in desperation. Because the most important thing is what's happening now – not what's going to happen in the future. And whatever happens later will always be influenced by what we're doing right now."

Sabina stayed silent, letting Diva's words absorb into her mind. They were starting to make sense. She understood now that she'd been doing exactly what Diva had warned her against. She'd been clutching tightly to all of her visions – the good ones and the bad – and hadn't focused on the present moment. She'd taken for granted that her visions would come true so she'd stopped bothering with any of the things in the present that would actually make that happen – like making up with her friends. And it had led her into a total mess.

She'd spent this whole time obsessing about what was going to happen that she'd missed what was already happening. She'd missed *so* much. She'd thought that because the Leeshes were popular, they wouldn't mind if she used them – but they had feelings, just like she did. Nor had Sabina realized that Faye needed her help just as much as she needed Faye's. When Harry and Ria had tried to call her out on it, she hadn't even been able to see that they were right – she'd been rude to them instead. Just like she had to her mum – all because she'd started dating Manish, and it didn't fit with what Sabina had seen in her vision. Oh, she'd made such a *mess* of things...

"Sometimes we need to make a mess so that we can grow," said Diva. "Nobody grows when things are super neat and tidy all the time."

"Did you just read my thoughts?!"

"Don't be so hard on yourself, Sabina," said Diva, ignoring her question. "You made mistakes, but you're able to see them. That's the most important thing. And your heart was always in the right place. That's why you were able to access your powers – because you have real integrity."

"My mum said something about integrity this morning! It's why she didn't want me to do the talent show. But what actually *is* integrity?"

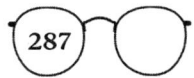

"Real integrity is when what you do, what you say and who you are, are all aligned."

Sabina stared at her teacher for a few moments, then sighed. "No offence, but I feel like my life was a lot simpler before you came into it."

Diva grinned. "None taken. But I'm not so sure it was. You see, life is always full of opportunities for growth. It's just that most of us choose not to see them and stay in our comfort zones. But you were brave enough to do things differently."

"I wish I'd stayed in my comfort zone…"

Diva shook her head. "That wasn't your path, Sabina. As I said when I met you, you're destined to do things differently. And you *don't* need a crystal to do it. All you need to do is come back to yourself and stay in your present reality. Good luck!"

Chapter 30

Sabina was waiting for the bus home from the talent show when she spotted the Leeshes, still dressed as Taylor Swifts, carrying a huge trophy.

"You won!" she cried. "I mean...congrats."

Alicia scowled. "No thanks to you. Liar."

"How did it feel to fail onstage?" asked Felicia. "I hope it was worse than when Alexis dumped me."

Sabina took a deep breath, then walked towards the Leeshes. Suddenly, she knew exactly what she had to do, and what she had to say, to be aligned with who she was.

"I am really sorry about what I did. It wasn't fair of me. I lied to you both when you didn't deserve it. There's no excuse, and I don't expect you to forgive me. You were right – I was using you. And it was really cruel of me. I'm sad I did it, and I hope I never do it again to you or anyone else. But I want you to know I'll always be grateful to you both for finding my dad, even if he never replied. And for being there when nobody else was. So thank you."

The Leeshes both looked taken aback. They exchanged looks.

"That was...a lot," said Alicia finally. "You aren't even going to try and pretend you didn't lie? Or use us?"

Sabina shook her head. "No. I did. And it was wrong. I'm sorry."

"Wow," said Felicia. "It's kind of cool you're not trying to defend yourself like Alexis always did."

"It was a decent apology as far as apologies go," said Alicia begrudgingly. "*Not* that we forgive you!"

"I don't expect you to," said Sabina sincerely.

"Well, I suppose we are over the worst of it," admitted Alicia. "Watching you fail onstage helped. And Leesh and I have decided to focus on our friendship and not our love lives. So long as you promise to never lie again, we'll be your friends again."

Sabina's eyes widened in surprise. She hadn't expected the Leeshes to forgive her – but she was so glad they had! Except... well...she wasn't sure that she'd forgiven *them.* She wasn't the only person who'd made mistakes. They'd treated her badly too.

Sabina stood up straight as Diva's words about integrity echoed in her ears. It was time for her to be brave. "Thank you so much for accepting my apology – and I promise I won't lie again. But…for us to be friends, I need you both to apologize to me too. I mean, you used *me* for my powers. You manipulated me. And…well…you can both be quite mean sometimes. It's not nice."

The Leeshes gawped at her, totally lost for words.

"Did she just ask *us* to apologize to *her*?" Felicia asked Alicia.

Alicia stared at Sabina in silence. Sabina squirmed under the intensity of her gaze. But then Alicia grinned. "I like that you're not scared of us. Not everyone has the guts to call us out. But you're right. We were pretty mean. It's in our nature. But I'm sorry if we hurt you."

Felicia nodded eagerly. "Me too! I'm sorry. Because I actually really like you – you're so fun! You didn't deserve for us to manipulate you like we did. We'll *never* do it again."

"Okay, cool it, Leesh," hissed Alicia.

Sabina swallowed a laugh. "Thank you. Both of you. I accept your apologies."

"Yay, group hug!" squealed Felicia, pulling Sabina and Alicia into a hug. "Love that we're all friends again! Leesh, do you have a spare hairband so Sabrina can match with us?"

Sabina felt another wave of integrity wash over her. "There is one condition though. Two actually. If we're going to be friends, you need to call me by my real name: Sabina. And from now on, I'll wear what *I* want to wear. No comments on my personal appearance. Ever."

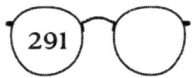

Alicia rolled her eyes. "Fine, *Sabina.* And...sorry about your dad. His loss."

"Totally," agreed Felicia. "I wasn't a fan of his short-sleeved shirt anyway. Oh wait – is it okay to comment on your dad's personal appearance?"

"Oh my God, Leesh," muttered Alicia, as she dragged Felicia into their awaiting limo. "See you later."

"Bye, Sabiiina!"

Sabina closed the front door behind her in relief. It felt so good to be home – and to not lie or pretend any more. Even apologizing to the Leeshes had made her feel a hundred times better. She felt bad for ever calling them the Leeches – she'd labelled them as judgemental when she'd been judging them the whole time. At least they'd been their authentic selves, which was more than she could say for herself.

"Sabina?" her mum called out from the kitchen. "Is that you?"

"Mum!" cried Sabina, running into the kitchen, before halting. There was a man with a moustache sitting next to her mum, sipping a cup of chai. Her heart swelled with joy. "Dad? You came!"

Her mum's eyes softened. "Oh, sweetheart. No. This is Manish."

Sabina felt her world come crashing down. She'd *so*

desperately wanted her dad to return – to prove that he loved her, that she was worthy of his love. She needed to know that he'd made a mistake in abandoning them, in *abandoning her*. But it hadn't happened. Her dad hadn't come; he hadn't even replied to her. And Sabina now realized he probably never would. Because she could clearly see that Manish (and his new moustache) was the man from her vision. Not her dad.

It was like Diva had said – she'd been so focused on the future that she'd only seen what she wanted to see.

Tears slipped down her face, and she tried to brush them away. She didn't want to cry in front of Manish.

He stood up quickly. "I'll leave you both to it," he said. "It's a pleasure to meet you, Sabina, and I look forward to maybe meeting again in the future." He kissed the top of her mum's head, whispering, "Take care, darling," and Sabina noticed her eyes light up with happiness.

When the front door shut behind Manish, Sabina burst into loud, confused tears. Her mum ran up to hug her.

"Oh, Sabs. I'm so sorry. I didn't realize how hard this all was on you."

"*I'm* sorry!" sobbed Sabina. "I hid my powers from you, and then I lost them onstage at the talent show. So now I won't get the prize money and you'll lose Beauties!"

Her mum peeled Sabina off her in surprise. "What? You were doing all this to save Beauties?!"

Sabina gulped back tears. "Yes! I saw you lose it in a vision and you were crying. I didn't want to you to lose your dream. You've worked so hard for it."

"Oh, honey," said her mum, squeezing her arm tightly. "That's my job to handle – not yours!" Her eyes welled up with tears. "I can't believe I was so harsh to you about doing the show! I should have known you weren't trying to exploit your powers for TikTok."

"I don't care about being famous – or being popular. Not any more, anyway. I just wanted to help you."

Her mum brushed a tear away. "Oh, Sabs. This is my fault. I'm sorry. I shouldn't have kept things from you. Then Manish wouldn't have come as a shock, and you wouldn't have tried to save the business. Because the truth is...I'm actually okay with Beauties closing down."

Sabina jerked upright. "What?!"

"Beauties *was* my dream at first," explained her mum. "But I think I'd always idealized running a business. The reality wasn't anything how I'd imagined – it was so much harder!"

Sabina couldn't help but think of what Diva had said about how it was better to stay in the present than daydream about the future. Maybe her teacher really did have a point.

"I tried to save the salon," continued her mum. "But when I hired Manish, I started to realize that I wasn't willing to do all the work that Beauties needed to survive. I was sacrificing too much – like my time with you. I've missed you so much,

Sabs. And Manish helped me realize that I'd rather spend more time with you than running a business."

Sabina felt something melt within her. Maybe Manish wasn't as awful as she'd thought... "I've missed you too, Mum. But does that mean you're giving up on your dream for me?"

Her mum shook her head. "I think that my dream has changed. Failing is actually quite freeing. Now I can start again and do something different!"

Sabina had never thought of failing as positive. And she'd failed *hard* lately. If her mum could see her failure as a good thing, then perhaps she could too. "What will you do instead?"

Her mum bit her lip. "Don't laugh, but I'm thinking that maybe I could retrain as a therapist. I know we were joking about it, but I really do feel like I'd enjoy it."

"That's so cool!" cried Sabina.

"Do you think I'd be good at it?" asked her mum anxiously.

Sabina rolled her eyes. "Obviously! I'm the one who suggested it, remember? Besides, it means I can get free therapy."

"Do you *really* want your mum as a therapist?"

"I want her as my best friend again," admitted Sabina. "I *hated* not telling you things. And, Mum, there's *so* much I haven't told you. Harry and Ria are mad at me. So is Faye. Even the Leeshes were – that's why they sabotaged my performance and took my crystal. But I've apologized to them now."

Her mum's face fell. "I can't believe you've been going through all this alone! This is exactly what I was scared of."

"Scared?" echoed Sabina.

"Of everything changing! I know I was the one who pushed for us to move here, and lately I've been panicking that I did the wrong thing. Faye is lovely, but Alicia and Felicia seem so different to you. And when you said you wanted to do the show, I thought maybe I'd forced you to change into someone I didn't know."

Sabina hadn't realized her mum was scared of change too – she'd thought that was just her. But…it really didn't make sense to be so frightened of things changing. It was part of life. "Mum, change isn't always bad. I have changed, yes, but maybe for the better in some ways. And you're changing too, aren't you?"

Her mum laughed, wiping away tears. "Oh baby, when did you get smarter than me? You're right. We're all changing, and it's scary, but it's the only way for us to grow. And it sounds like you're *really* growing. Apologizing to the Leeshes is huge!"

Sabina smiled. "It was…" Then she sat up straight. "Also, Mum, there's one thing I haven't told you yet. Don't be mad, but…I emailed Dad. Well, the Leeshes did it for me."

Her mum inhaled sharply. "What do you mean? Are you… sure it was him?"

Sabina pulled out her phone and showed her mum the

profile, as well as the message with no response.

"That's him," said her mum, her voice tight. "Rohan."

Sabina burst into tears, letting herself feel the full pain of the rejection. It was her dad – and he hadn't replied. "I thought he was coming back for me. I saw you and him kissing in a vision, but now I can see it wasn't him – it was Manish."

Her mum wrapped her arms tight around her. "I'm so sorry, Sabina. It sounds like it's all been so confusing for you. I wish I'd been there to help you interpret your visions. And… to talk about your dad."

"Like what?"

"Your dad…he was a wonderful person. And I always wanted you to know that. But I suppose I was trying to protect you from the fact that…well…he was also a bit of a coward. He isn't brave like you. He couldn't face up to reality. That's why he ran away before you were born, and…I'd guess it's why he isn't replying to you now. He's scared."

"But I'm scared too! And you just told me you are as well."

"I know. But we still put ourselves out there. That's why I think we're braver than Rohan. And I want you to know that this is his loss, *not* yours. You're an amazing, incredible girl, Sabina. I am SO lucky to have you as my daughter. And he is missing out more than he can ever know."

"But he doesn't love me," said Sabina in a micro-whisper. "It makes me feel like there's something wrong with me. That I'm…not good enough."

Her mum squeezed her arm urgently. "Never think that, Sabina, please. Your dad's absence says everything about him, and *nothing* about you. You are more than enough exactly as you are. You don't need your dad to know how wonderful you really are. You don't need *anyone*'s approval but your own. You're Sabina Patel and you're a star."

Sabina let her mum's words sink in, like a warm hug. "Thanks, Mum. Even if I've made lots of mistakes?"

"You're only human," said her mum. "We all make mistakes. And the good thing about them is they can be fixed. You just need to apologize."

"I will! I just can't *make* people forgive me."

"No," agreed her mum. "But being brave enough to apologize and face up to things is the most important thing of all. I'm sorry your dad can't do that…but I'm so proud that you can. It must be from my genes."

Sabina made a face at her. "Maybe I inherited my messiness from you too. And my impatience, and—" She shrieked as her mum cut her off by tickling her. "Stop!"

Her mum let her hands fall by her sides as she looked into her daughter's eyes. "I really am proud of you, Sabina."

"Even though I don't seem to know anything at all, and I just proved it to hundreds of people from the middle of a stage?"

"*Because* of that," said her mum firmly. "None of us really know anything, and we all mess up. But you can admit it. Love you infinity."

"Love you infinity, too."

"Now, how about we go and meditate together?" asked her mum. "No crystals. No chakras. Nothing fancy. Just me and you – breathing side by side on the cushions?"

Sabina's face burst into a giant smile. "Yes, please! I can't think of anything I'd like more!"

Chapter 31

Sabina yawned happily, stretching out in bed. She felt more relaxed than she had in days. She'd had so much fun with her mum last night. They'd stretched together, giggling as they tried – and failed – to do complicated balances and headstands. Then, when they'd sat down to breathe, Sabina's whole nervous system had settled into a state of complete relaxation. She'd been worried she wouldn't be able to meditate again, but after a couple of minutes, she'd drifted off into total peace, where the only thing that mattered was the sound of hers and her mum's breath.

"SABINA!"

The door burst open and Sabina saw two blurry figures standing there. She recognized their voices, but without her glasses she couldn't be sure. She groped around her bedside table, but they weren't there. She stood up, immediately

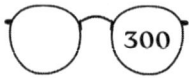

stubbing her toe on something. "Ow!"

"They're on the windowsill," said a gentle voice, handing her the glasses.

Sabina didn't dare to breathe until she had her glasses on. But when she put them on, she screamed in excitement.

"Ria! Harry! You're here!" Sabina sprang out of bed and wrapped her arms tight around her friends. "Oh my God. I can't believe it. This is the best thing that's ever happened to me."

"I wish I could say the same," said Harry, peeling her arms off him. "Next time you hug me, I suggest brushing your teeth first."

"Sorry," said Sabina happily. "I'll do it now. I just can't believe you're both here!"

"Of course we are – you invoked a FRIENDSHIP SOS," said Ria matter-of-factly.

"Oh, of course." Sabina's smile faded. "So...you're only here because I made you come?"

"Pretty much," said Harry, his face deadly serious. But then he let out a tiny grin. "And because we saw the viral clip of you running off the stage at the talent show. We wanted to get the inside story on what actually happened to Sabrina the Teenage Witch."

"There's *another* viral video?!"

"Let's not worry about that now," said Ria hastily, giving Harry a look. "It sounds like you've had a lot going on, Sabs.

With all your friends being mad at you. And everything with your dad..."

"Don't remind me," sighed Sabina. "It's been such a mess. Although I've made up with my mum. And the Leeshes! I apologized."

"Charming," huffed Harry, crossing his arms. "We're still waiting for ours. I listened to your voice message twice and there wasn't a *single* sorry in it."

"I'm SO sorry," cried Sabina. "Like, beyond sorry. I was really selfish and wrapped up in my own stuff. I wasn't a good friend and I don't know why I said that thing about you both not changing. It's not like I've been very mature – I've been more of a child than ever."

"We are all technically still children," pointed out Ria with a grin. "So...maybe that's okay?"

"Don't let her off the hook that easily," said Harry sternly. "Please continue with your apology."

Sabina swallowed a smile. "Of course. I really am sorry. I have no excuse. I just...I missed you both so much. I was really lonely. And I...got a bit lost. I was so caught up in the future, and when I was popular and people suddenly noticed me and thought I was amazing, it...made me forget who I am."

"Popularity does that," said Harry airily. "Take it from the most popular person you know."

Ria and Sabina both made faces at him.

"I forgive you, Sabs," said Ria. "Who knows what *I'd* do if I had to move to a weird village and go to a posh school without you both? I'd probably become a psychic mean girl too."

"Thank you," said Sabina, hugging her friend gratefully. "And if you think this part of the village is weird, wait till you see the nice side. There's zero graffiti, hardly anyone of colour, and everyone *smiles* all the time!"

They all shuddered.

"I suppose I underestimated how much has been going on for you lately," said Harry begrudgingly. "So…I forgive you too." Sabina squealed, but Harry raised a hand. "So long as you promise to never change like that again."

Sabina hesitated. "I actually think I might *have* to change again – we all will. It's part of growing up. But I promise I'll handle it better next time!"

"Deal," said Ria. "Me too."

"Fine, me three," said Harry, as they all interlaced pinkies. "Okay, now you *really* need to go shower. And brush your teeth. We've got a village to explore!"

"I can't wait," cried Sabina. "But…there's actually someone else I need to speak to first."

"Another apology?" asked Ria.

"Yep," said Sabina. "An urgent one."

Harry sighed theatrically. "Okay. So long as we can come too."

"We're here," announced Sabina's mum, pulling up outside the hall in her Ford Fiesta. "Out you get! Manish and I will collect you when it's over."

"Thank you," chorused Harry and Ria as they piled out of the back seat.

"Enjoy!" said Manish longingly. "Chess is *such* a wonderful game. You know, I was a school chess champion back in my day."

Sabina hesitated. It had been a long drive out to the chess tournament, and Manish had behaved very appropriately throughout. He'd supported Sabina, Harry and Ria's music choices, he'd bought them all chocolate at the petrol station, and he hadn't said a thing when it had taken her mum ten minutes to parallel park. In short, he'd proved himself worthy of being given a chance.

"Mum, if you and Manish want to come watch, then... you're welcome to come in with us."

"Are you sure?" asked her mum, glancing at Manish, whose eyes had lit up with excitement. "I know you need some time to adjust. I don't want to rush you."

Sabina shook her head. "It's okay. Manish, I didn't like you at first. But I didn't give you a chance either. And...I'm ready to get to know you. With an open mind. But if you hurt my mum, I will literally ruin your life."

Her mum suppressed a laugh as Manish gulped nervously. "Of course, I wouldn't expect anything less. But will your friend mind if we all come to her competition?"

Sabina shrugged. "It's open invitation, and I can't imagine there'll be that many people – it's only a chess competition."

But when Sabina, her mum and Manish joined Harry and Ria in the hall, she realized how wrong she was. The ginormous hall was completely packed. It was even busier than the talent show!

"Wow," said Sabina in awe. "I can't believe Faye's going to play in front of so many people."

"Yes, and she's starting in ten minutes," said Harry testily. "Come *on*!"

Sabina followed Harry and Ria as they made their way backstage. "How do you both know so much about Faye's schedule?"

"Her socials, obviously," said Ria. "You know she follows us too?"

Sabina felt her heart light up with hope. Maybe there was still a chance her dream of hanging out with her, Harry and Ria would still come true! Then she thought of Diva's words and remembered it was okay to have dreams, but not cling onto them too much. She'd just have to wait and see.

"There she is," said Harry, pointing to Faye at the back of the green room, studying a complicated-looking textbook. "We'll leave you to it."

"You're not staying?"

"You need to do this alone," said Ria. "Good luck!"

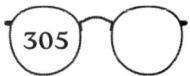

Sabina slowly walked towards Faye, her heart racing. She had no idea how she was going to react. "Faye? Hi!"

Faye's eyes rounded in surprise. "Sabina. What are you doing here?"

"I...came to support you," said Sabina. "And apologize."

"Here?" Faye frowned. "I'm about to go onstage and try to become the under-sixteen county champion. This is not the best timing."

"Oh," said Sabina, feeling foolish. "I'm sorry. About this, but also about everything else too, Faye. I've been a bad friend. A really bad one. I've blamed the powers this whole time, but now I know it wasn't their fault. It was mine."

Faye nodded. "I know." She turned back to her textbook.

"That's it? There's nothing else you want to say? I'm ready to hear anything you want to tell me – even if it's harsh. I deserve it."

Faye sighed. "I knew you'd do this once your powers were gone. I saw the video – it was obvious what happened. You lost the crystal and without the meditating, your powers faded."

Sabina looked down, shamefaced. "Yes. I *really* should have listened to you."

"But you didn't. You chose the Leeshes over me – don't try and deny it, you did. And maybe it was so you could win the prize money for your mum. But you still did it."

"I'm sorry, Faye. I made some terrible choices. Like the

cheating. And hiding things from you. Do you think you can ever forgive me? I'll do whatever I can to make it up to you."

"There's no need. I already forgive you. But I need to prepare. I only have five minutes left."

"Yay!" cried Sabina. "Thank you so much! I'm *so* glad we're friends again."

"Oh, we're not," said Faye. "I forgive you but I'm not sure I can be *friends* with you. Friendship is built on trust and loyalty. And you haven't really been there for me."

Sabina's face fell. "What? I... Can you give me a chance? Please?"

Faye shook her head. "I don't know – I don't have time for this now. You need to leave. I don't want anything to ruin my chances of beating Hvar."

Slowly, Sabina turned and walked back to her family. She understood that Faye wasn't ready to be friends again. It just broke Sabina's heart to hear it.

Chapter 32

Faye had won every single game she'd played so far, and now it was the final against Hvar. Manish was practically jumping out of his seat in anticipation. Sabina's mum, Harry and Ria were all less engaged – after three hours of chess, they were yawning and losing their focus.

Sabina had kept her eyes glued on Faye the whole time, but she hadn't been able to fully concentrate on the chess because she was too busy feeling her heart break. She wished she could go back in time and be a better friend to Faye. She wished she'd listened to her, shown up for her when she needed her, and made things up to her when there'd been a chance. Unlike now.

Sabina felt tears pool in her eyes. She didn't know what to do. Did she have to accept things as they were? Or could she try and fix things so Faye would be her friend again? Sabina tried to think what Diva would say. She'd probably tell her to stay in the present moment. To not try and control the future. And to come back to herself.

So, Sabina decided to do exactly that. She closed her eyes, and right there in the audience of Faye's big chess competition, she started to meditate. She began by breathing deeply, until her worries and her pain faded away. There was still a bit of pain in her chest, but Sabina could see now that she wasn't the pain – she was simply *experiencing* the pain. It made her remember that it would go away one day, and a new feeling would come instead. She just had to breathe through it all and not get too freaked out.

That was when Sabina felt her chakras start to light up. At first, she tensed in fear. Would she accidentally unleash some new powers again? But then she remembered it was never because of the chakras or the crystal that she'd got her powers – they'd been inside her all along. And if her powers ever came back, she'd know how to handle them this time – she'd simply need to stay aligned in integrity, and not get caught up in the future. Easy!

Sabina allowed herself to breathe, slowly connecting with her chakras. As she did so, a phrase for each one came to her. She said it aloud in her head, with her eyes still closed.

"I am safe," for the red chakra at the bottom of her spine.

"I am creative," for the orange one beneath her belly button.

"I am powerful," for the yellow one under her ribs.

"I am loved," for the green one by her heart.

"I am honest," for the blue chakra in her throat.

"I am present," for the indigo light in between her eyebrows.

"I am me," for the violet brightness at the top of her head.

Sabina stayed there, eyes closed, legs crossed, breathing deeply, as a soft light enveloped her. Her anxiety drifted far away and she felt total peace. She breathed it in and exhaled out her worries. She was okay - and no matter what, so long as she came back to herself, she always would be.

Sabina opened her eyes, coming out of her meditation with a smile on her face. Then she frowned, blinking in discomfort. Everything was so *bright*! Had they upped the lighting in the hall? But as Sabina's eyes adjusted, she realized that it wasn't the lighting after all.

It was her super sight.

It was back!

With her glasses on, she could see absolutely *everything*. Faye's tooth poking out as she bit her lip in concentration. The intricate details of the black and white pieces on the chessboard. And the tiny black dot inside Hvar's ear.

Wait. What WAS that?!

Sabina leaned closer as her eyes focused on the black dot.

It looked like an earbud. A really tiny one. Did Hvar have a hearing aid? And why was he talking to himself? It was really subtle – Sabina could only just see his lips moving. But he was definitely saying *something.*

She turned to the others. "Is it normal for Hvar to have a tiny black earpiece in his ear?"

Manish jerked upright. "What?!" He squinted at the stage. "How can you see that?"

Sabina exchanged a glance with her mum, whose eyes widened.

"It's back?" she mouthed.

Sabina nodded in reply, unsure what to make of the fact that her powers – or at least one of them – seemed to be back.

"Sabina, if you're right, this is serious," said Manish. "He could be cheating."

Harry and Ria gasped loudly.

"Oh my God, the drama!" shrieked Harry. "I knew Hvar was a cheat. You can tell from his facial hair."

"We need to do something," cried Ria. "We need to speak to the judges. Do you know who's helping him?"

Sabina sat up straight. "I might be able to check. Harry, can you pass me the programme with everyone's names in it? Just put it down on the chair for a second."

She took a deep breath and closed her eyes, connecting with herself. She started to say her intention, but this time, she phrased it differently. "Dear powers, please help me find

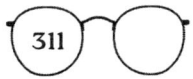

out the truth about Hvar. Thank you so much for whatever you choose to show me."

She slowly reached out to touch the page of the programme with Hvar's smug face on it.

Everything started spinning, the chess hall and the people around her, until it stopped. She was still in the hall, but this time, she wasn't sitting next to her friends and family. She was next to an old man with a beard. He was *also* wearing a tiny black earpiece, and Sabina could see him speaking into it!

She leaned in closer and heard him whisper: "Knight d5."

At that exact moment, Hvar moved his knight on the chessboard. And then he said: "Checkmate."

The audience erupted in cheers and Sabina blinked. She was back in her seat.

"Oh my God," gasped Harry. "Did you have a vision?"

"Your powers are back?" cried Ria.

Sabina nodded. "Yes. And I saw an old man in the fifth row on the right tell Hvar to move his knight to d5. He did. And then he said, 'Checkmate.'"

Manish made a strangled sound. "We need to do something!"

Her mum leaned across to her. "Sabina, are you sure about what you saw?"

Sabina hesitated. Had she misinterpreted what she'd seen, like when she thought she'd had a vision about her dad, and it hadn't come true? She took a moment to breathe, and then she felt her yellow chakra light up. She trusted herself. "I am," she said firmly.

"Right," said Manish. "Let's go!"

All of them raced to the judges' table, where Manish had a word with the top judge, whose face paled. She said something that Sabina and the others couldn't quite hear and then went over to speak to Hvar. He looked furious as the judge spoke, and they exchanged heated words, until a scowling Hvar finally pulled a black wireless earpiece from his ear.

It was official – he'd cheated!

"Oh my God," whispered Sabina. "Does this mean…"

"I've won," said a faint voice behind her. Sabina whirled around to see Faye. "I should have known he was cheating. There was no way he'd have lasted so long on his own."

"Sabs, we need to show the judges who the person helping Hvar is," said Ria. "Before he gets away!"

"He's on the end of the fifth row," replied Sabina. "The one that looks like Gandalf. I'll catch up with you later." She turned to Faye as everyone raced off. "Congratulations. I always knew you'd win."

"How did you know Hvar was cheating?" asked Faye. "It was you, wasn't it?"

Sabina nodded. "I meditated while you were playing. I mean – I totally watched all your games until then! But I was sad, because of how things went between us. So, I meditated to make myself feel better. All my chakras lit up, and when I opened my eyes again...my powers were back."

"Back?!" repeated Faye. "All of them?"

"I think so," said Sabina. "I saw his earpiece with my super sight, and then I had a controlled vision to check who was helping him."

Faye inhaled sharply. "Wow. So do you think your powers are here to stay?"

"I have no idea," said Sabina honestly. "And...I don't really mind either way. I'm starting to see what Diva meant when she said they were a gift. I...kind of want to treat them with more respect, you know? Rather than try and control them so much."

"Interesting," said Faye. "I can't wait to put this extra information into my paper. If...you don't mind, that is?"

"Of course not," said Sabina. "I owe you that. And I really am sorry, Faye. For everything. From the bottom of my heart."

"I know you are," replied Faye. "And...I don't think you *do* owe me any more. You took down Hvar - my ultimate nemesis. His chess career is over now. And I won. All because of you."

Sabina shook her head quickly. "No, no. Not because of me. Because of *you* and your talent!"

"True," agreed Faye. She took a deep breath and settled her brown eyes onto Sabina's. "I forgave you earlier, but I wasn't ready to be your friend again. Mainly because you'd hurt me by being selfish and thoughtless."

Sabina swallowed uncomfortably. It did not feel great to hear Faye's truth.

"But then you still helped me," continued Faye. "You showed up for me, which means a lot to me. It's...making me realize that life isn't as black and white as a chessboard. Things are complicated. And none of us are perfect. *Especially* Hvar."

They both turned to look at him, surrounded by booing chess fans.

"I guess what I'm saying is...I'd like to be friends again," said Faye. "If you're still keen?"

Sabina wrapped her arms around Faye and hugged her tight. "Yes, yes, yes! Thank you so much, Faye, I'd love that!"

Faye blushed pink. "Okay. Good."

Just then the top judge approached Faye. "It's time for you to receive your trophy," she said, eyes twinkling. "Congratulations, Faye Collins!"

"Your victory speech!" cried Sabina.

"I'm nervous," admitted Faye, biting her lip.

"You've got this," said Sabina. "Just be yourself. And remember, I'm here if you need me."

Sabina beamed proudly as Faye walked onto the stage to collect her trophy and the entire auditorium erupted into loud applause. It took ages for the cheers to die out – everyone was extra emotional about the young twelve-year-old girl who'd beaten a cheating sixteen-year-old boy – and then Faye approached the microphone.

"I just want to say thank you," she said. "To myself, mainly, because I'm really good at chess, and I've practised a *lot*. I hope my achievement inspires other girls to keep playing chess because we CAN beat the boys. I'm proof of that!" She had to pause as everyone started clapping and cheering again.

"Also, I'd like to thank someone else – the person who worked out Hvar was cheating. Sabina, will you come up, please?"

Sabina froze, disbelieving. Then she realized Faye was standing up on the huge stage all alone, waiting for her. She quickly clambered up the stairs to join her. "Faye," she whispered. "Do you really want me up here?"

"Of course," said Faye. "We're friends, right?"

They hugged tightly and the entire audience cheered loudly, as Sabina and Faye laughed happily. Sabina smiled as she looked into the audience beyond Faye's shoulder. She could see Faye's parents cheering madly. Harry and Ria were bang in the middle whooping louder than anyone. And next to them were her mum and Manish...kissing!

Sabina gasped as it hit her.

THIS WAS HER VISION.

She hadn't ever seen herself winning the talent show – it had always been Faye winning her chess competition! She'd just seen what she'd wanted to see – which was her winning, with her dad in the audience. Sabina's insides twisted at the memory. She'd wanted it *so* badly. But then she breathed deeply. What mattered was the present moment – her reality. And her dad wasn't in it. He never had been. As much as that hurt, Sabina also felt incredibly grateful for everyone who *was* in her life. Her friends, who'd all shown how generous they were by forgiving her. Her mum. Even Manish.

Sabina had so much to be happy about. And she knew that she was perfectly enough, just as she was, with or without her dad.

"Come on," she said to Faye, grabbing her hand. "Let's go find everyone!"

They'd barely made their way down the steps before they were smothered in hugs.

"Faye, I know we've never met, but you're *incredible*," cried Ria. "Your chess skills! Your speech!"

"The bit when you thanked yourself was *iconic*," declared Harry. "Obsessed."

"Congratulations, darling," said Sabina's mum, squeezing Faye's shoulder. "We're all so proud." She turned to Sabina. "Of you too, Sabs."

Sabina smiled and hugged her mum, her heart feeling like it was about to burst. She felt so good that she decided to be magnanimous, and reached out to shake Manish's hand. "Thanks for your help," she said, before their palms met...

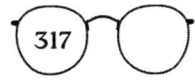

A jolt of electricity ran through Sabina's veins and everything started to spin, until she was no longer in the auditorium. She was outside in a bright, sunny garden. There was loud music playing. Everyone she knew was there dancing – Faye, Harry, Ria, even the Leeshes, while Manish was twirling her mum around the grass dance floor. Her mum looked *beautiful*!

She was wearing a floaty white dress, with flowers in her hair, and she was beaming. Manish was smart in a suit and behind him was Sabina. Her future self was wearing a simple white dress, with thin straps, and trainers. She was laughing as her mum and Manish reached out their hands to dance with her. The sun shone onto their hands and the metal of their rings glinted.

Rings! They were both wearing *wedding rings*!

Sabina blinked and the next thing she knew, she was back in the auditorium, holding Manish's hand. He gently released it from her grip.

Sabina couldn't believe what she'd seen. Should she tell her mum? Or should she try to stop it? She wasn't ready for a stepdad yet!

But then she remembered everything she'd learned from her powers the last time around. She wasn't going to obsess about the future – she was going to let it unfold in its own time. Anything else would lead to more complications and drama, which Sabina was officially done with.

Besides, she was way too busy enjoying the present moment to worry about what was going to happen next. With all her favourite people by her side, it was too good to miss out on.

"Let's go for a celebratory dinner," she said to everyone. "I know a place that does *really* good charcoal pizza!"

Acknowledgements

Thank you to everyone who helped me write this book – in so many different ways!

To start with, I'd like to thank my agent Chloe Seager, for always being so supportive, encouraging and taking care of all the things that mean I can earn a living by writing books.

I also owe a massive thank you to everyone at Usborne – my editors Rebecca Hill and Charlotte James for all your valuable insights which have made this a much stronger book, Beth Gardner for all things marketing, Jess Feichtlbauer for your fab publicity support, and everyone else who's been involved in the design and the general publishing of this book. Also thank you to my former editor Alice Moloney for the initial support and enthusiasm.

Thank you as well to Miriam Indries, my yoga teacher in Greece. Sabina's story was first inspired by you telling us how ancient yogis believed that unlocking their third eye chakras could lead to gaining psychic abilities – so thank you for sharing that knowledge with me.

Thank you to my mum for teaching me yoga and meditation at such a young age. Back then, I probably didn't appreciate it as much as Sabina did – but I do now.

And thank you to all my loved ones who've been there for me whilst I've been working on this book – I'm so grateful. Special thank you to Coco, for being the best cat ever, and to younger Radhika for reading so many books that it meant I had no choice but to become an author one day.